LOVE,
JACARANDA

ALSO BY ALEX FLINN

LOVE, JACARANDA

ALEX FLINN

HARPER TEEN
An Imprint of HarperCollinsPublishers

HarperTeen is an imprint of HarperCollins Publishers.

Love, Jacaranda
Copyright © 2020 by Alex Flinn
All rights reserved. Printed in the United States of America.
No part of this book may be used or reproduced in any manner whatsoever
without written permission except in the case of brief quotations embodied in
critical articles and reviews. For information address HarperCollins Children's
Books, a division of HarperCollins Publishers, 195 Broadway, New York, NY
10007.
www.epicreads.com

Library of Congress Control Number: 2019044022
ISBN 978-0-06-244786-9

Typography by Molly Fehr
20 21 22 23 24 PC/LSCH   10 9 8 7 6 5 4 3 2 1

First Edition

To my mother,
who gave me so many books,
Daddy Long Legs among them.

The world is full of happiness, and plenty to go round,
if you are only willing to take the kind that comes your way.
—*Jean Webster,* Daddy-Long-Legs

Viral Video

When I was little, my grandma used to say, "Think before you open your big mouth and get in trouble." Usually, she was right. But this time, opening my mouth without thinking changed everything.

I work as a bagger at Publix, two days a week after school and most weekends. You get to know the customers, who wants you to fill up their reusable bags and who can't lift anything heavy, who sneaks you a dollar and which ones want to remind you of Publix's fabled "no tipping" policy after you bust your butt loading bags of ice into their Mercedes SUV.

Mr. Louis is one of the good ones. Every Sunday, he comes in after church. He's about seventy, maybe older, skinny guy with a shiny bald head, a limp, and a Haitian accent. He used to teach music, so he always asks me about chorus, my passion. So, even though I was having a bad day with aching feet and a smashed phone I couldn't afford to fix, I smiled when I saw him.

"How is the school chorus going, Jacaranda?" he asked me.

He always brought two reusable bags, which he'd washed and even mended a couple times. I tried to put the heavy items like milk in the one that was in better shape, so it wouldn't break through from the weight.

"Good," I told him. "Trying for a solo in the spring concert." This time he had eggs, which made things tricky. I wanted to put them in their own plastic bag, but he was very picky about always using the reusable ones. But he loved talking about music, and so did I.

"You don't say." He nodded. "I am glad to hear they still have concerts in our schools. The government always wants to cut, cut, cut the arts."

I wondered if that was why he'd stopped working. No, he was old. I said, "Well, we made it through this year. We'll see about next. Do you mind if I put the eggs in a plastic bag?"

"I do mind," he said. "I brought reusable ones for a reason."

"We recycle. You can bring them back." Though I knew what he would say.

"Reduce, reuse, recycle—in that order. Those eggs will fit in my bags."

"Okay!" I nestled them in next to the toilet paper for cushioning.

"Your mother must be very proud," he said.

I winced since I don't hear much from my mother. But I turned it into a smile. "Yes, sir. Thank you, sir."

"What is the song called?"

"Well, I'm trying for all the solos, but the one I hope to get is called 'Lost in the Night.'" I added a can of mixed veggies to the bag with the milk. "You be sure to get your vitamin D, Mr. Louis.

It's important for bone health at your age."

He waved his hand. "I get plenty. How about you sing me some of that song?"

"I can't do that here, sir. I have a very strong voice, and it's a loud song." I added some yogurts to the bag with the eggs.

"I wouldn't mind."

"They would." I gestured to everyone else in the store.

"Then sing something else. Make an old man's day."

I laughed, remembering that when I was little and my grandma was alive, I used to stay with her when my mother was "busy" (meaning high). Granny's kitchen was always clean and smelled like Pine-Sol and cooking. She sang all the time, and one of the things she sang was this old Publix jingle. I missed her. So I started singing, "Publix, where shopping is a pleasure!"

The cashier, Maria, looked at me weird, but Mr. Louis clapped and said, "Sing it, girl!"

The second time, I put a little Beyoncé energy into it. If Bey was, you know, a bagger at Publix. "Publix, where shopping is a pleasure." I riffed on that a few more times, channeling Gaga next, "Pa-pa-pa-Publix! Where shopping is a pleasure!" Then I really began to improvise, looking around and singing about everything I saw.

Little Maria rings up your food
Come to Publix and lighten your mood
I'd come every day if I could
Come to Publix, where everything's good.

Publix, where shopping is a pleasure!
Publix, where shopping is a pleasure!

Mr. Louis was laughing. He began singing along with me, adding some beebops and skee-wahs, like accompaniment. The old guy was good!

Bread starts baking at seven each day
Come to Publix and you'll wanna stay
Andrew's in charge at the deh-lay
Too much salami, you'll get a big bell-ay.

Publix, where shopping is a pleasure!
Publix, where shopping is a pleasure!

By then, everyone had stopped what they were doing. Some guy was even filming, and lots were clapping along.

Come get some sushi rolled by Haruko
Fish is brain food, so eat it and you'll know
Publix is tops from head to toe
The bakery manager's name is Jo.

Publix, where shopping is a pleasure!
Publix, where shopping is a pleasure!

On the last one, I gestured to Mr. Louis. "Big finish!" We harmonized, "Publix, where shopping is a pleasure!"

We finished, and everyone clapped. That's when I started being a little self-conscious. I looked down and waited for Mr. Louis to pay while I packed up the last of his BOGO Oscar Mayer wieners. I hoped no one noticed me blushing. I put the bags in his cart.

"Shall we go?"

I always took the old people's groceries all the way out to their cars, even if they only had two bags. Especially Mr. Louis with his limp. So there was no way out of it now.

"Yes, ma'am." He followed me.

I tried to act normal. "How are your grandchildren?" I thought I remembered their names. "James and Patricia?"

"Oh!" He grinned wide. "Patricia is finishing kindergarten, and she is already reading books—thick books." He held his fingers an inch apart to indicate how thick her books were.

"That's wonderful. And what about—?"

"Excuse me, miss." It was the guy who'd been filming me. He was out of breath, like he'd been chasing me. "You have a beautiful voice."

"Thank you." I started to turn away. Creepers trying to pick me up in the parking lot was nothing new, and they're always hella old. This one looked in his twenties and was wearing a University of Miami T-shirt, but I've had guys twice that ask for my number. Not happening.

"I was trying to see your name." He glanced at my chest. "Is it Jacqueline? Jocelyn?"

"It's Jacaranda, like the tree." I didn't want to give out my name, but it was on my name tag for all to see, and I didn't want him to tell the manager I got salty.

"Jacaranda, like the tree?" He looked puzzled.

"The purple trees?" I said. "They're in bloom now. And they were blooming when I was born. That's why I'm named that." My sixteenth birthday had just passed, not that I had a party or anything.

"Oh, uh . . ." College Boy looked like he was going to say something else.

"I have to help this gentleman with his bags. If you'll excuse me." I saw Mr. Louis's old Civic, parked real far. He should get a handicapped tag.

"Sure," the guy said. "Thanks."

I put Mr. Louis's bags on the floor of the backseat, where he liked them, and he handed me a dollar. I tried to refuse, but he waved me off.

"Thank you," I told him. "You tell Patricia to keep reading."

"I will."

I pocketed his dollar and went into the store, where the rest of my shift was uneventful. I'm always dead tired at the end, and that day, my phone was busted, and I wouldn't be able to fix it 'til I saved up. So I didn't talk to anyone until I got to school Monday. When I walked into English class, people stood and began to clap.

"It's the famous Jacaranda!" someone said.

"Too famous to answer her phone," my friend Ally said.

"What are you talking about?" I was dimly aware that, in the background, someone was singing the Publix jingle pretty well.

Hey, wait.

Someone stuck a phone in my face, and I saw auburn curls

and a green uniform. It was me. The caption on the video said, "Publix Bag Girl Has a Set of Pipes," and it had a couple hundred thousand views.

I'd gone viral.

Well, I guess you've seen it.

Then it got a little embarrassing. I didn't have work Monday, but Tuesday, as I was walking through the parking lot, some guy started honking at me and yelled, "Sing, sister!" out the window. Then, when I walked up to the door, I saw someone had put up a whiteboard sign saying, "Jacaranda will be in at 3:00 today." I noticed that someone had smudged out where they'd originally written "Not" before "be in."

Whaaaa-aaat?

When I clocked in, Bev in Customer Service said, "Mr. Howard wants to see you. Now."

Was I getting fired? For singing? My throat tightened at the thought. I love my job! It's the most stable thing in my life.

"Where is he?" I managed. Mr. Howard was usually out and about, all over the store.

But Bev said, "He's in his office with some lady." Weird.

I shuffled in. Deep breaths. I was just having fun. They'd never specifically told us not to sing while bagging groceries, but it was probably one of those things that's assumed. Still, the song was very pro-Publix. They couldn't get that mad.

It was all I could do to put one foot in front of the other.

When I walked in, Mr. Howard was at his desk across from a skinny brunette lady with high-heeled shoes and a black dress.

Her legs were crossed gracefully, so I could see that the shoes had red bottoms, which even I know are expensive.

"Jacaranda Abbott!" She rose to her feet as she said it, like I was someone important. She was very tall and elegant, and I felt like I should curtsy or something. Instead, I said, "Yes, ma'am?" real quiet. Did they bring this lady in specifically to can me?

"Jacaranda." Mr. Howard was grinning and shifting in his seat like there was a bug in his pant leg. "This is Vanessa Lastra. She came all the way from New York City to offer you a very important opportunity."

"So you don't work for Publix?" I'm pretty sure they only have Publixes in the South.

She laughed, a tinkly laugh, and sat back down. "No."

"So I'm not fired?" I felt light as I said it, but it was sort of bad, because I felt so light I thought I might fall over. Why was this lady here? Was she a lawyer? Was my mother getting out of prison?

Ms. Lastra held out her hand. She must have noticed how freaked I was because she pulled me down into the seat next to hers then took both my hands.

"Jacaranda, I work for a private educational foundation. A member of our board, a wealthy gentleman who wishes to remain anonymous, saw your video and asked me to call Publix. After learning about your situation . . ." She looked uncomfortable.

"My situation? You mean, that I'm a foster kid and my mom's in prison?" I mean, I knew what my situation was. Why cha-cha around it?

"Yes, that situation. After learning about that, and in light of your talent, this gentleman—I'll call him Mr. Smith—would like to send you to a prestigious boarding school up north to study musical theater."

Boarding school? I didn't know those existed outside of books.

At that point, I was glad I was sitting down. Otherwise, I'd have fainted. Still, I had to take deep breaths, and while I did that, she explained some details. Like, she'd be my guardian instead of Laurie, my foster mom, who'd keep me until I left in September. The school had seen the video and was interested in having me as a student. But they asked me to write a thousand-word essay about why I wanted to go there, to make sure I wasn't being coerced into it (like that would happen!). The foundation would pay for it. "Mr. Smith" told them to pay room, board, and everything else. I'd even get an allowance, like a rich kid. Ms. Lastra said other stuff, important stuff, but all too much to take in at once.

You're looking at the essay, obviously. It's way longer than a thousand words, but I think it's hard to make it shorter when I have so much excitement in my words, so I thought I'd tell you the whole story. But I still haven't gotten to the why-I-want-to-go part.

I want to go to Midwestern Arts Academy for a few reasons.

The first is that, starting in middle school, I've always taken chorus. It's the best part of the day, sort of like a little vacay right in the middle of school. It's when all the bullying and craziness about who has the better sneakers or the less-nasty backpack stops, and we all sing together in harmony—something our government should do more of. But Miss Rojas, the chorus teacher, says this is her last year, and they aren't going to replace her, so I'll probably have to take Personal Development since I can't afford to rent an instrument for band.

Also, I'm good at singing. I write songs too. So being able to do that on a regular basis *and* be around people who think music is actually important would be a dream come true.

But the biggest reason is, I've been alive sixteen years, and this is the first time since my granny died that anyone has ever noticed me, especially. Some people get noticed for good things, like getting high grades. Others get noticed for bad things. I bet there's a lot of people who get noticed by their families because their parents think they're cute or smart, even if they aren't. Old people like Mr. Louis might notice me a little, but he's got his own grandkids to love and care for. I had my first taste of being noticed with that viral video, and I want it to keep going. I want to be special.

Please take me. I'm way out of words now.

To: Johnsmith247@dll.com
Date: September 5, 9:00 a.m. Eastern Standard Time
Subject: Introduction

Dear Kind-Gentleman-Who-Sends-Teens-to-Boarding-School,

I wanted to introduce myself and thank you. Vanessa says you are the person responsible for my being sent to school. I asked her if I could write to thank you and let you know how I'm doing. She said you probably wouldn't read it, but if I wanted to write occasionally, like once a month, that would be lovely. She said I could write to John Smith, not your real name, because you want to remain anonymous. She set up an email account for it.

ANYWAY, I'm here on the plane to Midwestern Arts Academy in sunny (I'm guessing not really) Michigan.

Thank you for my "allowance" (I'm putting that in quotation marks because I've never had such a thing in my life, and it seems like something someone else would say, not me). The amount I'm getting each week is—WOW—what I'd make in a month of working at Publix, and considering Vanessa took me shopping and bought me clothes and shoes and makeup and an Apple laptop (!), on which I'm typing this letter, and a new phone, and there's supposed to be a bunch of stuff waiting for me at the school too, sheets and dance clothes and books and blankets, I don't even know what I'll spend it on. I promise it won't be drugs.

JK. I don't do drugs. You were probably wondering about that, since my mom's in prison. She's not in prison for drugs either. She's in prison for the attempted murder of her boyfriend, Oscar. She shouldn't be. He would have killed us both, so it was self-defense. I lived there, so I know. But she wouldn't even have had boyfriends like that if it wasn't for drugs, so I stay away from them.

Change of subject: I've never flown before. I bet you probably go on airplanes all the time, but this is my first. I've also never been out of Florida. I've never seen snow or red leaves, except in pictures. Vanessa took me shopping for a goose-down jacket and boots. They're also being shipped to the school, since they don't exactly sell that kind of thing in Miami.

By the way, Vanessa is really nice. She told me to call her by her first name and also says I should call her if there's an emergency, like if I get kicked out of school. But she assumes I won't be. She didn't say I should call her just to talk, so I'll put everything in these letters. Maybe she'll read them. Hi, Vanessa!

I asked Vanessa what you looked like, old or young, tall or short, fat or skinny, black or white. All I could get out of her was that you are tall, and she laughed when I asked if you were bald, so I guess you aren't. Vanessa is very good at keeping your secrets.

Anyway, the plane. We had to get up at the butt-crack of dawn (Is "butt" a bad word? I feel like I shouldn't use bad words because you're probably old). My flight left at 6:00 a.m., and I was checking a bag. Two bags, actually. I now own two matching suitcases plus a carry-on bag and a laptop (!) bag. The thought is insane to me! You know what I used to move my stuff to my foster home? A Hefty bag. One was enough, too.

I woke up five times before it was time to get up anyway, since I was so excited.

When I got on the plane, I had a middle seat, with two big men on either side. In the front of the plane, a baby was crying. It didn't bother me. I've lived in apartments with thin walls. Babies are like white noise to me.

What wasn't white noise was this guy in a suit who was having. A. Fit. I mean, he was yelling louder than the baby. "Can someone please quiet that baby down?" he yelled to no one. "CAN SOME-ONE PLEASE QUIET THAT BABY DOWN?"

Working at a supermarket, I've heard some privileged rants, but you never get used to it.

He yelled it about five times until I just . . . wanted . . . to . . . !

Finally, the flight attendant lady said, "He'll quiet down once we take off, sir."

"How could a stewardess possibly know that?" he demanded, as if the mere fact that she does this every day of her life wouldn't make her more of an authority than him.

The poor flight attendant tried to answer, but he kept yelling, ragging on her, saying he couldn't stand sitting there. Any seat, anything farther back would be better.

I said, "He can switch with me."

Well, he wasn't too happy with that when he saw I had a middle seat, but I guess he realized he'd look bad if he said no, so he took it. I got to move up ten rows and sit in an aisle seat that had "in-seat entertainment," a little TV with free movies. But I didn't watch a movie because I was too busy looking around, thinking, "I'm on an airplane!" I made friends with the baby and even offered to hold him so the mom could get settled in. His name was Ashton. He calmed down real quick after we were in the air.

But it made me wonder, if you were on this flight, would you be that rich guy who couldn't handle being around a crying baby? Obviously, you're a much better person than that man, because, odds are, he isn't volunteering to send kids to boarding school. But are you someone who flies all the time and gets bored with it, or do you still see the magic in life?

Oh, we're landing, and the flight attendant is telling us to put up our tray tables. I'll send when I'm on the ground . . . assuming we make it. I'll write more later.

I know you probably think it's silly, but writing to you, having you care enough to send me to school, it makes me feel like I'm part of your family, like I belong to someone, even though I don't know your name. I'm even going to sign it with love because I love you for sending me here!

Also, I don't have anyone else to write to.

Love, (Miss) Jacaranda Abbott

To: Johnsmith247@dll.com
Date: September 5, 3:41 p.m. Eastern Standard Time
Subject: I'm here!

Dear Mr. Smith,

This place is BEAUTIFUL. I admit that when I heard the school was in Michigan, I pictured Detroit, or what I've heard about Detroit, which sounds a lot like Miami only without the sun or the beach or the palm trees or pretty much anything that makes Miami a cool place. But this place is green and beautiful, and there's a lake and even hills. When we were driving from the airport, I saw some beautiful trees, and I asked the girl in the next seat (a tiny dark-haired girl with an instrument case she said was a flute) what kind they were.

She looked at me funny but said, "They're cherry trees."

Then I felt ignorant. "We don't have cherry trees where I'm from."

She laughed. "Where are you from?"

"Miami. We have mangoes and avocados. There's a lady on the corner who sells mangoes from a wagon all summer."

After I said that, I wanted to stuff the words back into my

mouth because people selling mangoes on the street didn't exactly make me sound like I lived in the classiest part of town (I don't), but the girl said, "I've never had a mango. What are they like?"

"Kinda like peaches. Only bigger and more tropical."

"Now I have to try one." She pointed to the cherry trees. "They're so pretty, though. In the spring, they have pink flowers all over. I'm Daisy Murtaugh-Li, by the way. Daisy like the flower."

"Cool." I wanted to say I was Jacaranda, also like the flower, but I've decided that I don't want to be identified as Jacaranda the Publix Girl and have everyone be able to figure out the whole rest of my history, so I said, "Jackie."

"What do you play, Jackie?"

"I'm in musical theater."

She said her roommate was in musical theater. She made kind of a stank face when she said "roommate," which made me wonder what that was about, but she kept talking, telling me everything about the school. If everyone here is as friendly as Daisy, I'll be good.

We got to campus (which is also beautiful and woodsy, like a summer camp in a movie), and Daisy ran into some people she knew, so I was alone, but she said she'd look for me at dinner. At least I know someone. Starting as a junior, I was worried about that. I found my dorm and went to check in.

"Where are you from, Jacaranda?" the lady at the desk asked.

When I said Miami, she squinted like she was trying to think of something. I wondered what she knew. That I was here on scholarship? That my mom was in prison, so they had to worry, lest I murder my roommate in her sleep?

Do you like my use of the word "lest," by the way? I've been reading John Green novels to up my vocabulary for this place.

But after a second, she hummed a few bars of "Where Shopping Is a Pleasure."

"Yeah." I looked down.

"You have a beautiful voice," she said. "They said you'd be in my dorm. I'm Angie your dorm advisor."

"Does everyone know I'm the Publix girl?" I asked her.

She thought for a second before saying, "Oh, I doubt it. There are kids here whose parents are famous." She nodded toward a girl in the back of the line and told me her mom was some actress I've never heard of. But I acted impressed.

I told her I was going by Jackie, in any case.

Angie said as long as I worked hard, I'd be fine. She handed me a marker and told me to use it to change the name tag. I had no idea what she meant, but I took it. She said don't worry.

I wondered, will it be that easy here? Is it enough to be talented? I hope so.

But on the way to my room, each step seemed like a mountain, and not just because I was dragging two suitcases. What would my roommates and suite mates be like? What would they think of me? I thought I got off easy, because I didn't have to audition for the school. But this was the audition, right here.

Do you think it's wrong that I don't want to talk about my past? Because I don't, not even to you. I want to turn my back on everything that came before today, shut out all the bad memories. I want to be like other girls, like everyone else here except me. I hope you don't mind. You're probably not even reading this anyway, so you won't.

I stepped off the elevator and into a long hallway with closed doors all along each side. On each door were cutouts of stars and moons and planets with names on them. My room was number 107. When I got there, my name, Jacaranda, was written on a cutout of Saturn. I turned it over, took the tape off the other side, and wrote "Jackie" on it with the marker. Then I taped it back up. A cutout of the moon said "Abigail."

I thought maybe I should knock, in case Abigail was already there, so I wouldn't scare her. I settled for rattling my key as I put it in the lock. I needn't have worried. When I walked into the room, it was empty.

I pulled my suitcases inside and let the door shut behind me.

I am entirely alone for the first time in at least five years.

Love, Jacaranda

To: Johnsmith247@dll.com
Date: September 5, 4:35 p.m. Eastern Standard Time
Subject: Roommate troubles?

Dear Mr. Smith,

So this just happened.

I was lying on the bed, minding my own business and contemplating the enormity of the fact that I, Jacaranda Abbott, am going to live in this beautiful place with gleaming wooden floors, music coming through the walls, and a semiprivate bathroom (we share it with the room on the other side—Angie said it's called a Jack and Jill bathroom) and only *one* roommate instead of as many as three I've had in the past when suddenly . . .

I'm pausing for dramatic effect here, but also to thank you for my room décor. Vanessa bought everything, but I know the foundation paid for it. When I arrived, it was all piled on the bed closer to the window. I have a fluffy lavender comforter—something called a duvet (it's French—ooh-la-la!) that goes over a real feather quilt. My sheets are lavender-and-white pinstripes. I have pillows in a deeper purple, and a fluffy white rug for when I get out of bed on cold mornings, and even a dorm fridge in a matching shade of lavender because that's a thing that exists and that Vanessa thought I needed! I've long believed that lavender should be my signature color because of my name, but to decorate a whole room in it . . . I've never had so much as a bath mat! It was always someone else's old castoffs or from Goodwill, so nothing matched. These are from Pottery Barn. So classy!

Anyway, picture this serene environment. Imagine me lying on my beautiful bed. Then, suddenly, this shrieking person bursts through the bathroom door.

"Abigail!" She ran up to me. When she saw my face, she jumped back.

"WHO ARE YOU?" she shrieked. "WHAT ARE YOU DOING HERE?" She looked around. I couldn't tell if she was trying to find someone to report to or something to hit me with. She was a tall blonde. Very white, if you know what I mean, with blue eyes and skin that's probably never seen the sun. Literally no one in Miami looks like this. She opened her mouth like she was going to scream again.

I froze. I should have explained that it was MY room and I had every right to be there, but first off, I was having trouble believing it myself and, secondly, this girl was LOUD.

Then the bathroom door flew open again, and another girl was in there, yelling, "What's wrong? What's wrong?"

Then, just as the first girl started talking, the new girl said, "Jackie?" Daisy from the bus.

She seemed glad to see me, and she turned to the screamer like everything was perfectly normal and said, "This is Jackie. She's new."

Okay, so this should have been the part where the screechy girl apologized, right? You'd think? Or at least looked embarrassed. But she started explaining how she was looking for Abigail, who was supposed to be there. I glanced over at the other bed, as if to say, "There's two beds in this room." I still hadn't actually spoken words.

She must have figured it out too then, because she said, "I guess you're her roommate." Then she said she and Abigail were supposed to be roommates, but there must have been some mix-up 'cause they were only suite mates and she'd contacted Abigail over a month ago to correct the problem, but Abigail hadn't gotten back to her. Probably Abigail got smart and didn't want to room with the cray girl. I mean, she hadn't even told me her name yet.

I stared at her until finally she said, "I'm Phoebe Pendleton-Hodgkins."

Like the disease, I guess. Then she said we should switch rooms.

Remember how I'd just unpacked everything?

Deep breaths.

When I worked at Publix, there was this girl, Jasmine, who always tried to convince me to give her my Saturday shift because, she said, they must have gotten our names mixed up. I stood my ground with Jasmine. I stood it with Phoebe too. I said, "I don't think so. We should stick with our assigned rooms for now. I don't want to rock the boat."

She stormed off in a huff, saying something about talking to Angie.

"Nice meeting you?" I said, and Daisy laughed.

"She's usually not that bad," Daisy said.

I stared at her, and she said, "Okay, she's pretty bad," and added that they probably put Phoebe in the room with her because they were roommates last year, and Daisy is the only one who can stand her. Daisy said she gets along with everyone.

And then, as if to prove this, she asked me if I wanted to go to dinner with her and her friends. So I have dinner plans in an hour!

I wonder, though. When Phoebe Hodgkins-Disease saw me in the room, she was so sure I didn't belong here. Do I? And is it obvious to the world that I don't? Do I have "Mom in Prison" stamped across my forehead?

Love, Jacaranda

To: Johnsmith247@dll.com
Date: September 5, 5:23 p.m. Eastern Standard Time
Subject: I know this is way too many emails.

Dear Mr. Smith,

Turns out, Abigail isn't returning. Phoebe is shattered, and because I didn't switch with her, I have my very own private room. At least, Angie says, until someone can't get along with their roommate and gets switched. But she said that would be at least a month.

But for now, I'm going to be all alone for the First. Time. Ever. This means:

1. I can stay up all night if I want, and no one will complain. I once had a roommate throw a full soda bottle at my head because I was studying!

2. I can talk to family and friends until all hours without anyone judging me. (JK. I don't have any family and friends.)

3. No one will be in my room:
   a. Crunching Takis
   b. Keeping the lights on when I want them off
   c. Engaging in disgusting personal grooming rituals that I won't describe

d. Practicing giving an oral report

e. Fighting with their boyfriend

f. Sneaking guys through the window and NOT fighting, if you know what I mean

g. Crying

h. Walking around naked

i. Doing drugs

Daisy is knocking on the door between our rooms, asking if I'm ready for dinner. I am!

Love, Jacaranda

To: Johnsmith247@dll.com
Date: September 5, 9:18 p.m. Eastern Standard Time
Subject: And one more

Dear Mr. Smith,

I promise not to write 5 times a day all year. I guess you can ignore it. I'm used to being ignored. But, if you ignore it, you won't get to hear all the exciting things that happen.

Like, tonight, we had chicken divan. That's what it said on the cafeteria menu sign.

That might not sound very exciting except these were boneless, skinless chicken breasts, the kind that cost $7.99 per pound. I may know people who buy boneless, skinless chicken breasts, but I'm certainly not related to any of them.

Of course, I didn't say anything. I took the chicken divan as if it was perfectly mundane.

A digression: I've always been on free lunch at school. It wasn't bad. I mean, I never got Lunchables or a bento box lovingly prepared by my mother like the rich kids, but on the other hand, I always had lunch. I went into the cafeteria, gave my number, and no one had to know my mom hadn't put the money in my account.

Then, one time in fourth grade, we had field day, and instead of going to the cafeteria, the PTA bought pizza and juice boxes and cupcakes, and there was enough for everyone, especially since most of the kids were so juiced about missing class and running around that they barely touched the pizza.

I was excited about pizza. We never got it at home unless it was frozen Totino's, but as I was going back for another slice, the teacher, Mrs. Mirabal, called my name and the names of some other kids from my neighborhood. I didn't want to lose my place in line, so I ignored her.

Mrs. Mirabal repeated, "Jacaranda?"

She gestured, and I saw one of the lunch ladies standing there with a tray that was, I guessed, mine. I shook my head. She said they were legally required to give us our free lunch even on field trips.

When she said "free lunch" I looked over at my friends, Vershona and Cristina. They'd stopped talking, so they'd definitely heard. Now they knew I had free lunch, and I knew they didn't. I took the tray, but my stomach hurt, and I didn't eat anything, not even the plastic cup of peaches that I usually liked so much I ate my friends' peaches too. It would be more dramatic to say I never ate peaches again because I was so upset, but I'm not in a position to turn down food. It just never tasted as good anymore.

Today, when I lined up behind Daisy, one of her friends, this guy named Blakely (that's his FIRST name), who is maybe the best-looking guy I've ever seen in person (picture a 16-year-old Chris Hemsworth), said, "Mmm, white mystery sauce! Anyone figure out what it is?"

Daisy shushed him. "You're going to give Jackie a bad impression of the food here."

"The food gives a bad impression of the food here," he said.

Daisy said it wasn't that bad. To me, she added, "Blakely's family flies to Scotland to eat fermented lamb with kelp."

I had no idea what those words even meant. Blakely laughed and said, "They didn't serve the lamb and the kelp together, Daisy."

I pretended to get the joke. At least, I thought they were joking. Do rich people like you eat kelp? I told them I was sure the chicken would be fine.

When I tasted it, it was juicy and soft and a million times better than anything from the school cafeteria in Miami. Still, I tried not to act like I enjoyed it too much or eat too fast or in any way act like someone who hadn't always had enough to eat. These were people who worried about their carb intake. I once ate bean burritos from Taco Bell every meal for a week because that was all we could afford. This was back when they were on the dollar menu.

But no one was watching me, so after a few minutes, I relaxed. It was a big reunion for Daisy's friends, who hadn't seen one another all summer.

In addition to Blakely, there was a girl named Shani, who played the drums, which I thought was cool, and her boyfriend, named David, a tall black guy with short dreads, who was in musical theater. They chattered away for a while, and then they all turned and looked at me.

"So what's your deal?" David asked.

I looked at him. I didn't want to discuss my "deal," considering it involved an incarcerated mom and a life without boneless chicken breasts.

"Are you rich, or are you a prodigy?" he asked.

I said I didn't think I was either.

"Everyone's one or the other," Blakely said. He explained that everyone there was either a rich kid with so-so talent whose parents could pay the tuition and justified sending them away because it was so artsy, or a prodigy whose parents scrimped and saved and got financial aid so they could go there. So, apparently, even the "poor" kids have enough money to afford some tuition. They also had parents who knew this place existed.

"So which are you?" David asked while Shani shushed him.

I laughed and said I definitely wasn't rich.

"So, a prodigy," David said. Then he started asking me how long I'd taken voice lessons, what kind of dance I did, and where I'd studied acting. To change the subject, I asked if they did anything special for the first night, like at Hogwarts.

They all laughed, and Daisy said, "They have the sorting ceremony tomorrow."

"But you're rooming with Phoebe, right?" Shani said. "So you must be Slytherin."

Blakely said Phoebe was definitely a Slytherin, and David told a story about how her mother called and complained when she didn't get a solo part in the musical, even though the family had endowed the school or something. He imitated her, making her sound like a snooty cartoon character. So I guessed Phoebe was one of those rich kids without talent. I'd started to ask him when I saw Daisy waving her hands wildly, and they all went silent. I turned. Phoebe was behind me.

"Hi, guys." Her eyes were a little pink, like she'd been crying. Daisy asked her to sit down, and Phoebe said she wouldn't want to interrupt our conversation. She glanced at David.

I knew she'd heard what he had said. She looked at me. I saw her eyes blaming me, even though I just got here.

I've had enemies before, and more often than not, it was because of something I didn't do. The boy who got stuck being partners on the bus because all his friends paired up without him. The girl who had her own room before they took on another foster kid. Not to mention all the people who somehow blamed me for stuff my mother did.

I didn't deserve those enemies, and I don't deserve this one. So I said, "Please sit with us. We're going to be suite mates."

She sat, mumbling something about guessing she had to sit somewhere.

They didn't have a sorting ceremony, but the headmistress, Miss Pike, made a speech welcoming everyone back and talking about the "exciting, diverse" campus and all the usual things principals everywhere talk about. Then there were performances. First was a string ensemble, well, one of the string ensembles, since they have three. They were incredible, and next, a vocal group performed. Phoebe got up for that, which I guessed was why she said she had to be there. It was a small group, an a cappella jazz ensemble of twelve guys and girls. They were amazing. It sounded like instruments, even though there weren't any. They were all really professional. Phoebe didn't have any solo lines until the last part of the medley, which was "Hallelujah" by Leonard Cohen. She sang the verse that ends, "I've seen your flag on the marble arch / And love is not a victory march / It's a cold and it's a broken Hallelujah." Mr. Smith, her voice was clear as a sunny day in June, and she put in all the anguish the lines needed and still sounded good enough to give me literal chills. I was sitting on my hard, wooden bench, slack-jawed, my throat closing from the beauty. It was that glorious.

She must have known she killed it too, because afterward, she actually had a pleasant expression on her face.

And I was thinking about what David had said, about the rich kids and the prodigies. I assumed Phoebe was the first type and I was the second. But if Phoebe was an example of the people without talent, what must the prodigies be like?

Whoa, it got real, real fast.

Phoebe is way better than I am. They probably all are, and when the school realizes it, they'll send me home.

I can justify that to myself by saying she's had more training than I have or more time to practice because she wasn't working at Publix or hiding from her mother's scrub boyfriends or moving from one sketchy apartment to another. That's all true. For sure, she's had more advantages. All of them have. But I still have to compete with them, and it's going to be hard. In my old school, I was special. In this school, everyone is special, and I'm just one of them—one with a lot less schooling too.

Can I even do this? Do I even belong here?

And, on that note, I'm going to sleep. In my own bed in my own room, all by myself for the first time in pretty much ever.

I hope they let me stay.

Love, Jacaranda

P.S. Are you Will Smith? I figure probably not, but I've been dying to ask. After all, you are rich enough to send a total stranger to school, so maybe . . .

To: Johnsmith247@dll.com
Date: September 8, 8:37 p.m. Eastern Standard Time
Subject: It just keeps getting realer

Dear Mr. Smith,

I'd like to tell you about my first day of classes. But, unfortunately, I have to write a 500-word essay about George Gershwin because I didn't know that he wrote the song I was singing. Because people apparently know that stuff here?

More tomorrow or whenever I come up for air.

Love, Jacaranda

To: Johnsmith247@dll.com
Date: September 10, 9:28 p.m. Eastern Standard Time
Subject: Update

Dear Mr. Smith,

Almost a week since I arrived at Midwestern Arts Academy. Every day, I take my regular classes (language arts, history, algebra, and French) in the morning. In the afternoons, I take:

Monday/Wednesday/Friday
    Period 5: Musical Theater Workshop
    Period 6: Dance (ballet on Monday, Broadway jazz on Wednesday and Friday)

Tuesday/Thursday
    Period 5: Drama
    Period 6: Music theory/class piano

I thought music theory or dance would be hardest, since I've never taken either. But they put me in beginning music theory with mostly ninth graders. It's a little embarrassing, but I'm learning. And I'm not even in the lowest dance class, because some people are just plain uncoordinated.

No, it's musical theater where I struggle.

Why?

Apparently, there are all these Broadway musicals everyone has seen and are *actually bored with* that I've barely heard of. Even if they are from Des Moines, Iowa, they all seem to have grown up taking weekend trips to New York to see plays like *Hamilton*, going to the national tour that came to their town, or at least having Tony Award–watching parties and downloading all the albums from the nominated shows.

Can I tell you a terrible secret? I've never seen *Wicked*. Or *Phantom of the Opera* either. Or *Les Mis*. But especially *Wicked*. Some people here have seen it seven or eight times. They saw it in utero. I'm dying to see it, but I'm pretending I already have.

Once, in Miami, we went on a field trip to see *West Side Story* at a local theater. I could barely concentrate because Christian Miranda was kicking my seat the whole time, and it was so loud with all those school groups there, but I still sang, "I like to be in America, okay by me in America" for a week until my mother's scrub-of-the-week boyfriend yelled at me to stop . . . or else.

On the first day of class, the teacher, who told us to call him Harry, an older black guy with a voice that makes everything sound like Shakespeare, told us the titles of the musicals we'll be doing scenes from. The only one I've heard of is *My Fair Lady*. He said we all had to sing for him, and that we should have an audition piece ready at a moment's notice, in case we had an opportunity.

Then he went around the room and asked for the titles. Most people had something ready. I hadn't done any Broadway stuff, but last year I sang "Someone to Watch Over Me" in a school concert, so when Harry got to me, I told him I'd sing that.

"From . . . ?" he asked, his voice booming like he was onstage.

It took me a second to realize he meant what show the song was from. No clue. I tried to visualize the sheet music my teacher had copied for me. Nothing.

"Do you *at least* know the composer's name?" Harry said, his voice rising on "least."

Behind me, I heard David whisper something that sounded like "gherkin." Which made no sense because a gherkin is a kind of pickle (this is Publix knowledge here). But maybe the pickle was named after the person who discovered it. So I said, "Gherkin?"

Harry scoffed. "What Mr. Sanders whispered was 'Gershwin,' one of the most widely known American composers, of whom you've apparently never heard." Then he told me I must never sing a song in this class or anywhere else without knowing the name of the show, the composer, and the lyricist.

People giggled and this girl named Brooke, a brunette with big eyes who sits behind me, whispered she couldn't believe I didn't know that. I said, "Yes, sir," trying not to cry.

He made me write a 500-word report on George Gershwin, no copying out of Wikipedia, because now he thinks I don't know better. I'm attaching the report in case you're interested in knowing more about Mr. Gershwin.

After class, David came up to me with this other guy, Owen,

and a girl named Nina, who had sung that day in class. She sang a song called "Show Off," and she also tap-danced! David said, "Don't worry about it. That guy's a jerk* to everyone. I wanted to go home my first week."

I would have wanted to go home, if I'd had a home to go to. As it was, I wanted to go back to my room, to my bed with its lavender-and-white sheets, and I wanted to stay there until they kicked me out for not attending class.

I probably shouldn't tell you this.

I sighed and said, "Everyone else knew who wrote their song."

Nina replied, "You went to public school, right?"

I could have let this be the reason for my cluelessness, let myself be the poor, pathetic public school kid. But it kind of made me mad. *Most* people go to public school. They can't all be ignorant. And, if they are, the government should give schools more money so that they can teach things like drama and music, because those things are important. I mean, how often do you hear someone say, "I stayed in school because I loved math so much"?**

So I changed the subject. I told Nina she was incredible. Everyone who sang that day was. "I'm kind of scared to perform Wednesday," I admitted.

"Don't be," Owen said. "You wouldn't be here if you didn't deserve it. I mean, your family didn't donate a building, did they?"

I knew he was talking about Phoebe, who, by the way, was *not* one of the ones laughing when I said "gherkin." She acts like I

---

* "Jerk" was not the word he used.

** I had a math teacher who said this, but we all thought he was weird.

don't even exist, though. The nights that I haven't been embroiled in a research project, Daisy and I have been going to dorm activities, like cookie-baking or movie night. Phoebe never goes. She didn't even want a cookie.

Anyway, I told Owen my family didn't even have enough money to donate a port-a-potty.

And I didn't end up singing Wednesday, which means I'm singing tomorrow, which means I should go to sleep, but Daisy is knocking on the door.

I'll write more over the weekend. Enjoy reading up on Gershwin!

Love, Jacaranda

To: Johnsmith247@dll.com
Date: September 11, 3:01 p.m. Eastern Standard Time
Subject: I'm sorry!

Dear Mr. Smith,

By now, I assume you've heard from Vanessa about our escape (or, at least, escapade). How bad did the school make it sound? Did we seem like drunken deviants? Because that is not the case, though I'm deeply sorry and drowning in a pool of self-loathing for disappointing you.

Here's the whole story:

As you know, I was sitting (innocently) at my desk at 9:30, planning an early bedtime, when Daisy pounded on the door and called my name.

I opened it to find both Daisy and Phoebe standing there, which was certainly a surprise. As I said, Phoebe hasn't even acknowledged me since the first day.

Daisy was stammering nervously and said she had to show me something downstairs. Phoebe nudged her and said, "Stop acting weird."

I asked if I should get dressed, since I was wearing a T-shirt and pajama pants. Daisy told me to put on shoes and take a jacket. I figured it wouldn't be long since our curfew is 10:00.

When we reached the lobby, five other new juniors were there, along with a few other girls, including Shani and Nina. I guess I was the last one, because once I was there, they walked outside. I noticed that no one was at the desk. Shani had offered to watch the door while Angie took a cigarette break. When we got outside, Phoebe and Nina and some of the others were holding bandannas.

"Time for secret junior initiation!" Nina said.

"What?" one of the other new juniors asked.

Nina explained that they have all sorts of rituals for new freshmen, but since we'd missed them, they came up with something special for the new girls in the junior/senior dorm. This sounded cool but also sketchy. Wouldn't we get in trouble? And what were the blindfolds for?

But Daisy was there. She whispered, "Don't worry. It's not a big deal," and I trusted her. Besides, they couldn't kidnap all of us, could they? So I let Phoebe put a purple bandanna on me. It smelled nice, sort of lemony. I wanted to ask her why she didn't like me, but of course, I couldn't. Acting super needy doesn't make people like you.

Also, I've learned that, sometimes, someone's in a bad mood and it has nothing to do with me.

We started walking. I tried to peek, but it was dark, and I couldn't see anything. Daisy put her arm around my shoulders. I knew it was her because she whispered in my ear. I started thinking about all the news stories I'd read about fraternity pledges drinking themselves to death in hazing rituals. But this is ARTS SCHOOL. That couldn't happen here. Still, I decided right then and there that I wasn't going to drink. (That's a good thing, right?) I asked Daisy if we'd get in trouble for breaking curfew, and she said she thought the school sort of knew about it.

I wasn't sure, but I wanted to make friends and have a "bonding experience." We walked pretty far without hearing any sounds. The ground was soft, so I guessed we were in the woods. Did I mention there are woods all around the campus? It was cool but not yet cold. Still, Daisy helped me zip my hoodie.

I relaxed a little. Daisy was probably right. The school must know. Finally, we reached the road. We walked about five minutes more, and then Phoebe ripped off my bandanna. "We're here!"

We were in front of a place called Hobie's Hideaway I'd heard people talking about at school. It wasn't so much a bar as a hangout where people went on weekends. I saw a sign outside, saying "Karaoke Thursday 9–12."

Was this my initiation, karaoke? People at my old school, especially in chorus, sometimes talked about doing karaoke at parties, but since I moved a bunch of times, I was never invited. I always thought I'd rock at it.

Except I hoped I didn't get expelled from school.

But what could I do at this point? Call someone? I didn't have my phone. Also, it sounded fun. So I pushed back my trepidation and went in.

Only when I saw the sort-of crowd (maybe twenty people, some dressed up in special outfits) did I remember I had on pajama bottoms with hot pink chameleons on them! I wished the chameleons could fade into the background.

A girl was onstage, singing the song from *Titanic* badly. I thought she should go down with the ship. But she got pretty good applause after, so what do I know?

We found seats at a long table in back. There were twelve or thirteen of us in all. Then Phoebe said, "Who's first?"

This girl who called herself Lucky, a creative writing major with purple hair and a nose ring, said, "We have to SING? I can't sing."

"Can we do it in pairs?" I asked Phoebe.

"I thought you were supposed to be so good," she said.

I don't know where she heard that. I certainly didn't say I was good. But I thought maybe I could help Lucky. Phoebe agreed— grudgingly—and Lucky and I went over to the corner to consult. A girl with very long blond hair who I think plays the violin lined up by the DJ. She kept saying she might as well get it over with because it was going to be bad.

Lucky looked unlucky, so I said maybe she didn't have to sing at all, just dance.

She shook her head and, at that moment, I knew what I was going to do. I said, "How about walking? Can you walk like this?" I imitated walking in kind of a stylized way. Lucky said she guessed so, so I showed her a box step, which we'd been learning in Broadway jazz.

"It would be better if we had a third girl," I said.

Phoebe overheard me and said, "No way. You're not all going together."

I told her it would look more balanced with three of us. Then, getting brave, I said, "Then you do it with us. You can dance. I've seen you." Because she's in my Broadway jazz class, and I think she's in the highest level for ballet.

"I don't do girl squads," Phoebe said.

This is actually something we have in common, but I was trying to be friendly. So I turned to Daisy and asked if she'd do it instead.

"Oooh, what are you doing?" she asked. "'All About That Bass'? 'Miss Independent'?"

The first girl was onstage now, singing "Single Ladies," so I told Daisy my idea and that they'd just have to dance behind me.

She turned to Phoebe. "You should so do this with us," she said, then added, "Pleeeeze!"

Phoebe turned away. Daisy gave up then and grabbed Lucky's hand to go find the video on YouTube.

Onstage, the girl was on her third repeat of "If you like it, then you should've put a ring on it." A girl named Kira from our group was behind her, so I got in line. I asked Kira what she was doing.

She giggled and said, "'Shake It Off,'" explaining that her older sister used to sing it all the time. The girl onstage finished her final "Oh-oh-oh, oh-oh-oh." Then Kira went up.

Daisy and Lucky joined me. "We're good," Daisy said. "You do your thing in front, and we'll try to stay together." She was jumping up and down from excitement, which made me excited too. Then it was our turn. I told the DJ my song: "These Boots Are Made for Walkin'." Too bad I was wearing Nikes.

"Do you know the lyrics?" he asked.

"By heart," I said.

"Nice pants, by the way." He pointed to the chameleons.

I went and sat on the stage. I said, "I'd like to dedicate this to my mother!"

That got a laugh. Daisy and Lucky got on both sides behind me and started pretending to walk in rhythm.

Weirdly, I know all the lyrics to the song, a sort of girl-power 1960s anthem about a woman walking out on a cheating man, because, when I was little, it was one of my mother's favorites. Any time she had a bad, lying, cheating, drugged-out boyfriend, she'd walk around our apartment singing it. I sang along. It is one of my best memories of her.

Maybe if she'd kept those walking boots in mind, she wouldn't be doing time.

But I missed my mom when I belted out: "One of these days these boots are gonna walk all over you!"

Daisy and Lucky were doing a good job, acting like go-go dancers, and the older people in the audience were whooping, saying stuff like "Go, girl!" and "Shake it!"

And right during the musical interlude, where the three of us go-go'd around the stage, I noticed some grown-ups had joined our group.

Specifically, Angie and Headmistress Pike.

Uh-oh.

But I figured there was nothing else to do but finish at the top of my lungs (to generous applause, by the way). Miss Pike was already lining everyone up. When I came down, she said, "Start walking, boots!"

Of course, you know the rest. We got dragged back to campus in humiliation. And this was not, in fact, a tradition everyone knew about. Someone had called the police and said they'd seen us being frog-marched to a karaoke club blindfolded. Luckily, the police recognized what was happening and called the school.

They called everyone's parents but mine. For me, they called Vanessa (not the worst possible consequence—she sounded like she was out at a club when I talked to her). The word "expulsion" was thrown around. But finally they said we'd only be suspended for one day and "confined to our dorm" on weekends for a month. Plus, we have to clean up the cafeteria after dinner. And we got a l-o-n-g lecture about the wonderful opportunity we were being given, so we couldn't do anything like that again, or we'd be expelled.

I was in tears during this, because it's particularly true due to my situation. But Phoebe spoke up. "It wasn't the new girls' fault. We dragged them there from their beds. I mean, look at her." And she gestured at my pajamas.

Miss Pike said we should have refused to go, which was impossible. But I calmed down and said I would never do anything wrong again. Daisy squeezed my hand and, when I looked at her, she gestured to her feet and pretended to be walking.

It was totally worth it, but I hope you aren't disappointed in me.

Anyway, that's why I still haven't sung in Harry's class. Hopefully Monday.

Love, Jacaranda

To: Johnsmith247@dll.com
Date: September 13, 4:16 p.m. Eastern Standard Time
Subject: Your way-too-generic name

Dear Mr. Smith,

Do I have to keep calling you Mr. Smith?

Forgive me if that's a rude question. But seriously. It's not very creative. As someone who never had a father or uncle or even a cousin to write to, I'd rather not write to a mysterious Mr. Smith. Plus, I tell everyone here I'm writing to a relative, because these rich kids all have relatives. When you're rich, everyone wants to be related to you.

When I was little, one of my friends had this Uncle Bob she talked about all the time. I used to wish I had an uncle (I have an aunt I lived with when my mom first got arrested, but you can guess how that worked out). But I don't have an uncle or a doting aunt, just you, who probably doesn't read this anyway.

If you're not Will Smith, are you Sam Smith?

I'm signing this "Best wishes" because it's hard to love an inanimate object.

Best wishes, Jacaranda Abbott

To: Johnsmith247@dll.com
Date: September 15, 5:01 p.m. Eastern Standard Time
Subject: Your rebel beneficiary

Dear Mr. Smith,

I'm famous! Well, again. But this time, I'm famous as the rebel who blew out of MAA in the middle of the night and led a girl gang to a bar to sing onstage. Very little of the story is true, but it makes me sound cool, so I let it go. Several people have asked me to perform "These Boots Are Made for Walkin'" in the hallways, the cafeteria, outside.

I've become intimately familiar with both the cafeteria dishwasher and the girls from that night. We've bonded, scraping plates and sweeping the floors. Someday, when we're once again allowed to leave campus, we plan to go shopping or to Starbucks to get a Frappuccino.

And I finally sang in Harry's class. I thought I was going to be the only one to sing on Monday, but it turned out that Phoebe also hadn't sung yet. So Harry pulled us both aside and said, "Which one of you young convicts wants to sing first?"

I looked at Phoebe. She looked down at the floor. I remembered her glorious voice on "Hallelujah" the first day. I've heard enough of my classmates to know that some are better than I am, and some are not. Phoebe's definitely in the first category, so why follow her? I told him, "I'll go first" at the very same moment she said it.

Finally, Harry pointed to Phoebe.

I sat. Phoebe walked up to the front of the room. She looked kind of terrified. She drew in a long, shaky breath and stared at each one of us individually. Then she glanced down.

Harry said, "Whenever you're ready, Miss Hodgkins."

Another shaky breath. Then she said, "I'll be singing 'Glitter and Be Gay' from *Candide* by Leonard Bernstein." The accompanist started the piano part, and a second later, this voice came out, singing, "Glitter and be gay / That's the part I play / Here I am, Oh sorry chance!"

Maybe she was supposed to look miserable. The song was about how sad she was. She even sobbed a bit on a line that ended with "bitter circumstance."

But her voice, Mr. Smith! It was like nothing I've ever heard. Okay, maybe Mariah Carey back when she was good. It went up, up, up to the stratosphere. She was laughing, "Ha-ha!" and it sounded like opera, only funnier, and then she went down to her lowest range, and that was strong too. There was a spoken-word section, where she bemoaned her cruel fate. Then the music came back on, and she was laughing again. This was the hardest song I've ever heard, and after the momentary terror, she was singing it like a boss, ending with a series of incredibly high notes, one after the other.

Finally, it was over, and I burst into applause. I mean, she's like a tall Kristin Chenoweth (see, I'm learning—I now know who that is). The rest of the applause was only polite, which I didn't understand. I mean, sure she's a pain, but she's REMARKABLE.

But maybe that's why they don't like her. Jealousy is a thing around here, in the caring, accepting womb that is MAA.

I went up to sing next, which, at this point, was anticlimactic. I introduced it as "Someone to Watch Over Me" by George Gershwin from *Oh, Kay!* (Again, I'm learning.)

Harry smiled encouragingly.

Mr. Smith, I know the song is about a girl who wants a husband or at least a boyfriend, but it made me think of you. The lyrics talk about a shepherd for a lost lamb, and I feel like *I'm* the lost lamb, and you're the shepherd, keeping me from being eaten by wolves. What would I have done without you?

Anyway, I thought about all that while I was singing, and I tried to think about other things, *singing* things, like doing a cool run on the part that goes, "To my heart, he carries the key—he-e-e-e-e carries the key!" What I tried not to think of was Phoebe, who was slumped in her chair, right in my sight line, in abject misery. She couldn't possibly have thought she was bad! She had to be doing it for attention! And suddenly, jealousy hit me too. How dare she be so good and act like she's not! I looked away and finished. Owen and David stomped their feet in support, and David even whistled. But some of the girls were doing golf claps. I sat with a smile.

Harry said he would put up the list of who was in what scene by the end of the week. Everyone started buzzing about who would get which part, but I don't know any of them, so I wasn't in on it.

After class, Phoebe bolted before I could tell her how well she'd done. We had dance, and since it was ballet day, I didn't see her again until dinner. Then she avoided eye contact. What is with that girl?

In music theory, we're learning major scales and key signatures. I'm practicing scales, but it's slow going. The practice rooms are across campus, so it's hard to go there at night. Most people in my theory class took piano as children, so I'm way behind. But I'm working very hard!

In other news, I saw my first leaf starting to turn red, and it made me feel a little giddy. Soon they'll all turn, and the campus will be a riot of color.

Thank you for sending me here!

Now I'm going to dinner and to sweep the floors and scrape plates.

Love, Jacaranda

To: Johnsmith247@dll.com
Date: September 16, 8:17 p.m. Eastern Standard Time
Subject: My mother

Dear Mr. Smith,

I haven't written to my mother since I came here. Before I left, I wrote as if everything was perfectly normal, as if I wasn't flying across the country to come to this school and I didn't have a new guardian and a benefactor and a bed with lavender-and-white sheets.

Why haven't I told her? It's not like she can do anything about it. Yet it's hard to sit here at my nice desk in my room with a lavender duvet and think of her reading my letter on her prison bunk.

But I'm going to write to her tonight. As soon as I finish this email.

And write a three-paragraph essay in French.

And do 30 algebra problems.

And study the key signatures for music theory. Daisy told me a funny mnemonic device to memorize the order of sharps on the staff. It's FCGDAEB. Fat Cows Get Drunk After Eating Babies.

This makes no sense if you don't know music, but it's definitely helpful!

And watch *The Sound of Music* . . . which is three hours long.

Maybe I'll write to her tomorrow.

I miss her sometimes. I miss having a mother.

Love, Jacaranda

To: Johnsmith247@dll.com
Date: September 17, 8:25 p.m. Eastern Standard Time
Subject: I've never eaten a lobster

Dear Mr. Smith,

Are you Kevin Smith? This is an important question, because if you're a famous filmmaker, you could probably help me in my career.

Nvm.

Today, after dinner, Lucky came to my room to work on a history project. She took in the bare walls and pristine bookshelves. I have one poster, and it says, "What would Beyoncé do?" I'll buy more, but I'll never match Daisy's walls. She has collages of every family vacation since she was five. Most other rooms are the same. Lucky said, "Your room's so empty."

I waved it off, saying I didn't like having a lot of possessions. I left out the fact that, if you'd moved as much as I have, you didn't let stuff weigh you down.

Lucky nodded. "Oh, yeah, my parents weren't into stuff either. Like when I was little, they preferred giving experiences as gifts, instead of a lot of Barbies or whatever. They didn't want me to get spoiled."

No risk of that with me. When I asked what she meant by experiences, she said they went on vacations or to the opera or sent her to writing camp.

So, basically, they took her to Europe instead of buying her a $10 Barbie. Barbies are cheap. "Experiences" are expensive. I've had a ton of Barbies. Rich people love donating them to toy drives. But you can't get theater tickets from Toys for Tots.

Don't worry. I didn't say any of that. I probably didn't think it until after she left.

There are so many things everyone here takes for granted. I'm not even talking about how none of them ever had the power turned off, had to remember not to flush because there was only one flush per toilet since no one paid the water bill, or saw anyone shoot up. They all grew up watching television shows like *Shake It Up* and *Austin & Ally*. They've all seen every episode of *SpongeBob*. They've all had Netflix passwords since forever and cell phones since they were nine. None of them have ever not had unlimited data or not repaired a cracked screen. Some of them get a new phone when the screen cracks!

They've all eaten crab, lobster, and sushi. They know how to pronounce "quinoa."

They've all seen *The Nutcracker* at Christmastime, even the Jewish kids.

They've all taken piano lessons, ballet lessons, or been on a team, and they were all in Girl or Boy Scouts.

I'm trying to improve myself. I used part of your allowance to buy myself Amazon Prime so I can watch the movie versions of the musicals people talk about. That way, I'll be less ignorant. I watched the entire works of Rodgers and Hammerstein. *The Sound of Music* is my favorite. How can people here think it's boring? I cried when Captain von Trapp sang "Edelweiss" and was so scared when they were fleeing the Nazis! *Carousel*, on the other hand, I could do without. A woman returning to an abusive man and saying it doesn't hurt when he hits her comes too close to my reality. After *The King and I*, *South Pacific*, and *Oklahoma!*, I watched *Sweeney Todd*, which kept me awake, and *Hairspray*, which was adorable and empowering and had Queen Latifah in it, and *Les Misérables*. Who knew Wolverine could sing? Every night, after homework and practice, I see another movie. Tonight, it's *My Fair Lady*. We're doing a scene from it in class. I stay up late and use earbuds so no one can hear.

The first weekend I'm allowed to leave, I hope to finally eat some kind of shellfish.

Wouldn't it be embarrassing if I was allergic?

Love, Jacaranda

To: Johnsmith247@dll.com
Date: September 17, 11:09 p.m. Eastern Standard Time
Subject: You are Henry Higgins

Dear Mr. Smith,

OMG, I love *My Fair Lady*! It is like my life story. Have you seen it? Of course you have. Maybe you're even old enough to remember when it premiered.

In case you haven't, it's the story of Eliza Doolittle, a poor flower seller on the streets of London with a hideous cockney accent. (Okay, that part isn't exactly like me.) One day, Henry Higgins, a fancy linguistics professor, sees her and bets his friend, Colonel Pickering, that he can teach her to speak like a lady and take her to a fancy ball with no one suspecting she isn't a princess. He moves her in with him, gives her beautiful clothes, and fulfills his mission. She's perfect at the ball! Then Eliza gets her feelings hurt because Higgins acts like she didn't do anything, like it was all about him. She storms off to marry a silly but rich guy named Freddy because what else can she do?

But there's music! And costumes! When Eliza goes to the race-track, everyone is dressed in black and white and fancy hats. And when Freddy falls in love with Eliza, he sits in front of Higgins's house day after day, singing about how beautiful the street is, because she lives there (which they didn't call stalking then). Eliza dances with Higgins then sings about how she wishes she could have danced, danced, danced all night. Good thing no one could see me dance around the room!

The ending is enigmatic. Eliza is clearly in love with Henry Higgins, and he with her. But they come from different worlds. It ends with her going back to his house, and I guess most people assume they live happily ever after. But I'm not sure. When Eliza goes back, Higgins doesn't say he loves her or admit she triumphed at the ball. He says, "Where the devil are my slippers?" as if he just expects her to slip into staying with him, neither flower seller nor wife. It's a bit sad. Just like real life.

I would love to play Eliza in the scene we're doing, but she has to have a beautiful voice, a voice like Phoebe's. So I bet I won't, even though I am Eliza in my soul!

It's after midnight, and I should go to sleep, but "My head's too light to try to set it down!" That's from the play too.

Love, Jacaranda

To: Johnsmith247@dll.com

Date: September 18, 7:15 a.m. Eastern Standard Time

Subject: Phoebe

Dear Mr. Smith,

Remember how I said I loved *My Fair Lady* and wanted to play Eliza?

So this morning, I wake up to Phoebe SHOUTING into her cell phone in the bathroom between our rooms. There's very bad reception in there, so even though shouting doesn't actually help, people still do.

And what she was shouting was, "*MY FAIR LADY* . . . YES, THAT'S WHAT HE SAID . . . WELL, WHO ELSE WOULD BE ELIZA? THEY'RE ALL BELTERS. BELTERS! HE HAD TO HAVE PICKED IT FOR ME. I WAS BORN TO PLAY THAT PART."

There was a long pause and then Phoebe tried to lower her voice, maybe realizing the whole dorm shouldn't hear her. "No . . . No, I did fine . . . I SAID I DID FINE. I DIDN'T FLIP OUT . . . YES, I'M SURE. I DIDN'T FLIP OUT THIS TIME . . . Forget it. I can't hear you. Stop." And then she must have hung up, because I heard water running.

So, Phoebe thinks she's going to be Eliza. And she's probably right.

But I wish she was wrong.

Love, Jacaranda

To: Johnsmith247@dll.com
Date: September 18, 9:31 p.m. Eastern Standard Time
Subject: Exciting news!

Dear Person-Who-Is-Going-to-Be-So-Surprised,

Guess who is going to play Eliza Doolittle in a scene from *My Fair Lady* in the winter scenes production? If you guessed Phoebe Pendleton-Hodgkins because her voice is so perfect and she's so beautiful, you're . . .

SPOILER SPACE

WRONG!

We're doing the scene where Eliza finally learns to speak correctly, which includes the songs "Poor Professor Higgins" and "The Rain in Spain," and I AM PLAYING ELIZA! Owen is Henry Higgins, and David is playing Colonel Pickering. We all sing together, and we dance!

Phoebe was so sure she was going to be Eliza. But, in fact, she has an even bigger song, a solo from a musical called *Bandstand*. It's about veterans with post-traumatic stress disorder and is depressing, so perfect for her.

We are also doing several group numbers. I'm in one from *Titanic* (which I'm guessing is about the *Titanic*) and another from a show called *Something Rotten!*. But no one has more than one solo part, and some people don't have any. That girl, Brooke, the basic bitch who practically wet herself laughing when I didn't know my composer's name, was giving me side-eye in class, and Phoebe won't even look at me.

I hope you're proud!

Love, Eliza Doolittle

To: Johnsmith247@dll.com
Date: September 22, 9:13 p.m. Eastern Standard Time
Subject: Low of 50, high of 72 today!

Dear Mr. Smith,

Do you ever lie in bed in the morning, thinking, only to realize when you actually wake up that every single thought you had was part of a dream? That it wasn't real at all?

That's how I feel every day here. It's surreal that I was in Miami, leading a perfectly ordinary, somewhat-below-average life, and now, all of a sudden, I'm here!

Today at dinner, some poor freshie girl dropped her entire tray full of stir-fry vegetables and brown rice and an open milk container onto the floor. She was in tears, and people were doing the thing where they applauded, which I guess is the same in all school cafeterias. But I decided to walk right up to her. I recognized her from music theory class. I told her she should get a new dinner, and I'd take care of it. Then I told Daisy we should get some cleaning supplies because other people (coughPhoebecough) were pretending not to notice.

"Ugh, how are we going to get all this up?" she said. There were peas rolling all over the place and a river of milk heading for the cafeteria door.

Fortunately, I'm an expert on cleaning spills. I bet you didn't know that about me. I told Daisy we should get a couple of towels first, sop up the milk, and then we'd worry about the rice. Daisy looked at me like I was some kind of cleaning guru, but I said, "Oh, this is no big deal. At least there's no broken glass." Then I started to tell her about how, when I worked at Publix, this lady knocked into a display of red wine and broke three bottles.

But halfway in, I remembered that I wasn't Jacaranda, who worked at Publix. I was Jackie, who was leading a Witness Protection Program–like existence. I told everyone my parents are overseas (lots of people's parents are) to explain why I'm not going home for breaks!

Daisy looked shocked and said, "You worked at a supermarket?"

Oops. I started to hem and haw, but Daisy gushed about how cool it was that I'd been "allowed" to work. I guess she assumed it was a summer job. She's never done anything but babysit. She wanted to work over the summer, but her parents forced her to go to SAT prep camp, then on a family vacation to visit relatives in, like, five different states. This sounded great to me, having relatives who actually want you to stay with them! But, of course, I didn't say that. I commiserated with Daisy about her sad, sad life.

So now she's convinced my parents are cool hippies who want me to spend time with the little people.

While we cleaned, she started asking more questions about my family, but I was able to change the subject, quickly asking her how she got interested in playing the flute.

"It sounds silly," she said. "I had a lisp when I was little, and it made me shy. So my mom wanted me to do cheerleading to improve my confidence. But I'd rather have died." She made a face, and I agreed that I'd rather have died too. "But my mother still insisted I had to do an activity, so the next week, when the music teacher spoke to our third-grade class, I declared I wanted to play the flute. I said it would help me make friends, and that playing a wind instrument might help with my tongue placement. I was totally lying, but it actually all happened."

She joined the band and went to the summer camp they have at MAA. She made first chair, and after a few years, she auditioned for the school, and they offered her a scholarship.

So Daisy is one of the gifted middle class (okay, upper middle class), which is still a higher class than the working-at-a-supermarket class like me, but lower class than Phoebe. That's nice to know. But, when Daisy asked me how I ended up here, I said it was similar, that I loved singing and auditioned and got a scholarship. Then I became intensely interested in picking up stray grains of rice.

So the good news is, I'm making friends while being a drudge in the cafeteria. The bad news is, they don't know who I really am.

Do you think they'd like me if they did?

Love, Jacaranda

P.S. I realize Vanessa said I could write you a monthly update. But I'm just so excited to tell someone all my news! I don't want to be a burden, though, so I won't write until at least mid-October.

To: Johnsmith247@dll.com
Date: October 15, 7:02 a.m. Eastern Standard Time
Subject: Updates!

Dear Mr. Smith,

HELLO, STRANGER! LOTS to catch up on! But I know you're most interested in hearing about my studies, so I'll tell you the basics first.

In algebra and American history, we're working on . . . well, I won't bore you.

In French, we are learning about French-speaking countries and writing reports on them in French. Right now, I'm learning about Belgium. They're known for their waffles. I'm attaching my report in case you're interested. And speak French.

In language arts, we're reading *Death of a Salesman*, because we're not already reading enough plays. It's very sad. Have you read it? Willy Loman commits suicide so his son, Biff, can have opportunities. I wish I had a dad like that. I mean, not one who committed suicide, but one who loves me. Or one at all.

We're learning about intervals in music theory. An interval is the distance between two musical notes. So, C to E is a major third because there are one, two, three notes (CDE). They taught us different songs for each interval, to help us remember. Like a major third up is the first two notes of "Kumbaya," and a major third down is the first notes of "Summertime" (by Gershwin). I don't think I'll ever remember all this!

In drama class, we do a lot of improvisation, which I've never done before. Everyone else has done it since preschool.

Freeze and Justify is a game where two people start a scene and, once they get into a funny position, someone yells, "Freeze!" and takes someone's place to start a different scene. Lots of bathroom humor. I've been shy, but last week, when David pretended to do a karate kick, I yelled, "Freeze!" and took his place with Nina. I stuck my leg way up in the air.

I said, "Doctor, I can't get out of this position. I start a new job Monday!"

"What's your new job?" Nina said.

"I'm a . . ." I hopped around a few times, trying to think of a funny job. Finally I said, "I'm a phlebotomist—I take blood!" I stabbed at the air, like a doctor with a needle.

Nina started yanking on my leg. I shrieked and pretended to kick her in the head. Everyone laughed, and the drama teacher, Mr. Adams, a sweet, chubby-faced man, said, "Very good, Ms. Abbott. You're getting the hang of it!"

In musical theater, I'm learning the tango for "The Rain in Spain." Our scene is adorable. Everyone says so. Well, everyone but you-know-who, who came up to me last week and said, "Harry says he gave me *Bandstand* because he wanted to challenge me."

So, clearly, she'd complained to him about me getting Eliza.

She kept going. "Yeah, he knows I can sing Eliza. But 'Welcome Home' has a bigger range, plus it's more dramatic. It's really a stretch for me."

I told her it sounded like we both got the perfect thing for us. I didn't get salty and say what I really thought—that maybe Harry didn't think Phoebe would be realistic as a lovable underdog.

In ballet, we're learning *grand jetés*. It's a kind of leap where you do a split in the air. My room is not big enough to practice. I learned that the hard way.

The leaves have turned a glorious shade of orange. It's so beautiful I want to sit in a tree.

There, now you're all caught up.

Oh, and I wrote to my mother. Just yesterday.

Love, Jacaranda

To: Johnsmith247@dll.com
Date: October 15, 8:17 p.m. Eastern Standard Time
Subject: What I wrote my mother

Dear Mr. Smith,

You probably wonder why I waited so long to write to her. Maybe you think I have no heart.

But I do. Which makes it hard for me to write about something wonderful happening to me when I know nothing good is happening to her. All the things I write to you about, school and friends and chicken divan and even getting in trouble, probably sound like heaven compared to her life. They definitely sound like heaven compared to my old life.

When my mother was first arrested, she was in a correctional facility (fancy name for jail) in Miami. I'd seen this place on TV when some rock star was arrested for DUI on South Beach. My aunt took me to visit.

I remember staring at the massive, gray, windowless building that looked like the Death Star in the Star Wars movies, with barbed-wire fences all around. I remember wanting yet not wanting to go in. I brought my school ID, to prove who I was. And there were all these requirements for what we could wear, like certain colors so we wouldn't look like prisoners or guards, and I had to have shoes with straps, not flip-flops. My aunt complained 'cause she had to buy me sneakers, which I needed anyway. I'd just started wearing a bra then, and I remember they said it couldn't have underwire.

The smell was like old sweat and hopelessness. My mother looked happy to see me but also unhappy because she knew I'd be leaving and she'd be staying. She said we'd be together soon. That was five years ago.

I miss her.

After she got sentenced, she got moved to a prison upstate, and my aunt stopped being my guardian, so I never got to see her again. I've seen TV shows about prisons, like *Orange Is the New Black,* and I wonder if it's like that. I'm guessing it's not a comedy.

And I know for sure she isn't having chicken divan.

So the reason it took me so long to write was because it took a while to actually compose the letter. I had to make the most wonderful thing that's ever happened to me sound not-so-good.

Also, it's easier not to think about where she is. Otherwise, I feel guilty about being happy.

Love, Jacaranda

To: Johnsmith247@dll.com
Date: October 18, 11:08 p.m. Eastern Standard Time
Subject: I've been out with a guy!

Dear Mr. Smith,

Maybe you're not interested in hearing this kind of thing. I mean, I know you sent me to school, so probably you're just concerned with my education. Or maybe you're some old guy who doesn't want to hear about my love life. If so, delete this.

But I have to tell you for the simple reason that I can't tell anyone else. You see, it's a secret. I'll explain later. Also, you probably don't even read my letters, so you're safe.

The guy is Phoebe's cousin, John Jarvis Pendleton III! What a mouthful! Maybe you've heard of him? I hadn't, but apparently he is quite well known as a 17-year-old "eligible bachelor," a philanthropist, and computer genius. He laughed at all this, saying people only say that because of who his father is, but I'm getting ahead of myself.

Let me start at the beginning.

I was in my room, studying for my music theory test, using the keyboard you were nice enough to send after I whined about my inadequacies in piano. (Thank you!) I was playing intervals over and over. A perfect fourth sounds like the opening notes of the "Wedding March," so I was playing, "Here comes . . . here comes . . . here comes . . ." over and over. I was moving on to the tritone, which sounds like the opening notes of *The Simpsons* theme (where they sing "The Simp-sons") when I became aware of some fairly loud pounding on the bathroom door (this is how we communicate now—one of us goes into the bathroom and knocks on the bedroom door on the other side), and someone else beating equally loudly on my front door.

I opened the bathroom. Daisy was there, looking annoyed.

I gestured to the keyboard. She's been helping me with theory. Walking through my room to the other door, she told me Phoebe had a cousin visiting, and he wanted to take us to tea. Not coffee. Tea! Can you imagine? He insisted he wanted to take *all* Phoebe's suitemates, possibly as a buffer between him and Phoebe. Believe me, I sympathized. I started to ask why I'd want to have tea with Phoebe's cousin when Phoebe herself barely speaks to me. But then Daisy threw open the door, and I stopped talking.

I looked up, way up, and met the nicest eyes I've ever seen.

I didn't know that he was an eligible-bachelor-multimillionaire-genius-philanthropist yet. Phoebe mentioned that in the first 5 minutes, though. And to his credit, Jarvis tried to stop her. But, based on that and his looks, this guy should definitely have his own reality show. I respect that he doesn't. I suppose not everyone would think he's handsome. He's very tall, slim, and long-legged, with sandy hair and eyes the color of the sky after it rains, when the blue struggles to come through the gray. His eyes are a bit closer together than is considered ideal, but that flaw adds to his charm. Also charming was the way he held out his hand like it was a business meeting and said, "Jarvis Pendleton. Pleased to meet you."

"She knows who you are, Jarvis," Phoebe protested.

"How would she when we've never met?" Jarvis said. I took his hand. His fingers were slender but strong.

It was very. Very. Nice to meet him. He smiled, and I could tell he was sweet and modest, nothing like Phoebe. I assumed he didn't know how awful she was.

During the elevator ride, Phoebe recapped his stats and accomplishments. She called him "Kardashian-rich" right to his face even though he shushed her. When we hit the ground floor she said, "And he's never wanted to visit me in the two years I've been here, even when my parents invited him to the freshman showcase."

"Seriously, Phoebe, would you come to rural Michigan to see *me* in a play?" he said.

She laughed. "I would, particularly because I couldn't imagine you in a play. Would you sing?" It was the funniest I've ever heard Phoebe.

"You couldn't stop me," he joked.

We're now finally allowed to leave campus on weekends again, so we headed to the parking lot, where Jarvis had a sharp-looking white Infiniti, which Phoebe immediately dissed. ("A sedan, Jarvis! How uncool of you.") He said it was a company car from his dad's Detroit office, and he wanted to get something big enough to take out her friends, if she had any. I'm afraid I cackled. Phoebe was still grumbling about Daisy and me being there, so he gestured to me to take shotgun and stuck Phoebe in back to make her even madder. Ha!

Jarvis asked how I enjoyed being a new student and what I was taking. I still had intervals on the brain, so I told him about that. He said he loved theater but couldn't sing if his life depended on it, but now he'd think of me and tritones every time he heard the *Simpsons* song. We hummed it until Phoebe and Daisy both yelled at us to stop.

"'Maria' from *West Side Story* also starts with a tritone," I told him, and hummed it.

"My cousin doesn't care about intervals, Jackie!" Phoebe said from the backseat.

"Actually, I find the arts fascinating," Jarvis said. We'd stopped at a red light, and he looked at me. I could've stared into those eyes forever, tbh.

He took us to a tea place, which was Phoebe's idea, and has 54 different kinds of tea (I counted). He asked me what type I wanted to get, but I had no idea, so Phoebe chose a pot of chai. Cousin Jarvis ordered several plates of sandwiches and cookies and mini quiches because he said he couldn't decide. So my lavender mini fridge is now stuffed full of leftover wasabi eggs, caprese, and something called a "fig delight." Phoebe and Daisy plan to get together tomorrow for a picnic.

We spent lunch (or, I guess it was tea) talking about theater.

I mentioned I'd never been to New York City, and Jarvis said I should come spend Thanksgiving with Phoebe, and he would take us all to a play.

That perked Phoebe up. She said Jarvis's family could always get tickets to the best shows. I didn't know if that was an invitation to stay with her, which would be sort of horrifying, considering Phoebe doesn't like me. The school gives an entire week off for Thanksgiving, so spending a week with her in stony silence would be a lot.

Fortunately, Daisy piped up that she'd been wondering if I had plans, since my parents are abroad, and if maybe I could spend it with her. She lives someplace called Syosset, which is close to the city, so we could still visit with Phoebe and Jarvis. I said I'd ask.

So . . . can I go to Syosset for Thanksgiving? Otherwise, I'll have to spend it in my dorm, which wouldn't be bad, because there would be foreign students staying too. But I'd rather go with Daisy. I could probably also hang out with Vanessa a few days while I'm there, so Daisy wouldn't have to entertain me the entire time.

Once Daisy said that, Jarvis doubled down, talking about all we could do in the city. So I'm begging, can I pleasepleaseplease-pleasepleaseplease go?

I'll email Vanessa separately in case you aren't reading this.

I have another reason for wanting to go, besides the glamour and the hot guy and the theater date and not wanting to be alone in the dorm, except for people who *can't* go home because home is Tanzania. And, because I really REALLY want you to say yes, I'll tell you:

I've never lived in a happy home with a happy family. My last foster home was fine. I was there almost two years. But I wasn't up for adoption, so there was never a sense it could be permanent. And it wasn't. I moved four times in five years, which isn't a terrible record but isn't great either. One foster mom said I was "destructive" because I accidentally carved something into her table with a pen while doing homework. And before my mom went to prison, she still wasn't a very good mom. She had her drugs and her boyfriends, and I was, at best, third place. Daisy is so normal and well-adjusted with two parents, a brother, and a dog. I want to see what it's like, even if only for a week.

Anyway, think about it.

Phoebe finished reciting a list of shows she wanted to see and restaurants where we could eat, which was funny because I've never seen her eat much. (Today, she had one tea sandwich, which was the size of one of those travel soaps they put in my backpack when I first got into foster care.) Jarvis said he'd take it under advisement. He actually *said* "under advisement."

Then we talked about college. Jarvis is applying to all these fancy schools like MIT. I assume he'll get in because he's a genius multimillionaire. In fact, that's why he was in Michigan, to look at the University of Michigan, which I hear is supposed to be good. We had a second pot of tea, Moroccan Mint. It tasted like gum.

Too soon, it was over. We said our goodbyes, and I went back to my room.

Just as I was about to put on my headphones and start my intervals again, I heard a tap-tap-tapping on my bedroom door.

It was Jarvis. "Did you forget something?" I asked.

"Umm." He shuffled his feet. "I'm staying here tonight, I realized I'll be alone all evening, and I was wondering . . ."

I'm afraid I was staring at him. He looked down.

"Are you maybe free for dinner? I mean, I know you just ate, but we could go later."

"My curfew's at ten," I said, though I knew I was going. Of course I was.

"Seven thirty, then."

I nodded. "Seven thirty. Where should we meet you?"

He said he was actually only asking me. "My cousin and I get along fine, but a little Phoebe goes a long way."

I hesitated. I was nervous, getting into a car with someone I barely knew. Especially since he wanted to keep it secret so Phoebe didn't get mad. Maybe it's because of where I grew up, but I'm cautious. Sometimes rich guys think they can take liberties. I mean, not you, but you're old.

He must have seen my hesitation because he said, "How about this: I'll go to the restaurant, and I'll get a car to bring you there. That way, you don't have to ride with me."

I said I wasn't thinking that (even though I absolutely was). "It's okay," he said. "I like that you're careful. You don't know me. You can search my name online, but that won't tell the whole story either. Anyway, it's only dinner, and I'll be a perfect gentleman."

I gave him my phone number and agreed to be downstairs at 7:20. Then, as soon as I closed the door, I searched his name on my phone. One minute into it (about the time it would take him to get downstairs), he texted me.

Jarvis: Find anything interesting yet?

Me: What do you mean?

Jarvis: I assume you're googling me.

Me: No . . .

Jarvis: Search for the article about my report card.

Jarvis: That was a funny one.

Of course, I found the article. A New York paper actually published Jarvis's entire report card. He had straight As, not surprising, but comments on his conduct in two classes, with a note about his being too talkative and "inciting other students," plus another about spotty attendance.

A quote in the article said, "Reached for comment, Pendleton's father, John Jarvis Pendleton, Jr., stated, 'If my son can make straight As while talking too much and skipping class, perhaps that says more about the school than about him.'" He also suggested the school violated some privacy laws by releasing the grades in the first place. Go, him.

I spent about 20 more minutes searching. Jarvis definitely got around—there was a picture of him at the Golden Globe Awards with some movie star's daughter and a bunch of him at parties and Broadway premieres. But nothing about him getting a DUI or getting any girls pregnant or overdosing and having to be revived with Narcan. He seemed like a perfectly nice, normal multimillionaire. I forced myself to work on intervals until 6:15. Then I showered and put on a very chic emerald-green sweater dress Vanessa bought me and went downstairs.

When Jarvis said a car, I thought he meant a cab or some guy driving his Prius. But it turned out it was an actual Lincoln with a uniformed chauffeur. He took me to a fancy restaurant where Jarvis was waiting out front, wearing a jacket. I was glad I'd gone with the dress!

"You sure know how to treat a girl," I said, copying someone in a movie.

"I really wanted to see you," he said.

I shook my head. "Why?"

"You ever meet someone for the first time and already feel like you know them? Or you want to know them?"

I nodded. I'd felt the same spark. But I reminded myself that if he knew everything about me, he wouldn't be interested. Eligible-bachelor-multimillionaire-genius-philanthropists don't date girls whose mothers are in prison. Nobody's that philanthropic.

Still, it was only dinner. And, just in case, I confirmed that it was a secret meeting. What if the same people who unearthed his report card dug up dirt about me?

"Absolutely secret. Wouldn't want cousin Phebes to be jealous," he said. Then he asked me if I had any more questions about what I'd found online. I had to ask about the Golden Globes. He said it was fun because he loves movies but that his date wore some dress that was glued to her body, and she kept complaining about how uncomfortable it was. Then we spent a while discussing movies we liked. I hadn't seen most of the ones he liked, so after I finish watching every movie musical ever made, I'll watch those. Jarvis said he'd text me a list. He also said he likes musicals, especially old Rodgers and Hammerstein ones like *The King and I* and *The Sound of Music*.

He didn't over order this time but suggested lobster. I decided not to mention that I've never had a lobster before. Until the lobster showed up, and then it was obvious. But Jarvis was very patient. He showed me how to crack and eat it. I might have ruined my new dress, but it was definitely worth it.

Then he suggested we play a version of Truth or Dare, only the truth part since we were in a restaurant.

"That still sounds risky to me," I said.

He promised not to ask me anything sexual. "I just want to get to know you."

That also sounded risky, but I figured I could lie if he asked me anything too uncomfortable. So I said okay, if I could go first.

"Any tattoos? If so, what are they?"

He laughed at that one. "No tattoos." He said he was too young—he'll be 18 in April. And people knew him, so he couldn't lie about his age.

"So would you get one if you were older?" I asked.

He shrugged and said one time, when he was little, he was at the doctor's office, and there was a guy there who'd just turned 18. "The doctor told us he was lying to his mother about the fact that he'd gotten a tattoo. My mother said she thought it was nice that we could really talk about things."

Then I asked him if he was close to his mother, and he nodded. "My dad hasn't been around that much, and I'm an only child, so a lot of times when I was little, it was just the two of us. Nights when he'd go out, she'd send the maid home early and make eggs for dinner or order pizza, and we'd watch a movie on TV. That's probably why I love movies so much. I went through an astronaut phase when all I wanted to watch was *Apollo 13* and *October Sky* over and over again."

This was the point where he should have asked me about my family, and then I'd have to lie, but instead he said, "How about you? Any tattoos?" When I shook my head, he said, "If you were going to get one, what would you get?"

Thing is, I've actually thought about this, which is probably why I asked him. I said, "I don't think I'd ever get one. I don't like pain. But, at the airport when I was coming here, I saw a girl with one I liked. It was on her wrist, where people put things they want to be sure to remind themselves of, and it said, 'Art never comes from happiness.'"

"Chuck Palahniuk said that," he said. (I had to look up how to spell it just now—it's pronounced "Poll-uh-nick.") He nodded thoughtfully and touched my wrist, where the tattoo would go. He said, "Are you unhappy, Jackie?"

The real question! I thought about it. Here, in Michigan, with the fall leaves turning stunning shades of red and orange and music in my ears, it seems like I've never been unhappy. I shook my head. I said, "Do you ever think about how it would be if some omniscient narrator was narrating your life, like in a Dickens novel? Like whether the narrator would say you're pretty or ugly, interesting or just strange, happy or unhappy? Sometimes I don't know the answers to those questions. It would be cool to have someone truly objective around."

He laughed, but then his expression turned serious. "I know what you mean. People are always telling me I should be happy, but no one of quality is always happy. It's those bad experiences that make you grow."

I smiled and said I guessed I was growing.

"Should I ask you about it?" he said.

I told him no. "Right now, the narrator would say, 'Miss Abbott couldn't decide whether she was more enthusiastic about the lobster or her dinner companion.'"

Jarvis laughed and said he could accept being tied with the lobster. I loved making him laugh. I want to be the type of girl who can go out on a date with someone like him or even someone more regular than him and laugh and not have to worry about the future and all its ramifications. Like every other girl at MAA.

But I know I'm not like those other girls.

Soon it was 9:30. I was about to tell Jarvis he could drive me back, but he said the Lincoln was already out there. I was sorry it was over. I wanted to spend more time with him.

He must have felt the same way, because he touched my arm on the way out, and when I turned back, he said, "I'd like to see you again."

I said I'd like to see him too.

"Please come to New York for Thanksgiving," he said. "If you can't stay with Daisy, I'll get Phoebe to invite you." He said Phoebe's mom liked him better than she liked Phoebe.

I laughed at that and said I'd ask.

I wondered if he'd try to kiss me. I've been kissed before, by sloppy guys at parties, and once, this guy, CJ, who worked with me at Publix, kissed me in the parking lot when I was bringing in the shopping carts. I avoided him for weeks after that. But I never had a romantic first kiss under the moonlight like in movies, where the couple moves toward one another with an inevitability of mutual desire. I had a feeling kissing Jarvis could be like that. I mean, I *wanted* to kiss him, but I didn't want it to be all hurried, out in a parking lot with the driver watching. Also, my hands had butter on them, so I couldn't get them anywhere near his expensive jacket.

I stepped back.

He stepped back too. He said, "Don't worry. I'm not going to kiss you."

I must've looked at him funny, because he said, "If you come to New York next month, maybe you'll let me kiss you under the bright lights of New York City."

I said maybe, even though I knew I would. He glanced at the Lincoln and said I should get going. But he was still touching my arm, and I didn't want to pull away, because it was such a beautiful night and he was such a beautiful boy. I wanted it to last forever.

I stood on tiptoe to brush my cheek to his, which is the very least anyone from Miami would do at the end of an evening, even with a completely platonic friend.

I said I hoped I'd see him soon.

Then I turned and ran to the car before I could change my mind and miss curfew.

As soon as I got in, my phone buzzed with a text from him. It said:

Jarvis: Come to NY and I'll take you to 2 plays and an opera
Me: I'll try . . .
Me: What do you wear to an opera?

I saw the . . . that said he was texting. When he replied, it said:

Jarvis: Probably nothing they have in this part of Michigan
Jarvis: Maybe you can go shopping in NY.
Jarvis: I have to stop texting now because I'm going to drive
Jarvis: I'll see you soon though
Jarvis: I hope

I'm lying awake at one in the morning, reliving the whole perfect day. And I'm asking again, PLEASE can I go? I'll go visit Vanessa for part of it, so she can report back to you about me. I know you're paying for my education and not for me to kiss boys. But I'm feeling like part of my education is kissing boys, and besides, he said he'd take us to 2 Broadway plays, which is 2 more than I've ever seen and at least 50 fewer than everyone else in my class has seen, so that will be educational.

Please . . .

Love, Jacaranda

To: Johnsmith247@dll.com
Date: October 19, 8:33 p.m. Eastern Standard Time
Subject: Thank you!

Dear Mr. Smith,

Thank you!

Thankyouthankyouthankyouthankyouthankyouthank
youthankyouthankyouthankyou!

I heard from your travel agent (a profession that I didn't know still existed!) that she is getting the tickets, and Daisy and I should contact her so we can get a flight to LaGuardia together. And I heard from Vanessa that she'd love to see me the first weekend I'm there and "maybe shop." I wasn't begging for a dress, Mr. Smith. I've saved up my allowance, so I'll be fine, really. But I would love to see Vanessa, because it's as close as I can get to seeing you, and also, because she has better taste than I do and probably knows what to wear to an opera.

I wish I could also meet you. Could you join us at Starbucks for coffee? Just pop in and pop out. Would that be so much trouble?

In any case, I'll visit Vanessa.

By the way, I got 100% on my interval test.

Thank you again!

Love, Jacaranda

To: Johnsmith247@dll.com
Date: October 21, 7:59 p.m. Eastern Standard Time
Subject: Kindred spirit

Dear Mr. Smith,

There's a girl here named Falcon who used to live on the streets in Baltimore. A volunteer at a shelter saw her beautiful drawings and sent her portfolio to MAA. They accepted her, gave her room, board, books, even let her stay for summer camp. Another me.

Except, unlike me, she's being truthful about her past.

I saw her this morning, in the cafeteria, a small girl with wide brown eyes. She was sitting with one other girl, and they weren't really talking. But that might be because the art kids keep to themselves. I thought about introducing myself. In fact, I was on the verge of tapping her on the shoulder. But then Daisy called on me to settle a dispute about whether hash browns are better than home fries, and by the time we'd finished talking about that, Falcon had left.

I wanted to ask her whether people accept her, knowing her past, or do they get all weird?

But maybe I didn't ask because I was afraid to know the answer.

You probably know about my mother. Maybe you assume she's a horrible person, since she's in jail. Or maybe you think I'm being unfair to her. You never tell me what you think!

The truth about my mother is somewhere in the middle. She wasn't terrible, but she wasn't brave either. She fought to keep a roof over our heads, even if that meant living with some pretty scary men. But she never fought for me.

Still, I have some good memories.

Once, when I was in first or second grade, my teacher sent my coloring page home with a note for her to sign. It was for Memorial Day, and we were supposed to color a flag red, white, and blue.

Except this kid, Darius, stole my red crayon. I could probably have used someone else's. But I hated coloring pages. I hated always having to stay in the lines.

So I made the red parts purple, and yellow, and green polka dots, and I made the white parts orange—a whole rainbow.

My teacher yelled at me for not following directions. And for being unpatriotic.

I brought it home and held it up to Mom, tears in my eyes.

And she laughed!

She said, "Randa, don't ever let people say your picture has to be just like everyone else's."

And she hung it on the refrigerator.

Sometimes I forget the good times, but that was one of them.

Just thought you'd like to know.

Love, Jacaranda

To: Johnsmith247@dll.com
Date: October 27, 7:48 p.m. Eastern Standard Time
Subject: Drama drama

Dear Mr. Smith,

In drama, we are doing monologues from something called *Spoon River Anthology*. It's a book of poems about dead people in Illinois. They're sort of like their epitaphs, where they talk about important things in their lives. The one I chose is called "Elsa Wertman."

In it, she talks about how she was a servant, and her boss came into the kitchen where she was working, "and took me / Right in his arms and kissed me on my throat, / I turning my head. Then neither of us / Seemed to know what happened."

Okay, so I know what happened, but I guess they had to say it that way. It's a million years old, long before #metoo.

She got pregnant, and her employer's wife adopted the child and raised it, pretending it was the wife's, and Elsa had to watch him grow and be successful, never being able to admit he was her son.

But I couldn't get past the part where she says, "I cried for what would become of me. / And cried and cried as my secret began to show."

Doing it in class today, my voice broke, and I started to sob a little. Mr. Adams said, "You can't cry in the middle of it. Hold it in, at least until the end."

I started over, and I broke at the same place.

He waved his hand for me to stop and said, "People think it's such a big deal to be able to cry on cue. But it's a parlor trick. Acting is control."

I said I wasn't crying on cue. I was actually crying. "I can't help it."

He scoffed and told me to start over. Everyone was looking at their phones and talking. I got through it, finally, by not thinking about the words I was saying, so I was like a robot.

But, Mr. Smith, I've been that girl in the kitchen. I worked at a sub place before Publix, and the manager used to try and grab me. Once, while I was sweeping up some shredded lettuce, he came up behind me. "I can do that," he said, though he'd never offered to help before. He pretended to reach for the broom, not-so-incidentally brushing his open hand against my chest. I couldn't quit, because I needed the job. Or once, my mother's boyfriend-who-shall-not-be-named made a move on me. She stopped him, but then she got mad at *me* for leading him on, even though I was only eleven.

Women always blame other women. Even in *Spoon River Anthology*, Elsa says, "Mrs. Greene said she understood, / And would make no trouble for me." Why would she make trouble for Elsa? Why wouldn't she make trouble for her sex-offender husband?

So that's why I cried. My throat's getting full just thinking about it.

After class, Owen came up to me and said, "Don't get upset. Not everyone can cry on cue. I had to cry in a scene last year, and I pulled out an eyelash every time."

"That's why they looked so patchy," David said.

"Ha ha. My lashes are thick and luxurious enough to spare." Owen batted them.

And I went along with it because I knew they were guys and wouldn't understand.

By the way, speaking of guys, I'm also exchanging emails with another guy besides you. We text every night, way past lights out.

Shhh.

Love, Jacaranda

To: Johnsmith247@dll.com
Date: October 29, 7:59 p.m. Eastern Standard Time
Subject: Sorry

Dear Mr. Smith,

I'm sorry about my letter Tuesday. I didn't mean to burden you with hearing about my pervy sub shop manager. I'll try to keep my letters in the here and now.

I haven't told you about my voice teacher. Her name is Noreen, and she used to be an opera singer, and she frightens me a little. Okay, a lot. We spent the entire first lesson talking about how I stand (half an hour) and how I form the letter *E*. The second lesson, we discussed the shape of my lips.

It took three whole lessons before she gave me a song. It's a ballad from a musical about Bonnie and Clyde, and she said I should have an up-tempo piece from an older show. She repeated the same thing Harry said, about having audition pieces ready at a moment's notice.

Because, obviously, Broadway producers are going to be lining up to hear me, very soon.

Love, Jacaranda

To: Johnsmith247@dll.com
Date: November 2, 5:03 p.m. Eastern Standard Time
Subject: Broadway producers may be lining up!

Dear Mr. Smith,

We did our scene, "The Rain in Spain," in class today. It is the sweetest scene, where Eliza finally pronounces "The rain in Spain stays mainly in the plain" correctly, and Henry Higgins and Colonel Pickering lose their sh*t (excuse me) and start tangoing her around the room in delirium. This leads into Eliza's solo "I Could Have Danced All Night," which is how you know Eliza is falling in love with Henry Higgins.

But we weren't doing "I Could Have Danced All Night."

Until now!

That's right. Harry was so impressed with our performance. He kept saying, "Wonderful! Really first-class, kids." Then he turned to me and said, "Could you work with your voice teacher on a song, if I gave you something? Could it be ready for December 11?" I had no idea what he was talking about, but I've worked in retail, so I knew to say yes. Yes, of course I can. Then he says he's decided to add "I Could Have Danced All Night" onto the scene. He pointed to three girls who were playing servants and told them they'd be the chorus in that song too.

My very own song! I have a solo, just like Phoebe and Nina. I didn't look at Phoebe, afraid of what she'd say.

But on the way out, Nina said, "I'm so excited for you! Sometimes colleges come to our performances, to check us out. Or people from summer theater programs." She said Harry must be really impressed to give me a whole song my first year.

I've heard people talking about summer performing arts programs. So I asked Nina if the summer programs were expensive, and she said yeah, but they give need-based scholarships, so maybe.

For now, though, I'm so excited about singing "I Could Have Danced All Night."

Over the weekend, the school put on a haunted house and invited some local "disadvantaged" kids to come through it. The art students decorated the house, and the drama and musical theater students acted in it. Then the orchestra held a concert of scary music. Daisy's been playing "Night on Bald Mountain" in our bathroom for weeks.

Nina, Phoebe, and I played the three witches from *Macbeth*. Phoebe did our makeup—she's as talented at making warts as she is at hating on me! We stood in the common room of the senior girls' dorm, stirring a cauldron full of dry-ice smoke and saying stuff like "Double, double, toil and trouble" and "We're out of toads—maybe we can add these nice children to the pot!" When they screamed, we'd giggle wildly. It was so much fun!

I didn't dare mention it, but I was one of those "disadvantaged" kids growing up. More years than not, I was wearing a donated costume and going to some event at the Catholic church, even though we weren't Catholic.

After all the kids went through the haunted house, we carved pumpkins with them. I'd never carved a pumpkin before, but I researched it online, and I think I did okay. A little boy dressed as Aquaman hugged me and said I was pretty for a witch. I think it was the best Halloween of my whole life!

Jarvis texted me a photo of himself, dressed as Jack Skellington from *The Nightmare Before Christmas*, also carving pumpkins with a kid. Awwww!

I hope you had a happy Halloween too.

Also, BOO!

Love, Jacaranda

To: Johnsmith247@dll.com
Date: November 4, 11:34 p.m. Eastern Standard Time
Subject: Bed, bed, I couldn't go to bed!

Dear Mr. Smith,

Because I'm up at all hours, practicing "I Could Have Danced All Night." This song is a lot harder than it looks. It doesn't go that high, but the way the notes are arranged makes it difficult.

Maybe too difficult for me.

Love, Jacaranda

To: Johnsmith247@dll.com
Date: November 6, 8:10 p.m. Eastern Standard Time
Subject: Frustration

Dear Mr. Smith,

Yesterday, I spent ONE ENTIRE HOUR of my voice lesson working on the same eight notes of "I Could Have Danced All Night." ONE. HOUR.

Today, I spent two hours on my own, doing the same things. I still sound like someone is pulling out my fingernails. Phoebe was right. This isn't my part. I'm better at the jazzy stuff. It's what got me in here in the first place. I'm a belter.

Maybe Harry gave me this song to challenge me. If so, it's kicking my butt.

But Noreen says that the practice you do now will show a result in six months. "You have to practice and have faith."

But I don't have six months. And I have to sing this song in front of the class. And Harry. And Phoebe. On Monday.

Love, Jacaranda

P.S. I wish you'd write back! Is that so hard?

To: Johnsmith247@dll.com
Date: November 9, 8:17 p.m. Eastern Standard Time
Subject: Bad day

Dear Mr. Smith,

As predicted, Harry had me sing "I Could Have Danced All Night" in class today, and as predicted, his hand crept toward his ear at the sound of my shrieky high notes. He sent me to the practice room to work on it.

Five minutes later, he came back with Phoebe.

He said, "Okay, here's the deal: Two performances didn't meet expectations, and two performances might get cut from the show if they don't improve." He explained that he wanted us to work together. I could help Phoebe with her "deficient" low notes, and she should help me with my "earsplitting" high notes.

He left, and Phoebe and I stared at each other.

Phoebe said, "I guess Harry saw *The Parent Trap.*"

I looked at her blankly. She said, "Lindsay Lohan and Lindsay Lohan hated each other, so their camp counselor made them stay in the cabin together."

Another childhood experience I missed, I guess. I asked if that made them friends, and Phoebe sighed. "They turned out to be secret twins. That's the entire premise of *The Parent Trap*," she said, like she couldn't believe my weirdness.

You'd have been proud of me. I screwed up my courage and asked why she didn't like me. I mean, she couldn't still be mad about me not being Abigail, not after all these weeks.

She said, "You mean aside from the fact that you stole my role?"

"I didn't steal your role, and you haven't liked me since day one," I said.

She shrugged and said Daisy kept telling her how great I was, and now Jarvis was doing it too. And usually, when people told her she should like something, she didn't.

I was surprised to hear that about Jarvis. I mean, we've been texting every day, but I didn't know he talked to her about me. My face must have shown it, too, because she said, "Yeah, my cousin really liked you. I take what he says with a grain of salt, though."

"Why?" I asked.

"I don't know. He's strange. My father says it's a good thing he has a trust fund, because otherwise he'd give all his money to Greenpeace or some socialist political cause, and then he'd be out on the streets in a year."

I asked her why he had a trust fund, and she looked at me like I'd started singing country music. Apparently it's common knowledge that Jarvis's mother died of cancer when he was twelve, and she left him a ton of money in addition to his dad's.

I actually didn't know that, but I flashed back to what Jarvis had said about being really close to his mom and never getting a tattoo because she'd be disappointed. And how they'd eaten eggs for dinner and watched movies together when he was a kid. It made my heart hurt for him. I mean, obviously he's from a rich, important family, and mine is the opposite, but we both have a big hole in our lives where a parent should be. And obviously, neither of us brought it up.

I wanted to ask Phoebe more about what Jarvis said about me, but instead, I suggested we start working in case Harry came to check on us. Phoebe said, "How bad do those high notes suck?" as if she hadn't been listening and rooting for me to fail. So I said I didn't know—how bad were her low notes?

She rolled her eyes and admitted they were pretty bad. I suggested she sing for me.

I love her song, which is called "Welcome Home." It's super dramatic and inspiring, about soldiers who can't get past what they've seen in the war. It has this belty refrain that goes "Welcome home, my husband, welcome home my love, welcome home!" Seriously, I could have sung the crap out of this song, so Phoebe was probably right about Harry trying to challenge her. And he was trying to challenge me with *My Fair Lady.*

So here we were, Phoebe and me, stuck together and not even secret identical twins.

I could see the tension in Phoebe's jaw as she sang. "Stop!"

She looked offended, but I said, "You need to relax."

"How can I relax? This song is so miserable!"

I suggested maybe not to think of the lyrics at first. Then I made her get down on the practice room floor and do stretching exercises. Phoebe eyeballed the brown carpet that's probably never been cleaned and it looked like she gagged a little.

I made her take deep breaths through her mouth while she stretched. When she started to yawn, I said, "Okay, now sing 'Welcome hooooome!'"

"On my back?"

I yelled at her to stop thinking and sing.

She started to sing, and truly, it sounded way better. I was impressed, especially since I actually had no idea what I was doing. Maybe two months of voice lessons have really helped me! We went back to the beginning, and she sang the whole thing lying on her back.

"But I can't lie down onstage," she said, even though I could tell she was happy.

"No, but you can remember how it feels. Now, let's do mine."

She said, "Oh, that's easy."

I told her it wasn't easy for me, and she said she meant it was an easy fix. "You're having trouble with the end because it's right in your break."

"Break?"

She rolled her eyes. "The place where you go from chest to head voice. That's why it's hard even though it's not that high."

"So what do I do about it?"

"Sirens."

And, as I was about to ask what that meant, she started wailing like a fire truck! She went from the growly low range of her voice to the high part. She was so loud I was surprised everyone didn't run in there despite the soundproofing.

Then she made me do it. And, after about five times, she said, "Now, sing your song."

It actually did sound better. Oh, who am I kidding? I wrestled that song to the ground and made it an anthem to our combined tenacity.

We went over Phoebe's song one more time, and then (since we agreed Harry wasn't going to let us back into class yet) decided to do math homework.

Except I couldn't concentrate because I still wanted to ask her what Jarvis said about me.

Love, Jacaranda

To: Johnsmith247@dll.com
Date: November 9, 8:40 p.m. Eastern Standard Time
Subject: Jarvis

Dear Mr. Smith,

So, no lie, ten minutes after I sent that email, Jarvis called me. We've been texting, but that was the first time I'd heard his voice since he left.

He sounded super excited. He said he bought theater tickets for all of us for the Tuesday of my visit and was trying to get something else good for Friday and/or Saturday after Thanksgiving, but it was crazy with tourists, and did I like dim sum (I have no idea what that even is). And also, did I think I could see him at all the first weekend, without Phoebe and Daisy there, please? He said this all in one breath and then had to stop to inhale.

I said I hoped so, and I was excited about seeing him too. We talked for about 15 more minutes, and then I told him I had to practice. After years of watching my mother fawning over men, I know it's better to be the one who has something else to do and says goodbye first.

But secretly, in my heart of hearts, I was thinking, "HE LIKES ME!"

But I actually have to practice now. I'll write to you from New York. And, if you want to drop by Vanessa's, I'll be there from Friday afternoon until Sunday morning. I'll fit you in!

Love, Jacaranda

To: Johnsmith247@dll.com
Date: November 16, 4:28 p.m. Eastern Standard Time
Subject: My song

Dear Mr. Smith,

Just a note to say that, after a week of sirens, Harry said it was much better! I'm off probation and definitely in the show in December. It's December 11–12. You should come!

Phoebe's was fine too. But when I tried to congratulate her, she pretended not to hear.

Love, J

To: Johnsmith247@dll.com
Date: November 20, 5:35 p.m. Eastern Standard Time
Subject: I'M IN NEW YORK!!!!!

Dear Mr. Smith,

I'M HERE! It's so big! And loud! Okay, I sound like that song from *Annie,* but it's true. As Daddy Warbucks said, "I can't get enough!"

The second my plane landed, I had 12 texts from Jarvis. Was I there yet? How long would I be in the city? Could I get away from my aunt (I had told him Vanessa was my aunt) and see him soon instead of waiting until Tuesday? I was about to say no when I noticed a text from Vanessa, saying she'd forgotten a friend's birthday party Saturday night, and did I mind being on my own for the evening. So I texted Jarvis yes, I could see him tomorrow!

Daisy and I were waiting for our luggage when he called. Rather apologetically, he explained that he probably couldn't get tickets for anything new and hot ("shows Phoebe would approve of") on such short notice. He'd gotten tickets for all of us later in the week, but since I hadn't been to a New York theater before, were there any older shows I'd like to see.

Mr. Smith, I'm finally seeing *Wicked*! Tomorrow night with Jarvis! I CAN'T WAIT!

Love, Jacaranda

To: Johnsmith247@dll.com
Date: November 22, 2:49 a.m. Eastern Standard Time
Subject: One short day in the Emerald City!

Dear Mr. Smith,

It's true! I, Jacaranda Abbott, have now seen *Wicked*. It was sublime, as I knew it would be. And we had glorious seats. Jarvis's father's ticket broker outdid himself.

But first, THANK YOU for my shopping spree with Vanessa! It was NOT NECESSARY but so fun to have someone take me out and buy things for me, like having an actual rich aunt!

What a big, confusing place New York is! Do you get tired? I walked around Manhattan for one day and was exhausted. I thought, "Mr. Smith does this every day, and he's old!" Though, maybe one gets used to it. Vanessa seemed to think it was no big deal, and she was wearing high-heeled boots.

The sidewalks in Times Square were so crowded that I felt like I might be able to pick my feet up and be carried along by the crowd, and it reminded me of one time when I was six or seven, and my mother and whatever scrub boyfriend she had at the time took me to a holiday parade. It was so packed that I couldn't see out the sides of the crowd, or in front of me either. Suddenly, I felt like I was drowning. I lost my mother's hand. I tried to find her, but I couldn't move. I started crying. Finally, she pulled up on my arm. I saw the sky and drew in breath.

It must be like that all the time for New York children. I wonder if you grew up here. I asked Vanessa if she had, but she said she no. She's from Bogotá!

Vanessa even bought me an evening gown! I said it wasn't necessary, but she said if I was going to the opera with the Pendletons, *everyone* would be looking at us. She wanted to make me a hair appointment too, but Daisy and I will probably do each other's.

Anyway . . . the dress is bright blue, off-the-shoulder, and form-fitting but not *too* form-fitting, a little higher in front than on the sides. It is the most beautiful thing I've ever owned. I know I say that a lot, but seriously, it's true, and I'm going to wear it to everything, like Tiffany Haddish did with that white gown she wore at the Oscars.

You may not realize this, but before this year, most of my clothes weren't even new. That's not as bad as it sounds. There are great buys at Goodwill, and it's satisfying to take home a whole bagful of clothes for $25. Miami public schools have uniforms, so it really didn't matter. But one time, in middle school, this girl, Ashley, came up to me in the cafeteria and pointed to the polo I was wearing and said, "That used to be mine."

I looked at her like why are you talking to me, but then she said, "I know, because of this." And she pointed to this tiny bleached-out area, right on the bottom that you could barely notice, but she knew it was there. She said, "That's why my mother gave it to Goodwill, because it was good enough for poor people."

So, to go from that to buying Laundry by Shelli Segal at Bloomingdale's—wow!

Vanessa bought me three more dresses and two pairs of boots—one for snow and one just because they're adorable. I'm sending you a picture of the boots and another I took in the fitting room of me in the blue dress.

Do you like it? Do you think you would like me?

That was merely a rhetorical question. Don't feel obligated to answer.

Jarvis arrived at 7:00. His face was pink from the wind, and his eyes were bright. He looked so handsome! He opened his coat a bit to show me his green sweater. "In honor of *Wicked*."

I laughed and showed him my green dress, the same one from that first night (the butter came out), which I'd worn for just that reason.

"You look beautiful." He took my arm. And then he whisked me off into the night.

I was chilly, since there's been a sudden cold snap, and I didn't bring my warmest coat. Who could have imagined, a year ago, that I would be in a position of choosing between multiple coats! But Jarvis sneaked his hand into mine during the overture, and for a moment, I shivered. Then my entire body felt warm, like when you step into a hot shower.

I got immersed in the play. Mr. Smith, I would be so lucky to get to be on Broadway. Just imagine—up on stage with all eyes on me! I've seen hundreds of TV shows and movies, but theater is different. Being in the same place with a few hundred other people and sharing the experience with all of them at the same time—it's magical! I want to be part of it!

And did I mention he held my hand the whole time? He has this old-fashioned watch with a leather band, not something you'd think a rich person would wear, at least not a young person. I kept wanting to touch it.

After the play, he said he wanted to take me to dinner a few blocks away, instead of going to the touristy places near the theaters, and did I mind walking a bit. I said no, even though I was chilly. But Jarvis took my hand, and somehow I felt like there was a protective cocoon around us.

We went to a diner. They're all over the place here, so you probably know what they look like. This one was Paramount Diner. Maybe you've eaten there. It wasn't crowded, and as soon as we walked in, the waitress, a plump woman in her fifties, rushed up to us saying it had been a long time since she'd seen Jarvis, at least three days. He hugged her and called her Penny, which wasn't the name on her name tag. She asked if we wanted a booth or counter.

Jarvis looked at me. "If we choose the counter, we can sit next to each other."

I told him I wanted to sit next to him in the booth, and the woman, Penny, smiled like she knew what I was up to. "Smart girl!" she said, even after I explained that I was cold.

In the kitchen, someone was yelling in a language Jarvis said was Greek! Penny showed us to a booth, and we both sat on the same side. Then she handed us giant menus with maybe ten categories of stuff. I had no idea what to order. I asked Jarvis what was good here, and he said he came for the comfort food, but the gyros were supposed to be good. Someone opened the door, and I shivered.

"Are you that cold?" Jarvis asked.

I said I was fine. It was only when the door opened. But, before I could finish, he removed his coat and put it around my shoulders. I protested, but it felt so warm and nice, and it smelled like him, a nice woodsy scent. I don't think anyone's ever cared if I was cold before.

I snuck closer to him with the excuse that now he must be cold. He didn't object.

Are you scandalized by my behavior?

A different waitress came up, and Jarvis greeted her by name, Allison, which was also not the name on her name tag (Ellen). Weird! He asked how her kids were, whether Nicholas got his braces on, and she started chattering about how they hurt his mouth. But finally she took our order. I didn't get the gyro because I can't imagine eating a drippy sandwich on a date, much less in someone else's coat, so I got chicken. Jarvis ordered meat loaf!

"Why aren't the names on their name tags right?" I asked.

He laughed that I'd noticed that. "They're scared of stalkers, so they made up fake names. But I come here at least twice a week for home cooking, so they know me."

This guy has millions of dollars, and he eats cheap meat loaf and asks about the waitress's kid's braces.

During dinner, I probably talked too much, but I was still so excited about the show. I talked about Elphaba and how she felt different from everyone else because of her green skin. I said I thought Phoebe would make the perfect Glinda, both vocally and personality-wise. He seemed surprised by that, but I guess he doesn't spend much time around her.

I asked Jarvis if he ever felt like that. "Like you're green?"

He said he felt it all the time. "People know who I am, who my father is. But, really, I've never done anything notable. They think they know me, and wherever I go, they stare. Like them." He nodded toward a couple at the counter who, sure enough, had turned around to look at us. He gave a little wave, and they turned back.

I remembered how he told me to google his report card. I asked if that was why he didn't want to go someplace close to the theater.

"I mean, I love this place. But not having people pointing me out or taking my picture is a bonus." Allison/Ellen brought our plates then, and he inhaled appreciatively before saying, "Besides, where else can you get meat loaf?"

I laughed and said literally every single day at my school. I think it's a Midwestern thing.

"Do they really take your picture?" I asked.

He nodded and asked me if I ever felt green, and then dug into his meat loaf while I talked about being new at school and how much everyone else knows, compared to me. It's funny because he was as excited about meat loaf as I'd been about the lobster!

Jarvis said he wished we could spend more time together. I reminded him that we were going to a play on Tuesday and the opera on Saturday, but he said that Phoebe and Daisy would be there too. He wanted to spend time just with me.

I wanted to tell him I'd stay longer, but of course, I couldn't. I'd promised I'd be at Daisy's on Sunday, and I'm true to my word. I think it's important to be.

Later, Jarvis told the driver to circle the block so he could walk me into Vanessa's lobby. Then he walked around to my side and let me out and took my hand to escort me to the door. "Do you remember what I told you last time?" he asked.

I did, but I wasn't sure I wanted to admit I'd been thinking about kissing him. So I said, "You told me a lot of things." But I said it a little coyly, so he'd know I remembered.

He laughed and moved closer. His eyes were bright, emphasized by the cold. "So nothing stands out, then?" he said.

I smiled and said the lights of New York City sure were bright. "Can I?" he said.

I nodded, and he took me into his arms, sliding his hand under my coat, around my back. At that moment, I felt like my skin was sparkling, and he kissed me.

This is probably TMI, but since I have no one else to tell, I'm going to tell you: It was such a lovely kiss! I said I've been kissed before, but I've never been kissed like that. I don't know if anyone has. I felt like I was in a movie musical, like when Tony meets Maria on the dance floor, and he walks away, singing her name, and all of a sudden, the scenery changes behind him and he doesn't even notice!

I'm still thinking about it, even though it's 2:49 a.m. Good night!

Love, Jacaranda

To: Johnsmith247@dll.com
Date: November 26, 8:49 a.m. Eastern Standard Time
Subject: Happy, happy, happy!

My dearest Mr. Smith,

Happy Thanksgiving Day! I'm writing from Syosset, New York. I hope you're watching the parade, in person or on TV, surrounded by your loving friends and family. I'll be in Daisy's kitchen when the Snoopy balloon goes by!

I had an invitation to watch in person from a New York window, but I had to decline. More on that later . . .

Daisy's house is beautiful! Professor Murtaugh-Li (she told me to call her Diana, but I can't quite bring myself to) or, more likely, her housekeeper, has been cleaning so hard you can see your face in the granite kitchen counters. She's a law professor, but she gave her students Tuesday and Wednesday off so she could stay home with us and bake pies and cover every surface with autumn leaves, painted pumpkins, gourds, and drapes with the word "Thankful" stenciled on. Daisy and I helped. Yesterday, we prepared cranberry sauce from actual cranberries and learned to make turkey-shaped napkins for the Lis' thirty guests!

There's a fire in the fireplace, and the entire house smells of cloves and cinnamon.

I arrived on Sunday, and Daisy picked me up at the train station herself! She got her driver's license last summer, so she was very excited about driving. It was a little scary, but she drove slowly and carefully. When we reached the house, Professor Murtaugh-Li— Diana—rushed up and hugged me. She exclaimed over my boots! And my hair! She'd heard so much about me! Then she called upstairs, "Danny!" I was expecting the golden retriever Daisy has mentioned multiple times (to hear her tell it, the entire reason she came home this week), but it turns out the dog is Mulligan. Danny is Daisy's twin brother, who she's mentioned far less often.

After Diana called the third time, a tall boy lumbered downstairs, saying, "What, Mom?"

Diana said not to "what, Mom" her and to take my suitcase upstairs. I said it was fine, but Daisy said that Danny spends half his time exercising and the other half bragging about his strength (he's on the football team), so he could at least lift a little suitcase.

"Not everyone can be a flute prodigy, sis!" Danny retorted, but he said it affectionately. He picked up my suitcase like it was nothing and said he hoped I was nicer than Daisy's other friend.

"He means Phoebe," Daisy said, like I hadn't guessed. "They met at move-out last year."

I said we all had our issues with Phoebe, and Danny grinned and lifted my suitcase over his head, doing some squats to show off. Like Daisy, he has an infectious smile. Also, the kindest brown eyes, like a big teddy bear.

Daisy and I spent the afternoon gathering pinecones and sticks and spraying them with gold paint. Daisy's mom said we could put them out in baskets for Thanksgiving and then take them home to decorate our suite for Christmas. They're so pretty!

And that night, we actually played *board games*. We played a trivia game, which Danny, Daisy, and I won because Danny knew sports trivia and Daisy knew classical music. Danny high-fived me when I correctly identified the musical that takes place in River City, Iowa. Daisy said he was flirting with me, but I think he was just being nice. I want to be in a family that makes crafts and plays board games. Maybe someday when I have kids of my own, I will.

Tuesday, we met Phoebe and Jarvis in the city for a play, a very new, cool one that I didn't like as much as *Wicked*. Before the play, Jarvis took us out for Chinese. The place was called Kung Fu Kitchen, and Phoebe was angry about it.

"Ramen, Jarvis? Is this a joke? I've been eating gross dorm food for two months!"

"This isn't dorm ramen, dear cousin," Jarvis said. Then he looked at me and added, "I thought your friend might like to have authentic cuisine." He looked at Daisy for validation, and she said he was right, even though I happen to know she loves dorm ramen. Jarvis added that he was sure Phoebe's family could afford to take her wherever she wanted to go. Phoebe sulked and picked at her white rice the whole time.

Jarvis was right about the food, though. The dumplings were so good, crispy and soft at the same time! A few more days of eating with Jarvis will make me completely forget the girl who used to enjoy cafeteria fruit cups.

JK, I will always love peaches in syrup!

I was finishing up the last bit of my dumpling when I saw Jarvis looking at me. God, he was staring, because I'd been trying to pick up the last, tiny bit of sauce-soaked cabbage with my chopsticks so it wouldn't go to waste. I stopped.

"Sorry," I said.

"For what?" Jarvis asked.

"For eating like she grew up in a barn," Phoebe volunteered helpfully.

Jarvis shushed her. "I like watching Jackie eat." To me he said, "You seem like someone who grew up in a tower on a hill, and only now they're letting you come down and see and smell and taste everything."

He didn't know how far from the truth that was. I wasn't sheltered. I was too poor to have anything good. And yes, sometimes we lived off those ramen packets that sell 6 for $1.99. But it was sweet for him to say anyway. Phoebe said that was a nice way of saying I acted like I was raised by wolves. Jarvis shushed her again, and when he gave out the tickets for the play, he made sure to put himself on the end by me, with Phoebe at the other end. I saw him check the numbers.

Maybe I didn't like the play as much because I barely watched it. The whole time I was thinking about how close he was and how it had felt to kiss him. Not being able to kiss him now just made it more tempting. I bet he was thinking the same thing, because he leaned his arm against mine. I sort of nudged him back, and then we were touching and nudging each other throughout the second act. I hoped he couldn't feel my heartbeat or hear my breath quicken.

Afterward, as we walked to the train station, Jarvis asked if Daisy and I wanted to come back to the city to watch the parade. His father's office building is on the parade route, and he always hosts a giant party with a catered brunch to view it and lets Jarvis invite his friends. Phoebe would be there, of course.

Daisy shook her head, though, saying her mother was having thirty people over for dinner and counting on our help. I was a little disappointed about missing the opportunity to see the parade live. I've watched it on TV every year I could. Also, I wanted to see Jarvis. I bet holidays are hard for him. But he won't be alone—he said he was inviting other friends.

Today, the house already smells of turkey and pie. I've never had a Thanksgiving dinner with a big family and certainly never had anyone counting on me to help with the meal. Daisy and I are in charge of the stuffing, though Danny promised to help chop the celery. In fact, I'm due downstairs right now. The parade starts in ten minutes.

This year, I am thankful for you!

So HAPPY THANKSGIVING, and enjoy the parade, wherever you're watching!

Oops—Danny's calling me to help with the stuffing!

Love, Jacaranda

To: Johnsmith247@dll.com
Date: November 29, 5:31 p.m. Eastern Standard Time
Subject: I'm back!

Dear Mr. Smith,

Do you wish you knew me? I mean, in person? I wish I knew you. I write these letters as if you're a real person. I mean, I know you're a real person, but as if I really knew you. And yet, I might have passed by you on the street and never realized!

You don't have to write back to me, but could you send me a picture, so that I can see your face while I'm writing? I want to know what color your eyes are.

On the other hand, maybe *not* seeing your face helps me write to you. I wouldn't have told a real uncle or father about kissing Jarvis or how Danny flirted with me. (Okay, I'll admit he flirted.)

What do you think was waiting for me when I returned from break? Just guess!

A letter from my mother.

She's angry. She can't believe they'd send her daughter off to a different state when she wasn't there. Because she's such a great mother they should have consulted her. Like, what? Did she think

I was going into a holding pattern for fifteen years? That maybe I shouldn't graduate high school since she won't be around for the ceremony?

Wish she'd had all this concern for my welfare when she was around.

And to think, I felt guilty for not writing sooner! I missed her!

I'm sorry. I hadn't planned to write about this. It was going to be all about Thanksgiving dinner with two tables of Murtaughs and Lis, gathered hand in hand to give thanks. And how I gave thanks for you and for the opportunities you've given me . . . and that the stuffing came out okay!

As I was writing, Phoebe stuck her head through the door, and what do you think she said?

You'll never guess. Prepare to be amazed.

Phoebe: My cousin's obsessed with you.

Me: I don't think he's obsessed with me.

Phoebe: He called my mother and suggested we have you over winter break. He said he thought I should hang with you because *I* don't have enough friends. Can you believe it? Also, your family are out of the country. Actually, I guess he feels sorry for you because you'll be alone. That would be typical.

Me: Him being nice is typical?

Phoebe: No. I mean, yes. I mean—

Me (interrupting): You don't want to have me over. I can do something else. It's fine.

Phoebe: I didn't say I didn't want you to come.

I'm deeply confused by her behavior. First, she acts so unfriendly (downright hostile, tbh). Then she includes me in outings with her cousin. Then she acts mad that he likes me. But now she wants me to come and spend TWO FULL WEEKS at her house? I'm imagining the pleasant evenings with Daisy's family, playing Settlers of Catan in their comfy family room, and then I'm imagining the environment that made Phoebe into Phoebe! It sounds awful, and I'm saying that as someone who's lived in the much-maligned foster care system. In FLORIDA!

I told her I'd have to ask permission. I'll email Vanessa. Feel free to say no. I'm hoping Daisy will invite me again, but probably two holidays in a row is a lot to ask. I'd be happy to stay in the dorm. It will be peaceful, compared to Phoebe.

I forgot to tell you about the opera. I assume you've been to the Met, because it seems like a place where old, rich people swarm like ants on a mango. It's beautiful. The ceiling is gold; the curtain is gold. Everything is gold except the voices, which are liquid silver! I wore my blue gown, and Jarvis couldn't keep his eyes off me. Phoebe's and Daisy's dresses were gorgeous too. Phoebe bragged about the designer, but tbh, I don't remember who it was anymore. This old couple approached us and said how nice it was to see young faces at the opera. Our party did bring the average age down quite a bit!

Most people were all dressed up. There was even a gentleman in a cape, carrying one red rose, as if he was the Phantom of the Opera.

The opera was lovely but sad. It was called *Rigoletto* and was about a court jester and his daughter, Gilda, who falls in love with a despicable duke and then lets herself be killed in his place even though he's with another girl. So just like Julie Jordan in *Carousel*, another girl sacrificing herself for a man who doesn't love her back. But the soprano sang a beautiful song with runs and trills and high notes and generally sounded like Phoebe.

Should I try to be an opera singer, do you think?

Oh! Now Daisy is knocking on the door! Talk soon.

By the way, are you a rapper? Maybe you're not so old, after all? I notice a lot of rappers are actually named Smith, even if they don't call themselves that. In addition to Will Smith (who got his start as a rapper), there is LL Cool J (James Todd Smith), Ne-Yo (Shaffer Chimere Smith), and many others. It would be funny if you were a rapper when I've been picturing you looking kind of like one of those old guys on the Supreme Court.

Tua bella figlia, Jacaranda

To: Johnsmith247@dll.com
Date: November 30, 7:38 a.m. Eastern Standard Time
Subject: Thank you, I think

Dear Mr. Smith,

When I woke this morning, I already had a reply from Vanessa, saying I can visit Phoebe over break and telling me to contact her to make arrangements. She says I can stay with her some of the time if I like. She doesn't realize how much I would like that.

I should go. I have a test in music theory on Friday. We're learning to write down music (transcribing, it's called) when someone plays it, and if you can believe it, I am starting to be able to do it! Soon, I'll be able to write down my own songs! It's hard to believe that, only a few short months ago, I was struggling with the basic Every Good Boy Does Fine.

By the way, I wanted to remind you about my show on the 11th and 12th. If you come, please wear a red rose, so I'll know it's you. Well, you or the Phantom of the Opera. There's certainly no other way I'd recognize you, since you won't send me a picture!

Love, Jacaranda

P.S. Jarvis is VERY excited that I'm coming for winter break!

To: Johnsmith247@dll.com
Date: December 1, 1:57 a.m. Eastern Standard Time
Subject: Can't sleep

Dear Mr. Smith,

Do you ever lie awake at night, not sleeping because of worry? Like, you got through your entire day and were feeling sleepy, but the second your head hit the pillow, thoughts came? So many thoughts.

Maybe not. You're not in school anymore, so you can't worry about failing, and you're rich, so I guess you don't worry about things poor people worry about, like getting the electricity turned off. But maybe there's someone in your family you worry about? I just realized I don't even know if you have a family. I've been picturing you as a single man (unless you are, in fact, Will Smith), but you might have a wife and five children on your mind.

Anyway, that's how I'm feeling. It's after 1:00 a.m., and I can't sleep.

In musical theater class, Harry "reminded us" (I'm putting that in quotes because this is the first I've heard about it) that the week after the show are juries, and to be sure to prepare.

I think he was speaking mostly to me, because I'm one of only two new people. I was the only one who looked surprised.

"What's a jury?" I asked David later. The only jury I'd ever heard of was the kind that sent my mother to prison, and I was assuming/hoping it was nothing like that.

Well, it isn't exactly like it, but it's close.

"Your voice teacher didn't tell you about juries?" David said.

I said I guessed not.

"Noreen is such a flake." David said she probably forgot I was new and didn't know.

"Didn't know what?" I felt my chicken salad churning around in my stomach. The word "jury" certainly implied being judged.

And that is exactly what it is! Two weeks from now, we have to get in front of a "jury" of the voice faculty and Harry and perform two contrasting songs (one modern, one older; one fast, one slow) for them to judge. The songs are supposed to be fully blocked out and prepared.

David said I'd do fine. "You're working on songs in voice, right?"

I nodded, dimly remembering Noreen saying when I chose the song from *Bonnie & Clyde* that I also needed an older, up-tempo song. So I started working on this song called "I Got Rhythm" by my old friend Gershwin.

The idea of singing in front of Harry and three voice teachers is *terrifying to me*.

That sounds strange, considering I'm the one who sang a made-up song at Publix in front of the whole world (literally, it turns out). And since then, I performed "These Boots Are Made for Walkin'" in a karaoke club in my pajamas. But in situations like that, I can rely on being cute or funny or offbeat. Here, they'll be judging me on my singing alone. Am I good enough?

I know I'm a better singer than 90% of the population. But I'm competing with the other 10%. Maybe even the 1%. And that 1% has been taking voice lessons their whole lives.

"What if I mess up?" I asked David.

He said it would affect my grade in voice. "You'll get a B instead of an A."

And just as I was thinking that didn't sound that bad, he said:

"I mean, I guess if they didn't think you were making good enough progress, they'd ask you to leave. But that only ever happened to one girl I know about."

Except, turns out it was a musical theater student last semester. I probably got her spot!

And, of course, I have a scholarship to keep too.

This semester has flown by like the Canadian geese I see heading south. I've learned *so* much! I've learned improv, which I've never done before. And I'm working on a monologue, which I also have to do in class next week. I can play every major scale in two octaves, and also Minuet in G. And I can sort of do a *tour jeté*, if there's nothing in the way.

But this freaks me out. Which is why I'm up at 1:00 a.m. I practiced all afternoon and went back after dinner and sang until curfew and came back here in the freezing cold only to sit at my desk to do my other homework, which I finally finished at midnight.

But now I can't sleep. I keep thinking, what if I mess up? What if I do my best, but they still don't think it's good enough? What if they kick me out? Will I get sent back to Miami?

It's not that my life was that awful before. No one was beating me. I had enough food. School was fine. I loved my job at Publix. I was happy—happy enough, anyway.

But that was because I didn't know any better.

Now I know there's a place like this, a place where people care about music more than they care about algebra. At my old school, we were lucky if we even got algebra.

There are other good things about this place, too: the cafeteria, my beautiful room (still no roommate!), and Daisy and David, Owen, and Nina and Shani, and even Phoebe. I'd even miss Phoebe! But the arts are the most important.

I WILL DIE IF I HAVE TO GO BACK TO REGULAR SCHOOL WHERE THEY DON'T THINK ART IS IMPORT-ANT. It's like the schools don't care if their students have souls, as long as we can feed ourselves and not become a burden to society.

But I have a soul!

I'm going to try to go back to sleep. I'm reciting the titles of every musical I know to keep from thinking too much.

Yours, counting Rodgers and Hammerstein, Jacaranda

To: Johnsmith247@dll.com
Date: December 1, 7:01 a.m. Eastern Standard Time
Subject: Feeling better

Dear Mr. Smith,

Five minutes after I hit Send on that last email, I got a "You up?" text from Jarvis. And, unlike the usual "You up" text (which, I'm hoping I don't have to explain to you, is rude), this one was sweet because he's three states away and he just wanted to talk.

Jarvis and I have talked or texted every day since October. But usually before midnight, since Jarvis is a serious student who's applying to schools like MIT and Carnegie Mellon and needs his rest . . . as do I.

But today he said he was up late, worrying about exams. I'd been wondering if Jarvis even had exams, because we talk so often, and he never seems worried. But apparently that is just a good face he puts on, because AP Lit is killing him. He's behind on the reading, and he's been trying to read *Tess of the D'Urbervilles* and *Heart of Darkness* for two days. Now he can't sleep because he keeps thinking about what will happen if he fails and has to tell the colleges that accept him, and it will probably end up in the paper.

Also, he told me he has bizarre dreams about someone whispering, "The horror, the horror," which is from *Heart of Darkness*. It's near the end, so I guess that means he read it after all.

That was all one long blob of a text.

So I called and told him everything. He was so comforting. He said, "Not to belittle your fears, but I think you're underestimating yourself. They took you as a junior because they thought you were good enough. They wouldn't kick you out."

This made perfect sense when he said it, even though David had said roughly the same thing.

Then he added, "Besides, you must be good. Phebes is totally jealous of you."

Which I hadn't realized.

We talked on the phone for another half hour, and then I started yawning, ready for sleep.

"Do you want to leave the phone there, and I'll keep talking to you?" he asked.

I said no, I felt better. "You should try to sleep too."

But I still plan to practice for at least 2 hours after dinner tonight.

Love, Jacaranda

To: Johnsmith247@dll.com
Date: December 4, 9:18 p.m. Eastern Standard Time
Subject: Secrets

Joyeux Noël, Monsieur Forgeron!

Yes, that's "Mr. Smith" in French. I have an exam on Monday. And in the midst of all the stress and exams and juries and final performances, the junior/senior girls' dorm is doing Secret Santas. Except they're not Secret Santas. Because MAA is very nonsectarian, they're Secret Snow Fairies.

We're to leave our secret presents on specified days. Daisy says it's because otherwise, some people forget. "This way, if someone slacks, you can complain, and Angie can tell your person to be sure and get something the next day or they'll reassign them." Angie is in charge of this and is all-knowing.

I got Lucky for mine, which is lucky in another sense because I sort of know her. For the first day, we're supposed to get our person a card. But when I was in New York, I saw this cute deck of cards (Get it? Card = cards?) called "Writer Emergency Pack," which are illustrated with ideas for things to do if you have writer's block. It was a little more expensive than a Hallmark card, but I'll go cheaper on something else.

It's such fun! They sometimes did Secret Santa in school in Florida. The teacher would call up the kids who had a gift to participate, and I wasn't one of them. One year, one of the moms brought extra gifts for the kids who didn't bring one, which was nice, but then I felt guilty. Everyone knew which gifts they were because they all had the same snowman wrapping paper. It was always so shameful, being poor, even though it's a matter of luck when you're a kid. I mean, I didn't do anything wrong to be born poor, any more than Phoebe or Jarvis or any of the kids in my classes did something right to be born rich. But still, there was always shame.

Anyway, I left Lucky's gift in the floor lounge, on a chair she uses. She and her friends all watch reality TV together Tuesday nights. At breakfast the next morning, I heard her saying, "I got someone good!"

I also got someone good or, at least, interesting. My card is handmade, a pencil drawing on heavy paper of Times Square in the snow. Everything is black and white except the theater posters up above, which she filled in with watercolors, including *Wicked* in bright green. Inside, my Snow Fairy wrote, "I hope we can be better friends next semester!"

My Snow Fairy left it pinned to the bulletin board on my door. She put it in a big envelope, so she wouldn't have to put a pin through the drawing. I plan on buying a little frame for it and putting it on my bare walls. For now, I taped it up very carefully. I wonder who it is!

Our next gift is a playlist we make for the person and post on a special account over the weekend. The last Wednesday of the semester there's a party where we give our big gift and find out who our Snow Fairy is.

I'm also getting gifts for my friends. So far, I've found an adorable necklace with a collage of a flute and sheet music for Daisy. I know I need to get something for Phoebe since I'm staying with her over break (though I haven't told her yet—I'm a bit scared to), but I have no idea what to get her. The girl literally has everything. I googled the designer she wore to the opera that night, and her designs *started* at $1,000! What can I possibly get someone like that?

Also, do I get something for Jarvis? I'm sure to see him in New York.

Don't worry. These are just rhetorical questions. Don't trouble yourself to answer.

Tendrement (that's French for "fondly"), Jacaranda

To: Johnsmith247@dll.com
Date: December 7, 8:37 a.m. Eastern Standard Time
Subject: From the fairy front lines

Cher Monsieur Forgeron,

I'm sure I passed my theory exam. Well, not just passed, but did well. At least a B. I'm trying not to get my hopes up.

For my Snow Fairy gift for Lucky, I posted a playlist titled "Music for a Lucky Writer." It included all sorts of songs I thought would be inspirational. I even looked up writers who had created playlists for their work.

But then I got my gift. It was called "Just Jackie" and was musical theater, twelve songs, some old, some new, some slow, some fast, and every single one would be perfect for my voice! I wonder who this person is! I'm going to show the playlist to Noreen next semester, once I get through the horror ("The horror, the horror") of preparing for juries. Assuming I still go here.

Anyway, have to go. French exam today. Also, remember, there's still time to buy your plane ticket to attend my show December 11 or 12. Hint, hint.

J'écrirai bientôt.

Je t'embrasse très fort, Jacaranda

To: Johnsmith247@dll.com
Date: December 7, 6:05 p.m. Eastern Standard Time
Subject: Please Read—IMPORTANT!

Dear Mr. Smith,

GUESS WHAT???

Daisy invited me to go to Vermont for break. Her family has a vacation place there. We can go skiing and sledding and sit by a cozy fire and see Stowe, which is actually where the Von Trapp family (of *The Sound of Music*) lived in America!

The way Daisy explained it, Thanksgiving is when they have their big gathering, but Christmas is just the four of them, and they're each allowed to bring a friend. Danny's bringing some boy named Brent, who I think Daisy sort of likes. At least, she described him in detail ("Um . . . his eyes are, like, brown but with flecks of green and orange").

When I said I couldn't ski, being from Miami, Daisy said that was fine because her dad was a ski instructor in college, and he'd show me, or I could do ski school instead. She promised she and Danny would be happy to stay on the easier slopes for as long as it took. "I'm not that big on skiing. It's mostly about sitting in the lodge and drinking hot chocolate," she said.

"With Bre-ent?" I asked.

"Is that his name?" she said, even though she just told me about him.

She also told me we could take sleigh rides and ice-skate and that the town looks like one of those Christmas villages. She said her parents and Danny are all hoping I can come. It will be so much fun!

Can I please go? I haven't accepted Phoebe's invite yet, and she made it clear that she only asked because Jarvis browbeat her into it. I'll be really sad not to see Jarvis, but Daisy told me that if I have to stay with Vanessa a few days, I could do that and come up to Stowe with her father when he comes later in the week. Then I could see Jarvis too and have him all to myself.

Plus Daisy's father is the sweetest man. He's a lawyer but a nice, middle-aged estate-planning lawyer. And her mother is the perfect career mom that I hope to be someday. I would love to spend Christmas with a real family like that!

Please say yes!

Love, Jacaranda

To: Johnsmith247@dll.com
Date: December 7, 9:17 p.m. Eastern Standard Time
Subject: Re: Please Read—IMPORTANT!

Dear Mr. Smith,

I got Vanessa's email, saying that you think it's only polite to accept Phoebe's invitation because she asked first, and she'll find out I accepted Daisy instead.

You've chosen NOW to have an opinion?!?!?!

WHY?

Phoebe doesn't even LIKE ME! She's just asking because of Jarvis! I'm going to have to spend TWO WHOLE WEEKS being awkward around her and her sure-to-be-awful family when I could be playing in snow and having a perfect storybook Christmas!

Maybe I'll stay at school with the foreign kids. I hear there's a girl from Guyana, so I could work on my French.

I don't want to stay at school, though. I want to go to Vermont with Daisy, my best friend, instead of spending two weeks with a frenemy.

Pleeeeeeze!

Pleadingly, Jacaranda

To: Johnsmith247@dll.com
Date: December 8, 8:05 a.m. Eastern Standard Time
Subject: Fine

Dear Mr. Smith,

I am in receipt of Ms. Lastra's email, in which she states that you require me to go to New York with Phoebe, and she agrees it's only nice. She states that, as my guardian, you feel it necessary to instruct me in the proper way of handling invitations, so that I may know it for my later life.

I will do as required. I thank you for your charitable attention to my welfare.

I wish you a happy holiday. I will be limiting my nonrequired correspondence as I have a great deal of work to do.

Respectfully, Miss Jacaranda Abbott

To: Johnsmith247@dll.com
Date: December 16, 2:01 a.m. Eastern Standard Time
Subject: Phoebe for Christmas

Dear Mr. Smith,

You were right, and I'm sorry. Thank you for setting me straight.

The past week has been so difficult. If I were one of my classmates, I'd say "the hardest week of my life," but, well, we know that isn't true for me. If there's one good thing I can say for my childhood, it's that I'm not spoiled.

Still, it's been a lot of work. I've stayed up late every night, as late as I could without making myself sick and sending the whole thing crashing down.

Friday, the day of the show, I could barely concentrate in classes. I've worked so hard on "I Could Have Danced All Night." Sometimes I woke up singing it. I arrived at 6:00 for an 8:00 show. The cafeteria staff prepared a dairy-free dinner of stir-fry chicken and veggies (milk creates phlegm on the vocal cords, so half the cast hasn't had dairy in a month). Some people didn't even eat *that*. At 6:30, Owen called me. "Come on!"

"What?" I'd planned a leisurely 90 minutes of applying my makeup and staring into space.

He explained that before each show, they have rituals: first, a half hour of yoga, led by Owen, who can stand on his head and do something called "wounded peacock" (there's a Sanskrit name for it, which I can't pronounce). This involves standing on one hand, legs flung behind and up in the air. But we just did regular yoga, and by the end of it, the Savasana (corpse pose), I felt as one with my fellow thespians. Next, we did vocal warm-ups. Finally, a group chant, which was like a prayer to the theater gods. It was all very warm and fuzzy, as if we weren't hypercompetitive!

Then I went back to put on my costume for the *Titanic* number.

I was the first to the dressing room. At least, I thought I was. But when I got there, Phoebe was sitting by the mirror, no makeup, staring ahead, frozen, with this weird expression on her face, like she was Anne Boleyn headed to the guillotine.

When I tried to ask her why she missed warm-ups, she said, real softly, "I can't do this."

I was sure I'd heard her wrong. What did she mean, she couldn't do this? Phoebe's life revolves around theater. She's super talented and has been working so hard.

I said, "Everyone's counting on you." Wrong thing to say.

"I don't care," she said.

"You don't *care*?" I was sure I'd misheard her.

She took in a deep breath and let it out, shakily, like she was trying not to cry. Then she took another one. Finally, she said fine, she'd do the group numbers, but she couldn't do that solo. It was wrong for her voice. She couldn't hit the low notes. Her mother was in the audience, and people from colleges. "It's too hard," she kept saying, her breathing shallow and jerky.

Then other people started coming in, and she got up and walked outside, telling me to ask Harry to pull her solo.

Like hell I would! (Excuse my language.) I followed her, putting on my *Titanic* costume, which, fortunately, unfortunately, wasn't warm enough for Michigan in December. It kind of made me angry. I mean, yeah, she could just decide not to do a solo. No one expected anything of Phoebe. If she bombed at this, she could do something else, and if she bombed at that, she'd get another chance, because she's rich and everyone coddles her.

But I knew that wasn't true. She loves singing and theater. If she didn't do this, she'd regret it. I remembered that day I overheard her on the phone, saying, "I didn't flip out this time." Was this something that happened a lot? Did she not realize how talented she was, that she was better than most of us, even on a bad day?

I found her over by some trees behind the theater, taking deep breaths and shivering because she was only wearing a leotard and yoga pants. I wondered what to say. The logical thing was that she'd look worse by not singing than by singing and having it not be perfect. But I knew logic wouldn't work on her. So I said, "Sure. Go ahead. I'll tell Harry. But can we . . . I don't know, can we talk about what we're going to do over break?"

She looked at me suspiciously. I mean I was obviously trying to change the subject, keep her calm, not have her notice me looking at my watch. But I guess she appreciated the effort because after a minute of breathing, she said, "My family gives this great party on Christmas Eve. You're so lucky to get invited."

I turned away so she couldn't see my eyes roll.

She kept going, describing the people who were coming: "really important people, like producers, and we have a ton of food, and even Broadway performers. I'll loan you a dress if you don't have anything good to wear."

I ignored this. Being snotty is second nature to her and better than running away. Her breathing sounded more normal-ish now.

I said that sounded nice. "I've never been in a penthouse. How many stories is that?"

She told me 22 and talked some more about the party until finally, I told her I was looking forward to that but right now, I was freaking out about juries.

She said, "Oh, no, you'll be fine. You're so talented."

"You think so? I've always been jealous of you."

She seemed surprised. "Why?"

"Give me a break. You know you're good. That first day when I heard you sing 'Hallelujah,' I was ready to go home. I thought I didn't belong in the same room as you. And your song for this is so good too."

"You really think so?" she said.

"Absolutely. You're great at acting it out. I feel so sad for the soldiers you're singing about. That song is so meaningful, and I bet a lot of people would appreciate it. I mean, there's probably at least someone here who fought in a war. But if you can't . . ." I shrugged and let my voice trail off.

"I know you're right," she said.

"Look," I said through my chattering teeth. "What if you just do the group numbers and see how it's going? Your song's in the second act. There's no good time to tell Harry you're quitting, so you might as well wait until intermission."

She thought about it for a minute. "I guess that's true." She turned and headed inside. I followed her. But the funny thing was, dealing with her freak-out really kept me from freaking out myself. By then, there was only enough time to defrost myself and get dressed.

It went really well. I'm telling you this because you weren't there. But why would you come, when I was so rude to you? Still, I looked for a tall older man with a red rose in his lapel. Or maybe in his hand like that guy at the Met.

But you weren't there.

Who really surprised me by showing up was Jarvis Pendleton. He never mentioned he'd decided to take his aunt up on her invitation to fly to Michigan to see the show.

Anyway, I sang onstage, in front of people, and they applauded! My first solo!

It feels like a lifetime ago when I was in Miami. I was just some kid who liked to sing in the shower, if the water hadn't gotten cut off. Aside from Mr. Louis and maybe my chorus teacher, you were the first person who ever took me seriously as an artist. If it weren't for you, I'd be in foster care, going to my old school, taking Personal Development because there isn't any chorus. I'd be dreaming of being a Publix manager instead of a Broadway star.

Phoebe's solo ended up going really well after all. When she came into the dressing room, she said, "I saw people wiping away tears!"

After the show, sure enough, Jarvis was there. He stood at the stage door, carrying two giant bouquets of roses, white for Phoebe, pink for me. "For the stars!" he said.

I've never gotten roses before, not even from the supermarket, and I buried my nose in them, inhaling their scent.

Phoebe's mother, Mrs. Hodgkins, introduced herself. She was an icy blond lady who gushed about how wonderful everyone was. The show was wonderful, I was wonderful, Phoebe was wonderful, all equally wonderful. I tried to picture her at our apartment back in Miami, where the roof leaked on our beds and there was a rooster that crowed every morning at 4:00 and we only had one AC window unit in the 90-degree weather, and it let in palmetto bugs. Would she be so happy then?

I heard Phoebe mutter something about Valium, actually. She turned to Jarvis and asked him what he really thought.

He seemed kind of flattered that she even asked and said, "Gosh, cousin, you didn't stink up the place at all." But he had a smile that went all the way to his eyes, so I know he thought she was good.

"Gee, thanks," she said, but I could tell she was happy he'd come. I noticed some other girls looking at him too, and one even took his picture. Phoebe looked pretty proud.

Jarvis started talking to me about visiting over break. He's planned days of outings. He's going to take me to see all of what Phoebe calls the "silly tourist stuff," the Museum of Natural History, the top of the Empire State Building, and skating around the Rockefeller Center Christmas tree. His plan, he says, is to invite Phoebe along oh-so-sweetly, and when she scoffs at it, we can be alone together. I'm tired already just thinking of this trip!

Then, just as he was talking about taking me to see the Statue of Liberty, and Phoebe had gone back to being the eye-rolling mean girl I've come to expect, a lady came up to us.

"Ah, here are the two I've been looking for!" she exclaimed.

When we turned toward her, she handed us her cards. Her name was Wendy Lessing and she was on the admissions committee for the New England Conservatory, which has a summer program for high schoolers. She invited us to audition.

Phoebe took the card, not looking too interested. I said thank you but I didn't think I could afford a summer program. She said they offered scholarships and need-based aid, and someone as talented as I was should be able to get a full ride. She said we should ask Harry about it, and that they were having regional auditions in Detroit next month.

We both thanked her, as did Phoebe's mom, a little too enthusiastically. Phoebe said, "It's probably like those scams where a Nigerian prince contacts you to say you won a prize."

Jarvis said, "Maybe. But you guys *were* incredible." Phoebe turned away, but Jarvis grabbed my hand in his. "Especially you.

You were . . . I've seen the play a dozen times, but I never understood what it meant, how she felt." He bit his lip, like he was trying to find the right word. Then he lowered his voice and looked into my eyes. "You're astonishing, Jackie."

He held my gaze, and it felt like we were the only two people there, in the midst of all the clamoring families. It was as if I could feel his pulse, like we were connected through our veins. No one ever called me astonishing before.

I squeezed his hand. "Thank you."

The next day when I showed up for warm-ups, Harry said he heard his friend Wendy had talked to me and that I should strongly consider auditioning. "Strongly consider" is what adults say when they mean you'd better do it. She only gave her card to the two of us and to David and one other guy, Garret. Everyone's looking for more boys.

After Saturday's show, Phoebe came up and said . . . (pausing because this was beautiful) "I wanted to thank you for yesterday. I hope we get to be better friends next semester."

Hearing her say that made me think of the card, that beautiful card and the playlist and gifts I got from my Secret Snow Fairy, and I knew who they were from. I pictured Phoebe taking all that time to make that card, and . . . wow. Mind . . . blown.

I mean, maybe I'm wrong, but I don't think so.

"That's why I invited you for break," she admitted. "It wasn't because of Jarvis. I mean, he definitely has some kind of weird thing for you, but I'm sorry I was mean."

Whoa. This was as nice as Phoebe got by a lot. I'm sure it won't last. But I thanked her, and suddenly, I was hugging her. And she let me!

So, anyway, you were right. It would have been super rude to turn down Phoebe to go to Vermont with Daisy. Phoebe would have definitely found out, and any hope of friendship would have been gone.

Also, Jarvis is ridiculously excited. I'm ridiculously excited to see him. Going skating at Rockefeller Center sounds like something from a romance novel! I can't believe this is my life now!

Plus, Daisy said I could come to Vermont with them for Presidents' Day instead.

And I survived juries. What a relief! It turned out the four "jurors" were more Katy Perry than Simon Cowell. It felt like they were rooting for me. When I walked in the door, Harry turned to the two voice teachers I didn't know and said they were "in for a treat." They nodded and said, "Yes, you've told us."

I'm still waiting to get the results on Friday.

Fingers crossed.

Now I should go to bed, so I won't get sick over break. I have big plans!

Yours apologetically, Jacaranda

To: Johnsmith247@dll.com
Date: December 18, 3:15 p.m. Eastern Standard Time
Subject: Merry Christmas

Dear Mr. Smith,

Just a quick note because Phoebe and I are catching a plane.

I passed my juries! I mean, not just passed but got good grades—two Bs and two As—so all my paranoia was unfounded. I'm glad I worked hard though! I'm attaching copies of their comments. Apparently, I need to work on my posture. And Noreen, my own Noreen, marked me down for "spreading" my high notes. She was one of the Bs!

And I was right about Phoebe. She's my Snow Fairy. As the final big gift (which was supposed to be a $30 limit), she gave me a pair of beautiful earrings, silver with stones that look suspiciously like diamonds. She said I could wear them to the Christmas Eve party at her parents' place. I'm not going to google the designer because I don't want to know how much she spent! I think Lucky liked my gift, a notebook and a fancy pen. And Daisy loved the pendant and promised to bring back a snowball from Stowe!

I'm sending a small gift, a picture of me that Daisy took, in a frame I bought in New York. Maybe you can put it next to photos of your grandchildren. It's nothing compared to what I owe you, but know I was thinking of you. So check your mail. I'd send something more personal, but I don't know your sizes or what you like.

So much has happened this semester! I've learned so much! Thank you!

Phoebe is yelling for me to hurry up! I'll write soon.

Merry Christmas!

Love, Jacaranda

To: Johnsmith247@dll.com
Date: December 18, 6:27 p.m. Eastern Standard Time
Subject: Surprise!

Dear Mr. Smith,

Writing from the airport. The last thing I did before I left was mail two items, your gift and a card for my mom. And I picked up my mail at the campus post office. What do you think was in it?

A Christmas package from you! A big one too! I put it away for Christmas morning, so I'll have something to open when Phoebe is opening a roomful of treasures. I'm so excited!

There was also a letter from my mother. Two in one month. Probably just Christmas wishes. I sent her a card and didn't mention being mad about her last letter. I sent my love.

I stuffed both into my suitcase to open on Christmas.

Season's Greetings, Jacaranda

To: Johnsmith247@dll.com
Date: December 19, 12:42 a.m. Eastern Standard Time
Subject: I'm here!

Dear Mr. Smith,

OMG—this apartment! Phoebe said it was a penthouse, but it's actually two whole floors, every window with a view of gleaming city lights! All the furniture is black and white, with huge modern sculptures that look like something out of a Tim Burton movie! Phoebe's bathroom is larger than my dorm room, with a giant tub and another spectacular view.

Do you live someplace like this? Can I come see?

Sometimes, when I took the bus home from school, I'd look at the big houses in nice neighborhoods and wonder what people did inside. Did they have balls like in *Cinderella*?

Phoebe's mom is still super nice in her Valium way, but Phoebe's already annoyed with her because . . .

Today, bright and early, we are going out for brunch with a group Mrs. Hodgkins calls "the Thursdays." Apparently, they're Phoebe's friends she's known since their baby playgroup (which met on Thursdays). They all still get together. This is something rich people do. Phoebe said she couldn't believe she had to waste time going out with girls who hate her, when she's only home for two weeks. I texted Jarvis about it, and he texted back the 😶 emoji.

At least I get a fancy brunch at a New York restaurant called Red Rooster, where biscuits and gravy are $20. Isn't it funny how people in the city always want to pretend they're on a farm?

Love, Jacaranda

To: Johnsmith247@dll.com
Date: December 19, 10:18 p.m. Eastern Standard Time
Subject: The Thursdays—on Saturday

Dear Mr. Smith,

Jarvis wasn't wrong. Five girls, three named Emma, and two with names that sound like a bank or a law firm. They all look exactly like Phoebe, all skinny, all with perfect teeth, all with highlights that look like they were done at the same salon. It was like having brunch with the Rockettes. They greeted Phoebe like she was their long-lost sister, then their moms asked Phoebe vaguely condescending questions ("Sooooooo, you want to be a movie star?"), while the girls whispered to one another. Sometimes they glanced toward me as if I were a colorful species of iguana that had perched, unbidden, at their table. Then, when they figured out I wasn't anyone important, they ignored me. Which was fine. Brunch was delicious.

What wasn't fine was how miserable Phoebe looked. I tried to get her to eat some of her bacon ($9 for a side!). I mean, who can resist bacon?

She pushed it away and said, "Stop it!"

So I stole her bacon.

Then one of the Emmas turned to Phoebe and started chatting.

Emma #1: How's your cousin?

Phoebe (tries to look nonchalant): Which cousin?

Emma #2: You know which one.

Phoebe: My cousin Kenzie? She started horseback lessons.

Wells Fargo*: No one cares about your horse-faced cousin Kenzie in Westchester.

Phoebe: Well, I do. She's the cutest little thing.

Morgan Stanley*: She has buck teeth.

Phoebe: She does not . . . well, maybe a little, but she's 9. She'll get braces.

Emma #1: Your cousin Jarvis.

Phoebe (coyly): Jacob? Kenzie's brother? He's prepping for high school . . .

Emma #1 (interrupts): Jarvis! Jarvis!

Phoebe: Ohhhhhhhh, Jarvis. He's fine, I guess. We saw him at Thanksgiving.

Wells Fargo*: Does he have a girlfriend? Did he break up with that girl he was dating?

At that point, they all started chattering, asking questions. One of the Emmas (#3, I think) goes to school with Jarvis, so she had some intel about his girlfriend (ex-girlfriend?) Chaya, who, according to her, has cankles. Another said she heard he got in trouble for an Instagram post. A third said he'd taken some girl to the theater over Thanksgiving break.

---

* These may not be their actual names.

"He took me to the theater over Thanksgiving break," Phoebe said. They all looked relieved about that.

I'll admit I listened a little more intently than I had been (especially to the part about the girlfriend and her cankles) and stopped eating, even though my French toast was incredible, with caramelized apples and whipped cream. And then I looked up and noticed a sandy-haired head outside the window, tall enough to see from a distance. Jarvis?

It was Jarvis! He was at the restaurant!

I texted him (no one was paying attention to me anyway), RUN! Run while you can! Will text when coast clear.

I saw the sandy head tilt down, like someone looking at his cell phone. A minute later, he strolled into the restaurant. He walked straight up to Phoebe's mom, saying, "Aunt Caroline! Am I early? I came to pick up Phoebe and her friend."

We had NO SUCH PLANS. But I wasn't about to say that.

All of Aunt Caroline's friends perked up and started asking Jarvis the usual questions about where he's applying to college, and how his father is, while I sat there and thought about what a nice face he had. Even his eyebrows were just . . . perfect, especially the way they knitted together when he was thinking. Is that too much to say to you? The Rockettes all tried to get his attention too. Emma #3 waved at him. Jarvis nodded and smiled back and was very polite. He finally turned to Phoebe and said, "If you're not ready, I could come back later."

"NO!" Phoebe almost shouted, yanking me from my seat.

Bye-bye, French toast. Not that I'm complaining.

As we left, two Emmas and one of the banks (Morgan Stanley, I think) suddenly decided to invite Phoebe and me (and JARVIS) to parties they were having.

"Text me," Phoebe said as we sailed out onto Malcolm X Boulevard. I asked Phoebe if we were really going to their parties. She said, "It could be fun. They won't be the only ones there." The way she said it, I'm guessing there's some guy she wants to run into.

Jarvis wanted to show me around Harlem, since I'd never been. We walked a little, and at least I got to see the Apollo Theater, where lots of legends got their start (I'm sure you're familiar), but Phoebe kept looking behind us, worried the group would catch back up. So finally, Jarvis said, "Why don't we go to Rockefeller Center, to go ice-skating?"

Which was one of the 25 things he said we'd do together over break.

Surprisingly, Phoebe said yes. I told them that Miami girls can't ice-skate, but Jarvis said it was like roller-skating, and he'd hold my hand to help me.

I know you live here, so you're probably used to how magical it is, but this is the New York City that's in Christmas carols like "Silver Bells." Everything's covered in snow and hung with greenery and red ribbons. Jarvis stopped to give money to three separate bell-ringing Santas, until Phoebe finally made him stop. At Rockefeller Center, the giant Christmas tree was perched behind a gold statue of some kind of god! I asked Jarvis who it was, and he said Prometheus, the Titan who stole fire from the sun to bring it to mankind. I thought that was nice of him but also ironic to have a fire god at the ice-skating rink.

Jarvis was right. It was a lot like roller-skating. Still, he held my hand long after I stopped stumbling. It was very innocent, since Phoebe was there like a chaperone. Jarvis had gotten some special pass that allowed us to skip the lines. Halfway through, they told us all to clear the ice until only one couple was left. Then, the man knelt down on the ice.

"So romantic!" I said. My cheeks were cold, so that's probably why I felt a little weepy. I'm not *that* sentimental.

"Kind of cheesy," Phoebe said. "Proposing at an ice-skating rink? I'd want to go to Paris or something."

"Maybe they're from Iowa, and this is her dream," I said.

"You always have the nicest way of thinking about things," Jarvis said.

Phoebe said she thought the girl should get a worthier dream. Jarvis laughed and said he would tell Phoebe's future husband not to propose anyplace cheesy.

"Anyone I'd marry would know that," Phoebe said. "But I'm never getting married anyway."

I started to ask her why, but they were letting us back on the ice, and she skated off.

I wanted to stay forever, but soon, the session ended, and by that time, Jarvis was hungry.

"We had a big brunch," Phoebe protested.

"Which you didn't eat," I reminded her.

"Yeah, those girls always make me lose my appetite," she admitted, which I thought was funny since Phoebe never eats. She added that she was so glad she wasn't going to school with them anymore, and that people were so much more REAL at MAA. She smiled at me when she said that, and I felt bad for not liking her before. I sort of wanted to hug her. Then I remembered how mean she'd been that first day and I settled for smiling back.

Jarvis took us to the same diner, and there was the same love-fest at the door, especially when Jarvis introduced his cousin. We sat next to each other, with Phoebe on the other side. Jarvis ordered the meatloaf again, and I gave in to his pressure this time and got the gyro. Phoebe got a salad, but when my gyro got there, she picked at my French fries. I told her to help herself. The gyro was huge!

What Phoebe didn't see was, while I held my gyro in my right hand, Jarvis was holding my left hand. So I didn't have a hand for eating French fries (not that I'm complaining).

Our waitress that day was named Nikki, though her name tag said Grace. But halfway through the meal, Allison/Ellen from last time came in. When she saw Jarvis, she rushed to our table to show him Nicholas's school picture. "See his brace-face!"

Jarvis extricated his hand from mine to pick it up, which gave me a chance to eat a few fries. Ellen told him to keep the photo, and he pocketed it.

After she left, Phoebe said, "Jarvis, why does the waitress think you'd be so interested in her kid's braces? And want his school picture?"

I remembered her talking about the braces last time, too, come to think of it. But Jarvis shrugged and shook his head. He went back to his meat loaf.

"Did you buy her kid braces?" Phoebe asked.

Jarvis kept chewing. He took another bite of potatoes and ignored her.

"Jarvis, did you pay for the waitress's kid's braces?" Phoebe repeated, louder this time.

Jarvis stopped chewing long enough to shush her and say, "Okay, I may have heard her complaining about the cost and given her a good tip."

Phoebe laughed and said to me, "My cousin is a sucker for a sob story."

He said, "I eat here every day. They're like my family. And not everybody has what we have. Can you stop?"

I remembered what Phoebe had said about how Jarvis would give all his money to charity if he could. "I think that's nice," I said.

Jarvis grinned and said, "See, Phoebe. I'm *nice*. Don't know where that leaves you." He speared a forkful of meat loaf, and the conversation was over.

Phoebe didn't notice, but he leaned toward me when he said it, his leg pressing against mine. It was probably an accident on his part, but I swear, every muscle in my body tightened and the hairs on my arms stood up on end. Other girls might think he's handsome or like him because he has money. To me, paying for the waitress's kid's braces is . . . *hot*.

If you can work into conversation that you pay for my schooling, you'll probably have tons of girlfriends. JK—I'm sure you're married or, at least, too old to date.

Jarvis excused himself then, which gave me a chance to dig in to my gyro and fries while Phoebe tutted about Jarvis's foolishness (but I could tell she enjoyed bragging on him). Just then, I got a text. From Jarvis.

Jarvis: I want to see you WITHOUT Phoebe.
Jarvis: Ideas?

I texted him back a ♥.

When Jarvis returned, he said he thought we should go to see the Statue of Liberty, since I'd never been. Phoebe looked at him as if he'd suggested a *Star Trek* convention. A boat tour? In December? And with a million tourists? No thanks!

Phoebe said maybe Monday would be better than the weekend, but she wanted no part of it.

So Jarvis and I have a date for Monday!

Also, the gyro was excellent. If you're ever near the Paramount Diner, you should get it.

Maybe we can even meet there.

Love, Jacaranda

To: Johnsmith247@dll.com
Date: December 20, 11:30 p.m. Eastern Standard Time
Subject: Are you awake, I wonder

Dear Mr. Smith,

Are you awake, I wonder? I wish I could talk to you.

Today, because Phoebe had "suffered" through brunch with the Thursdays, we had a salon day. I said I couldn't afford it, but Phoebe's mom insisted that it was her treat. As she said it, her eyes swept over me in a way that took me back to my Goodwill store days, so I said okay.

I'm going to have to get famous someday, so I can pay back all the people who did nice things for me, including you. Especially you.

We got haircuts, conditioning treatments, facials, eyebrow waxing, and mani-pedis. I resisted Phoebe's invitation to highlight my hair and become an Emma.

I've never understood the whole idea of pedicures. Like, why would anyone pay a lot of money to get someone else to put on toenail polish, when they can do it themselves with a $5 bottle from CVS? Also, it's December, and nobody sees my toes. But after immersing my feet in bubbling, mint-scented happiness, I'm a convert.

While we were sitting there, Phoebe said, "If you could go back in time and tell your old self something, what would you tell her?"

A bit philosophical for Phoebe, with whom I've seldom had a conversation that wasn't about drama class or how much longer would I be in the shower. And, of course, it's an especially weird question for me. My younger self is a little girl, lying in bed listening to noises I'm trying to drown out.

But I guess "girl time" made Phoebe introspective.

"I know it's a cliché," I said, "but I guess I'd tell her it will get better, and the world is a beautiful place." I thought of MAA in the fall with all the orange and red leaves.

Phoebe gave me a weird look. She said, "I don't know. You seem like someone who's never had any problems."

This was obviously completely off base, and I guess my face showed it. "You're so confident," she said. "Like that first day, when I asked you to switch rooms with me, you just said 'no' like there was no other possible answer. You didn't hesitate, you didn't apologize. You weren't worried that I'd hate your guts."

"Are you kidding?" I said. "I was terrified."

"You didn't show it. I thought you were such a badass. You wouldn't let anyone push you around."

And by "anyone" she meant her. But with Phoebe, you take your compliments where you can get them. I asked her what she'd tell her younger self. She got very quiet, and finally, she said, "I'd tell her it's okay if not everyone likes her."

We were silent a moment. She looked at her phone and laughed, then held it up. "Look."

The lock screen displayed multiple texts from the Emmas, Wells Fargo (whose real name, I guess, is Wellesley) and Morgan Stanley (Morgan). All the texts mentioned Jarvis or "your cousin." They all wanted Phoebe and Jarvis to come to a party they were having.

"What will you tell them?" I asked.

She thought about it, then said, "I'll say I'm coming and bringing him. That way, they'll get all excited, and then I can text and say we aren't coming after all."

"Stone cold," I said.

"Hmm, you're right. I just won't answer." She side-eyed me. "You like him, don't you?"

I said he seemed nice, and she scoffed. "No, you *like* him. When he was helping you skate yesterday, you looked like a twelve-year-old with a crush." She made her eyes big and batted her eyelashes. I wondered if I really looked that way and if he noticed.

She continued. "The thing is, *everyone* likes Jarvis. I mean, he's practically Prince Harry, only without the wife—handsome, rich, charming, if he's not your cousin." She gestured to the phone, where yet another text was coming in. "But don't get your hopes up. He's taking you out, and idk, I guess he likes you. Maybe he'll try to get you into bed, but the girls he dates are, like, supermodels."

I've googled Jarvis a few—okay, a lot of—times, and Phoebe isn't wrong. Am I naive to think he'd be into someone like me?

I asked if he was really like that, the part about trying to get me into bed.

Phoebe shrugged. "*All* guys are like that. I mean, my cousin's ridiculously nice. But that doesn't make him the pope."

Then she looked in the mirror across from us and asked me if I thought they'd cut her hair too short.

So now I'm worried. Jarvis said he wants to spend time with me. WITHOUT Phoebe. Does that mean he expects something? Do rich boys always expect something? I figure you were a rich boy when you were Jarvis's age so maybe you know.

I know you won't answer this. Maybe that's why I feel so comfortable writing it. I'd be embarrassed to ask Vanessa. Do girls with mothers talk about this stuff with them?

Phoebe's right. I really like him. But I'm not ready yet.

Love, Jacaranda

To: Johnsmith247@dll.com
Date: December 21, 9:03 p.m. Eastern Standard Time
Subject: I had the loveliest day . . . mostly

Dear Mr. Smith,

The Statue of Liberty was closed. The ferry wasn't running due to morning fog. So, instead, Jarvis took me to brunch (people in New York seem to LOVE brunch) all the way across town in Central Park.

That's a big park! And a lovely restaurant, that looks like an old boathouse! Over brunch, we talked about our dreams. Jarvis talked about computer science, which I don't understand, but it sounds fascinating. Or maybe I just like watching his mouth move.

We discussed theater, and music too. Jarvis has seen or read every play ever written. He said that he thought that the characters' optimism was what made a tragedy tragic, whether it was Romeo and Juliet thinking they could make a life together or the mother in *The Glass Menagerie* thinking her awkward daughter might find a husband. I mentioned Willy Loman in *Death of a Salesman*, and how he was sure his screwup son, Biff, was one stroke of luck away from being the success Willy never was. Jarvis said, "Exactly!" I loved that he thought I was smart even though he's the smartest person I've ever met.

The weird thing about being with Jarvis is that people stare at him like he's part of the New York sights. I saw one girl take a selfie as she passed our table, angling her camera to get Jarvis in the background. He held his orange juice up in front of his face in a salute, right before the snap.

After brunch, we strolled down the walking path, looking at statues. There's one of Alice in Wonderland, another of Mother Goose. I commented that there were statues of pretend women like Alice, but all the statues of real people were men. He said he'd noticed that too! We came to this gazebo with benches all around. I said it looked like it was out of *The Sound of Music*, and he started to whistle "Sixteen Going On Seventeen."

"Yes!" I shouted, and I grabbed his hand. The second I did, my body went from freezing to burning. I paused for just an instant. Then I turned and ran to the gazebo, pulling him along after me, the way Liesl and Rolf did in the movie. Jarvis was laughing, and I said it was perfect for us because I'm sixteen going on seventeen, and he's seventeen going on eighteen. I took both his hands and spun him around, laughing.

He said, "We used to watch that every Christmas."

I wondered if "we" was him and his mother. But he changed the subject by putting his hand on my waist. "Jump up!" When I did, he lifted me up onto the bench, just like Liesl in the movie. He said he'd always wanted to do that, but the girls he knew would be embarrassed. "But you're not like that," he added.

I said I'd never heard of being unsophisticated framed as a good thing.

"It is," he said, "because you want to know things. I'd like to take you places, maybe even Europe or Asia someday, so I can see the excitement in your eyes."

Then I remembered what Phoebe had said about him just trying to get me into bed. Was he really saying those things just because he wanted something from me? I'm used to people wanting things from me, but I didn't want to believe it.

I asked Jarvis if he'd come here as a kid. He said yes, his mother had taught him to ride a bike there, and they'd gone to the zoo. Then he asked about my family.

And I told him.

Not everything. Not about my mother or her creepy boyfriends or the foster homes. But I told him we were poor and a benefactor was paying my way to school, and that I'd never known my father and didn't see much of my mother anymore either. I didn't tell him that she's in prison. I'm too ashamed. "You're the only one I've told all this to."

He raised an eyebrow. "Not Daisy? I thought you were best friends."

"We are, but . . ." I looked away. "I don't know. Her life seems so great. I don't want her to feel any sorrier for me than she already does."

"But you don't think that about me?" He looked pleasantly surprised, and I realized everyone probably treated him like a spoiled rich kid. I admitted Phoebe had told me about his mother dying.

"That must have been hard for you," I said.

He nodded and didn't speak for a moment, brushing a stray snowflake from my coat sleeve while I tried to think of a way to change the subject. But finally he said, "She wasn't sick long, not that they told me anyway. Maybe they knew earlier, but I didn't. She had cancer when I was very little, and she got better. And then she became sick again, and there was nothing they could do. She died right after my twelfth birthday. Now, I think that maybe she was trying to fit everything into a few years, since she knew she didn't have that many."

I asked him what he meant, and he said that sometimes, she'd come and pick him up from school for no reason and they'd have a picnic. Or once they drove up to the Catskills on a random morning in October, just to climb a mountain. She taught him to dance when he was 9 or 10 because she told him he might take a girl to the prom someday, and one year, instead of sending out cards, they made Christmas ornaments for everyone they knew out of Sculpey clay. "I rolled it out," he recalled, "shapes like snowflakes and candy canes, and she put them together and we baked them in the oven."

I could picture the little boy he'd been then, the one who'd had to grow up too quickly, like I had. "She sounds great," I said.

He explained how she taught him to be compassionate too. They'd make sandwiches to give out to people who looked hungry. That made me think of what he'd said to Phoebe about not everyone having what they had.

But then he said, "And one day, she went into the hospital, and then she died."

"I'm sorry," I said.

"I never talked about her. My friends don't bring her up. Everyone already knows."

"I'm sorry," I repeated, feeling stupid.

He squeezed my hand, hard. "I hadn't realized how much I wanted to talk about her."

It's funny because when I see what I've written, he sounds all dark and brooding, but in real life he was just open-faced, sunny Jarvis in a bright blue knit cap with his cheeks all flushed from the cold. I jumped down from the bench and put my arms around him. We're both damaged, I realized. We both have scars we're trying to hide.

I felt guilty about not telling him about my family. But, of course, having some saintly, dead-from-cancer mother isn't like having one in prison. So I kept my mouth shut.

Then he kissed me in that beautiful gazebo, surrounded by falling snow. Oh, how I loved that moment! He said we had to come back so I could see it in springtime. I liked all the promises he was making, even though they seemed too good to be true.

We walked around the park for a while, looking at every statue and sign, admiring poodles and flinging snowballs at each other until finally I said I was cold.

"Do you want to try the Statue of Liberty again?" he asked. "Fog's probably cleared."

I shivered, thinking about it. I guess I'm still a Florida girl at heart! I asked if there was anything closer. And indoors.

He mentioned the Metropolitan Museum of Art and the Museum of Natural History, both things I do want to visit. But I said, "You know, you don't have to keep taking me places and buying me things. We can just hang out. You know, inside."

He smiled and said (tentatively) that we could go back to his apartment to warm up. Actually, what he said was, "I . . . uh . . . I'm really suggesting that we go . . . um . . . watch TV and make hot chocolate or something. I wasn't . . . um . . . I mean, ah, the maid will be there, and . . ."

That's a direct quote. It was adorable.

To put him out of his misery, I said that sounded fine. I was dying to see his apartment!

And the apartment didn't disappoint. First of all, I didn't think an apartment could ever be bigger than Phoebe's. But it is higher, bigger, better in every way. And yet, it was eerily clean and sterile, like a law firm on a television show. There were fresh flowers in the entryway, which added to the law firm look. Jarvis definitely needs a dog! As we walked in, I heard a vacuum cleaner, but it was so many rooms away it wouldn't drown out conversation. That may be my dream, to live in a house so big you can vacuum and no one will be disturbed.

Jarvis took me down about three halls to introduce me to the maid, Milena, who smiled broadly and shook my hand. Jarvis told her we were going to make hot chocolate and sit in the family room. He took me to a room off the kitchen, the only room that *wasn't* like a law firm, with rugs and handcrafted objects. On one wall was a giant black-and-white photo of a younger Jarvis with both parents. They all were laughing, as if someone had caught them in a joke.

And when I looked over at him, he looked exactly as happy, staring at me.

We decided to watch *Elf.* Jarvis brought cocoa (Godiva from his perfect gourmet kitchen) and a blanket. I thought maybe he wanted to get under it with me, and it all felt more serious. But instead, he flopped down next to me, close but not intrusively so.

"Milena seemed excited to meet you," he said. "I don't usually bring girls home." I told him I was surprised, considering random girls were trying to take their picture with him at restaurants.

He shrugged. "I had a girlfriend for a while. She was the type of girl everyone thought I should be with—pretty, smart, rich . . ."

As he said this, I started feeling crazy jealous of this perfect girl I'd never met. I remembered Phoebe's friends mentioning he'd broken up with someone named Chaya, which sounded elegant. I pictured someone like a younger Amal Clooney, and smart like that too.

But Jarvis said, "I think she liked the *idea* of me more than she liked the actual me."

I asked him what he meant, and he shrugged. "Just too many times she thought what I liked was weird. My taste in music, the movies I like, computer science, which I'm planning to study in college—she thought I should study business instead. She thought diners were weird. Or not wanting to get trashed at a party. Or that I like to read biographies. The list went on. She'd act like she was joking, but she wasn't."

He started the movie, and we sat there watching Buddy the elf screw up everything he tried to do. I leaned against Jarvis. After a moment, I said, "But you *are* weird, you know?"

He frowned. "I prefer to think of myself as eccentric."

"Which means weird," I said. "Rich people are eccentric. Poor people are weird."

Mr. Smith, for a second he didn't react, and I thought I'd insulted him. Then he let out a huge laugh that Milena probably heard over the vacuum.

"True," he finally said.

"I like that you're eccentric," I said. "It makes me feel less weird." I snuggled closer. A moment later, he put his arm around my shoulder. He smelled of fresh air and snow, and something else I couldn't identify, but something good. They say smell is the sense most associated with memory. I wonder if that's true. Maybe someday, I'll be 80 years old and smell the snow and think of today. I wanted to bury my nose in his sweater, to remember that moment.

So I did it. I tried to be surreptitious, but he said, "Are you . . . sniffing me?"

I said yeah. "Is *that* weird?" Of course it was. We aren't dogs.

He grinned and said, "Totally. But carry on. As long as you're not saying I stink."

I told him about memory and about how he smelled like snow.

"Petrichor," he said. "It was a vocabulary word. It means the smell of rain in the air."

I buried my nose in his shoulder again. "Mmmm, petrichor."

He buried his in my hair. "You too." He nuzzled the top of my head as on TV Buddy arrived in New York City. We sat that way for a long time.

Then he said, "You ever feel like you want to do the right thing, but you don't know what the right thing is?"

"Sure. All the time." I wondered what made him think of that. I'd been debating telling him about my past, my mother. I didn't want to lie to him, but I wasn't sure if someone like him would even talk to someone like me if he knew. On the other hand, he's eccentric, so maybe.

"So what do you do?" he asked, and I felt him holding his breath.

He felt so warm, next to me. I said, "If it's not something that will hurt someone, I wouldn't say anything."

He exhaled. "I can't believe you're here. Like on my sofa instead of on the phone."

"Same." I turned toward him, and we kissed. A few times. It wasn't much more than kissing, but suddenly someone said, "Jarvis!" We both jumped.

It was a man, tall with sandy hair specked with gray. John Jarvis Pendleton Jr.!

Jarvis stood. "Dad!" He gestured toward me. "This is Jac . . . Jac . . ."

I stood too, my heart beating fast. I introduced myself, as if seeing a gazillionaire in his palace of an apartment was perfectly normal.

Mr. Pendleton took my hand but looked at Jarvis. "This is her? The girl?"

I wondered what he'd said about me, but Jarvis said, "Yeah, Jackie. Phoebe's friend. She's staying with Phoebe."

Mr. Pendleton nodded. "Oh, I forgot to tell Caroline we won't be there Christmas Eve."

"We won't?" Jarvis's chin jutted out. "Why not?"

Mr. Pendleton's eyes flickered to me, and he said they'd discuss it at another time. Then he left to go to some other room in the apartment, half a block away.

We went back to watching *Elf* then, Jarvis muttering something under his breath about Christmas with clients, and we sat a few feet apart. At the end of the movie, I said I should probably go back to Phoebe's. It seemed like Jarvis's dad wanted to talk to him. Jarvis nodded and suggested we walk back. "I want it to take longer," he said. I agreed, even though it was getting dark and colder, and I was weighed down with about ten books Jarvis had loaned me.

On the way back, we talked about what kind of dog breed we'd get (after I told him I thought he needed a dog, so his apartment would seem less lonely—I said a corgi, Jarvis wanted a Great Dane), our favorite holiday (we both like Halloween), and what extreme sport we'd do. I said definitely BASE jumping.

"Really?" he said.

"No, not really."

He said he'd done some free-climbing. He was serious, though. When we reached Phoebe's building, Jarvis said, "Sorry. My dad's kind of a douche."

I wanted to ask him what his father had meant by "the girl."
Like, had they discussed me? But instead, I said the expected
thing about being sure his dad wasn't that bad.

Jarvis said, "No. It's public knowledge. I'm pretty sure if you
found his Wikipedia page, it would say, 'John Jarvis Pendleton, Jr.,
entrepreneur and a bit of a douche.' If not, I'll add it."

He said he wanted to see me again while I was here. I thought
we definitely could.

But I'm NOT looking forward to some fancy Christmas party
at the Hodgkinses' without him! I'm hoping his dad changes his
mind.

Love, Jacaranda

To: Johnsmith247@dll.com
Date: December 22, 6:14 p.m. Eastern Standard Time
Subject: Girls get crafty

Dear Mr. Smith,

Today, I spent the entire day shopping and making decorations for the Hodgkinses' Christmas Eve party. I had to talk them into it. The Hodgkinses don't DIY, they buy. But after the twentieth time Mrs. Hodgkins sighed loudly about undelivered greenery from Maine, I spoke up. I figured it would solve three problems:

1. Make Mrs. H. less stressed out
2. Make Phoebe less stressed out
3. Give me and Phoebe something to do that doesn't involve shopping and spending money

Oh, and I'm going to add:

4. Get me to stop thinking about what, exactly, Jarvis Junior meant when he said, "This is her? The girl?" Like, do they DISCUSS me? And what do they say?

   Anyway . . . you can see how I'm overthinking this.

   When I said we should just make decorations, Phoebe looked at me like I'd suggested we form a metal band. Mrs. Hodgkins looked like I'd suggested we form a metal band and perform at her party.

"It'll be fun," I told Phoebe. Then I remembered the beautiful card she'd made, and I added, "You're the artistic one." She looked down and blushed, very un-Phoebe-like.

"What kind of decorations?" Mrs. Hodgkins asked.

Ah! There was the problem. Since I'm a Miami girl, they assumed I'd suggest flamingos in Santa hats or maybe a life-sized animated nativity scene in the living room. So I took out my phone and showed them the photos of everything Daisy and I made over Thanksgiving break. I figured that that would do the trick. Phoebe's hella competitive, so if I crafted at Daisy's, then they had to have BETTER crafts, CITY crafts, at her place.

I wasn't wrong. Half an hour on Pinterest later, we were out buying 6 Christmas trees, which we had delivered (I could get used to this whole "money is no object" thing), six stands, twenty pillar candles, and every string of lights and can of spray snow available in three Duane Reades. We sent Phoebe's brother, Fitz, out to buy white and silver spray paint since you have to be 21 to do that. Then we went to Central Park to gather twigs and pinecones to make centerpieces and giant wreaths for the walls.

"I feel like a vagrant," Phoebe said as she gathered twigs. "Or a bird." But she giggled and, with her face flushed pink in the cold and the sound of street Christmas music in our ears, she looked the happiest I'd seen her.

"Admit it, it's fun." We were throwing sticks into a Bloomingdale's Big Brown Bag because Phoebe refused to consider trash bags.

Phoebe nodded. "Abigail and I—when she was going to be my roommate—we talked about decorating our room a theme, like stencil stuff on the walls to look like Paris. But that didn't happen."

I started to say that Daisy and I would help her decorate, if she wanted. But I knew that wasn't her point. Instead, I asked her what had happened to Abigail. (But tentatively, because Phoebe is like this cat that used to sit outside our apartment when I was little. He'd purr when you petted him, then turn and scratch you a minute later.)

Phoebe got real interested in gathering sticks then. She picked up five. Six. Seven. Finally, she said, "When you were freaking out about juries, I thought about her."

I waited.

"She bombed her juries last year. I guess I should have seen it coming. She wasn't . . ." She stopped and thought about how to put it. "She wasn't at the same level as other people at MAA. She worked hard, and it wasn't fair. But they recommended she not return. She lost her scholarship, which she needed to stay at school."

I remember David saying a girl had gotten cut last year. Had I replaced her? Was that why Phoebe had hated me? "But was she coming back? Her name was on the door."

Phoebe said the school told her she could come back and do tech, and Phoebe thought her family had scraped together the money. "It's so unfair. *I* have a talent-based scholarship, and I certainly don't need the money." Normally this would be bragging for Phoebe, but her voice sounded strained and weak.

As the beginning of school got closer, Phoebe didn't hear from her. After Abigail didn't show up, Phoebe called her parents, and they said she'd been too depressed to send away. They'd spoken twice since then, but Phoebe felt bad because she was still at MAA, and Abigail wasn't.

"God, I can't imagine having to leave and go back to regular school," I said.

"I might never see her again," Phoebe said. "She lives in Kansas. I'll never go there."

"She could come to New York," I said.

"Yeah, everyone comes to New York." Phoebe examined a stick then rejected it. "But it won't be the same. Before, we were two people with the same dreams. We talked about college, maybe getting an apartment together someday. Now, it would be all weird."

I nodded. But, at the same time, I appreciated that Phoebe was saying she thought of me as an equal, someone with the same ambitions and similar talent. When I'd said I was worried about juries, Phoebe could have freaked me out by telling me her friend bombed them, but instead she'd said it wouldn't be a big deal for me.

"She was my only friend at school," Phoebe said. "I know no one likes me. You think I don't know that? You think I don't know how long you had to think about even coming here?" She looked away.

I said that wasn't true. I liked her. Daisy liked her. And, you know the funny thing? I wasn't lying. When I first met Phoebe, she scared the crap out of me. She was all the scary things—talented, beautiful, and rich. She knew she belonged. But now, I see she's as messed up as anyone. Except she has the added burden of having to pretend she isn't.

"We should decorate our suite!" I said. "We can even take the stuff we're making now."

Phoebe laughed. "You think I'm bringing 8,000 sticks on an airplane?"

But still, she proceeded to gather them. Then we stopped in the flower district and bought pinecones and florist tape and big glass vases.

Then we went back to Phoebe's apartment and spent the rest of the afternoon spray-painting sticks. Even Mrs. Hodgkins helped, after she supervised the building staff putting up six trees and all the lights.

We had to let the spray paint dry, so we left it all on the patio. Mrs. Hodgkins seemed pleased, and then Phoebe told me we were invited to a party tonight.

I assumed *we* meant just her, but I guess I was going as her houseguest.

If the girls I met the other day were examples of Phoebe's New York friends, I'd *much* rather sit home, literally watching paint dry. But I wouldn't want to upset our newfound bond.

So, I'm going to my first New York party!

I hope it's short.

Love, Jacaranda

To: Johnsmith247@dll.com
Date: December 23, 9:44 a.m. Eastern Standard Time
Subject: It was not short!

Dear Mr. Smith,

I made it back . . . finally. For a while there, I wasn't sure.

I'd like to say my first New York party was epic, but the only epic thing about it was how we left, and who I left with.

When Phoebe and I arrived, we pushed through the crowd in the living room to a wrap-around balcony full of more people, people drinking, people making out. A guy Phoebe seemed to know thrust a drink into her hand and one into mine.

"What is it?" I asked, eyeing it suspiciously.

"It's good," he said as Phoebe told me not to be paranoid. This wasn't Miami.

"No, it's New York City," I said, but she gulped down hers before I could stop her, then reached for mine. She switched her empty cup for my full one and went back to talking to the guy, whose name was Darcy or Dolby, something like that. I walked to the balcony railing and looked over, overwhelmed by the dark and the music. Phoebe had insisted I wear an outfit of hers, a short black suede skirt and a lace top that didn't provide much coverage, much less warmth.

I don't know how long I stood, watching the street below, random people walking by and one trash panda ransacking a dumpster. I wished Jarvis was there. I was dimly aware that Phoebe was now making out with Dolby or Dobby and the balcony was filling with more and more pressing bodies. Could it hold all of us? At least it was warmer now. Then I felt someone beside me.

"Stargazing?" he said.

I started to say no but then realized he was joking. There were no stars visible in Manhattan. I pointed to the trash panda instead. "Nature."

Laughing, he introduced himself as Preston and asked if I went to school with Emma (whose apartment it was). I said I went to boarding school for theater. He started yakking about his dad being an agent, but not the type who represents actors, the kind who represents books. Or "properties," as he called them. He was handsome, tall with dark hair, and not visibly drunk, which put him in the minority there. Tbh, I wasn't paying much attention, because I was looking for Jarvis. I hoped he'd walk through the door, sweep me away, and take me out for a gyro.

No such luck. Preston offered to refill my drink. I said okay. I didn't plan to drink it. Maybe this makes me a huge nerd, but I don't like drinking. I've been in too many rooms where I was the only sober person. Still, I watched Preston fill my cup with ice, then vodka.

"Straight vodka?" I said.

He laughed and asked if he should make me a cosmopolitan, or maybe a Moscow mule.

He was making fun of me. I took a tiny sip. It tasted bad.

He started talking about, well, himself, how he was going to Harvard next year, blahblahblah, obviously trying to impress me. I did look quite hot in Phoebe's skirt. I watched the ice melt. Preston moved closer.

Too close. It seemed like the balcony started to tilt. Probably my imagination. I said I was cold, and I wanted to go inside. He agreed, a bit too readily, and steered me into the living room. I dumped the rest of my drink over the railing. Probably, people down there thought it was raining. I hope that raccoon didn't get wet. Or drunk. Once inside, he maneuvered me to a spot on the sofa that was only big enough for one of us and pulled me down with him. He leaned into me, sliding his hand onto my bare leg.

I stood up. "I have to find my friend."

He stood, too, open-mouthed. Apparently, people didn't usually avoid kissing Preston.

"My friend Phoebe?" I said. "She's tall, blond, really pretty." I glanced around. This described about half the girls in the room. Where was she?

I texted her, then called. Straight to voice mail.

I pushed past Preston and searched for Phoebe, elbowing through crowds, glancing from one unfamiliar face to another. It wasn't like Phoebe to disappear with some random guy. Maybe her drink actually was drugged. I didn't know what to do or even, really, where I was. She hadn't been on the patio, so I pushed in the other direction, past a big line for the bathroom (still no Phoebe). I made another round. Maybe this *was* like Phoebe. How well did I really know her?

I checked my phone again. Nothing. Not knowing what to do, I texted Jarvis.

Me: At party. Lost Phoebe.
Jarvis: Where?

I sent my location. Then I wandered around for 20 minutes. She. Was. Nowhere.

Just as I was about to give up, the conversation near the door crescendoed. Jarvis! Someone said it. Then, again. Everyone stopped to herald his arrival. I pushed through the pressing bodies. I heard people offering him drinks, congratulating him, on what, I didn't know, saw hands reaching out to him. Everyone wanted a part of him. I finally caught his eye.

"Jackie!" His smile was the North Star. He reached for me.

"I haven't seen her in an hour, and she was drinking a lot." I didn't know if that was even true, but she'd had two drinks that I'd *seen*, so probably. I added that I knew I sounded paranoid.

He assured me I didn't. I was being a good friend. He took my hand. "I'll help you find her, and if she left, I'll get you home."

Home. Such a funny word. Because what does it actually mean? I've had so many homes, or maybe I haven't had any. Maybe my little room at MAA is the only real home I've ever had, the only one that's mine. At least, that's what my mind flashed to when

Jarvis said the word. My lavender-and-white bed.

People still kept coming up to him, congratulating him, talking to him. Each time, he asked if they'd seen Phoebe. "My cousin, Phoebe Pendleton-Hodgkins!"

Finally, someone said she'd gone into a room down the hall. Jarvis pulled me toward it and opened the door.

It was a study, and sure enough, Phoebe was in there, making out with the guy from before. Well, probably more than making out but less than . . . well, you know. I looked away, so I'm not sure. Jarvis yelled Phoebe's name and said, "Time to go!" The guy cursed at us to leave. Jarvis said, "Gladly, Duncan."

Duncan! That was his name!

"I'll take my cousin." Jarvis tugged her arm and asked if she had a coat. She looked red-eyed and kind of out of it and said she didn't know where it was.

God, her coat was gorgeous. It was a Canada Goose parka, which several girls at MAA have, but it probably cost as much as some of my Miami friends' cars. I looked around, but it was gone, and Jarvis had given her his. Phoebe was fighting Jarvis off, saying she wasn't a baby. He said, "Maybe not, but you're too drunk to consent to what you were about to do."

True. She was having trouble putting one foot in front of the other. Also, sober Phoebe would have stopped making out with the guy the second he took off his coat. He was wearing a Clemson football sweatshirt. Phoebe scorns both state schools and organized sports.

In the hall, there was another bottleneck of people, all wanting

184

Jarvis to stay and party. One girl grabbed his arm. I told him I could probably get Phoebe into a car myself if he wanted to stay. I've had a certain amount of experience maneuvering drunk people, but I didn't mention that. He said, "Yes. Yes, I'm absolutely going to send my petite girlfriend down to put my drunk cousin into a car while I party. That sounds like me." He looked insulted.

And all I was thinking was that he said "my girlfriend."

"Hey, I'm from the 305. Don't worry. I'm tough," I said.

He laughed. "And I'm from the 212, and the last of the gentlemen here." He launched Phoebe into the elevator and pulled me in after them.

Somehow, we got Phoebe into a car. By then, she was coherent enough that when I told her about Harvard-boy Preston touching my leg, she cackled, so I guess she wasn't drugged.

"Preston Stack isn't going to Harvard or anyplace else with standards. Maybe he could get into a trade school if he promised not to break anything there." Same old Phoebe.

Then she fell asleep on Jarvis's shoulder. He told me to take a picture and send it to her.

So that is how my first New York party went. Not that you asked.

We got Phoebe past the doorman, reasonably upright, and up to the 21st floor. By then she was complaining about her lost coat. Mr. and Mrs. Hodgkins were out, so Jarvis put Phoebe to bed without incident. Then I gave him a little tour of all the decorations we'd made, ending in the family room. He seemed impressed. "I wish I was coming."

I said I wished that too. But he's leaving today, going to some party in Westchester and spending Christmas Day with his father's girlfriend. He'd asked if he could stay in the city and go to Phoebe's. "But apparently, Dad said, I'm being a moody teenager."

He promised he'd be back the day after Christmas and had gotten us theater tickets. Then he rummaged in the pocket of his coat that he'd taken off Phoebe and said he got me something.

I didn't see what it was, but it was small enough for him to hide behind his back. He walked to the tree and nestled it among the mounds of Hodgkins presents. He sat on the sofa, which was the only thing in the room not covered in painted sticks, and motioned for me to sit beside him. I did, even though I WANTED TO KNOW WHAT WAS IN THAT PACKAGE!

So I'll have three gifts under the tree this year, yours and Daisy's and now, Jarvis's.

I got him something too—I made him something. I didn't know if it was too cheesy. I asked him why people had been congratulating him at the party.

"I got into MIT," he said. When I said that was incredible, he said, "I guess."

"Aren't you happy?" I asked.

He shrugged. "I don't know if I want to go there."

Because people just turn down MIT. "But I thought it was your top choice."

He said it was. But now that he'd actually gotten in, he wondered if he was smart enough. "I mean, you know half the people congratulating me think I got in because my dad could donate a building to the school. And who's to say they aren't right?"

"I say they aren't right," I said.

Have I mentioned that Jarvis is ridiculously smart? But now he was doubting himself, just like I doubt myself.

"Everything in my life is inevitable," he said. "I do well in school, I'll get into every college I apply to."

I said that was because he was smart.

But he kept going. "Lots of people are smart. But they don't all get in wherever they want. I will. I'll go to a good school, take the right classes, join the right clubs, get the right internships, probably go to law school. All because I'm Jarvis Pendleton, who gets what he wants."

Then he said, "Do you know that first night, when you stepped back and didn't let me kiss you? You were the first girl to do that since I started to look at girls."

I kind of smiled at that, since it was mostly the garlic butter that had kept me away that day. Also, how many girls has he kissed?

But I laughed. "I wouldn't mind a little inevitability in life."

"But it's so unfair. I could be taking a spot from someone more deserving."

"Life's not fair," I said, knowing the truth of that.

"And you're okay with that?" he asked.

"It evens out," I said. "People like you and Phoebe have the advantages of money. The rest of us have great life-learning experiences. You're a nice person, at least."

His face lightened, and he said, "I am nice, aren't I?"

I laughed. "So nice! You came to get me and drunk Phoebe

tonight. And you do other nice things too."

"I know it's silly—a rich boy whining about his privileges. But I'm not sure I want to go to Boston. It's so far away."

I was thinking Boston wasn't exactly Montana. Far from what, I wanted to ask him? Far from his father, who could get on a plane at a moment's notice? Or from his friends, half of whom would probably also go to Boston schools?

"Maybe I'd rather go to Michigan, if I get in," he said, and I remembered that's where he was visiting when we met. "Or Carnegie Mellon—it's one of the top computer science programs in the country. It's in Pittsburgh. Or NYU."

The schools he was mentioning were all top schools for theater too, the ones my friends wanted to attend. So I wondered if he meant closer to *me*. Because *I* was going to major in theater. And, even though I've only known him a few months, that didn't seem unreasonable to me. I wanted to be close to him too.

I thought about him calling me his girlfriend.

But he couldn't have meant that, could he? Jarvis Pendleton couldn't be throwing away MIT for some Publix bag girl he barely knew.

Barely knew and texted at midnight.

"When do you have to decide?" I asked.

He said he had until May. Then he took me in his arms. We sat there, quiet, until we heard the little ding of the elevator. The Hodgkinses were home. It was after one.

"Oh, no," I whispered. They'd think I snuck Jarvis in. Or, if we told the truth, they'd know how drunk Phoebe got. Neither good.

Seeing my distress, Jarvis reached over and switched off the light on the end table. He held his finger to his lips. I heard the elevator door open and close, Mr. and Mrs. Hodgkins talking in the living room. I held my breath. What if they came in here and found me sitting with their nephew in the dark, our clothes in a bit of disarray?

(Note: Just a bit of a disarray. I don't want to give the wrong impression.)

I heard them go into their bedroom and shut the door.

In the light from the city, Jarvis made an exaggerated gesture of relief, hand across forehead. Then he whispered, "The only question is, how do I leave? They'll hear the ding when the elevator comes."

We decided he had to stay the night. We'd wake up early and sneak him out then.

You see how very clandestine it all was.

"Can you stay here with me?" Jarvis whispered. It seemed risky, but probably not any riskier than just him staying there alone, so I agreed. But I went to put on something more comfortable than Phoebe's leather skirt and lace top.

When I returned, wearing yoga pants and an NYU sweatshirt and carrying a blanket from my bed, he'd already fallen asleep. He looked so sweet, like a baby. I watched him for a moment then covered him with the blanket. His eyes fluttered open. "I was hoping to see you in your jammies." He patted the space in front of him on the sofa. "Spoon with me."

I just fit. I could feel him behind me, kissing my hair as I fell asleep, and it was the nicest, safest feeling I've ever had in my life. I never wanted the night to end. I fell asleep in his arms.

We woke at 6:00. We were able to sneak out to the elevator while everyone else was still asleep. I went with him downstairs, past the doorman and out to the street. It was freezing, and I only had on the sweatshirt, but it was a nice, bracing feeling. I held him close and kissed him goodbye with all the sidewalk people trying to get around us, carrying briefcases and Christmas-wrapped packages, and the cold wind in my hair. He whispered that he'd see me on the 26th.

Then he stopped. "I want to say something to you, but I don't know if it's too soon."

I knew what he wanted to say. I wanted to say it too. I've felt it for weeks, since the night I was freaking about juries and Jarvis called and calmed me down. I lied when I told Phoebe I liked him. The truth is, I'm falling in love with him. And yet, it seems too scary to admit. Maybe I only feel that way because I have no one else. Or I'm starstruck. Or a silly girl.

But it isn't that. It's not his money or being starstruck that makes me feel this way. It's how I feel about myself when I'm with him. He makes me feel special the same way you choosing to send me to school made me feel special. I've never felt that way before.

But I've kept so much from him. He doesn't even know my full name! Probably he wouldn't love me if he knew where I came from. But maybe he would. He's so sweet and understanding. Phoebe says he's a socialist—maybe he wouldn't mind being with a member of the proletariat.

I put my arms around him and said, "I think I feel the same way. But let's not say it yet."

And then he kissed me again. He said, "I love . . . kissing you.

I loved holding you all night."

"Same." Then I ran my hand through his hair so he'd know there was a lot more in that "same" than just the one word. "Merry Christmas."

I turned and walked back inside, feeling like I was leaving my heart right there on West 54th Street. When I got into the lobby, I saw him, still standing there, like he'd been watching me walk away. I waved. Then I texted him from my phone. His Christmas gift, an audio file I made him, called *Jarvis's Christmas Gift from Jackie.*

Me, singing, "I've Got a Crush on You" by my old friend Gershwin. The Gershwins really get me. Part of the lyrics, by George's brother, Ira, go, "I never had the least notion that I could fall with so much emotion."

So much emotion!

My singing is all I have to give, and he's the one I want to give it to.

Then I snuck back into bed and pretended nothing had happened. I lay there, unable to sleep, just like Eliza Doolittle. Finally Phoebe woke up and asked me what had happened after we got home. I said, "Nothing much" and suggested she call Emma about getting her coat back.

Mr. Smith, I'm sending you a recording of me singing "I Could Have Danced All Night." It's my gift, but you sponsored it. I hope someday you'll come hear me in person.

Merry Christmas!

Love, Jacaranda

To: Johnsmith247@dll.com
Date: January 1, 12:11 p.m. Eastern Standard Time
Subject: New year, new problems

Happy New Year, Mr. Smith!

I'm sorry I haven't written before. I hope you haven't been worried.

You see, I returned to school early, the day after Christmas.

But let me back up.

Jarvis left on the 23rd, full of plans for when he came back. He texted me on Christmas Eve about how boring it was at the client's mansion (sigh!) and on the 25th, with Christmas wishes.

I opened your Christmas gifts. THANK YOU for the beautiful presents. The jade green cashmere sweater is my favorite color and just the right size! I needed the gloves—mine are not warm enough for the Michigan winter. I've already eaten the fancy chocolates. They are my first, best, grown-up Christmas gifts, and I will cherish them forever. Well, except the chocolate, which is gone!

Thank you also for the generous Delta Air Lines gift card. I appreciate that I can buy my own airline tickets and not have to ask permission. But, you'll see, I've already used part of it.

I had another present to open that morning, the little blue Tiffany box Jarvis left under the tree. It held a sterling silver ring with the infinity symbol and a card, signed "Love, Jarvis." I would have been so excited to open it, a ring from my wonderful boyfriend! It should have been my best Christmas ever. Except . . .

Except there was that other envelope in my suitcase. I saw it when I took out your gift.

Do you remember? The letter I found in the school mail and stuck in my suitcase, right before I left? My mother's letter that I put away for Christmas?

I opened it. But it didn't contain warm Christmas wishes or love. She's still upset about my leaving. "How can they take my baby all the way to Michigan?" she asked.

But, also, she had good news. Apparently, a women's advocacy group has taken on her case. They think her attempted murder was self-defense (it was) and that they can get her out of prison. Then I can come home and we can be together. Wasn't I so happy, she asked?!?!?!?!?!

I should be happy, Mr. Smith. I am happy. Of course, I don't want my mother imprisoned for a crime she didn't commit. I'm not a monster! I love my mother and miss her.

But, Mr. Smith, I also don't want to leave MAA!

I especially don't want to go back to Miami and live with her and her boyfriends and her addicted, irresponsible behavior. I'll be seventeen in April, but that's not old enough to live independently.

And then I started thinking of my friends, of Phoebe and

Daisy, all of them, and especially Jarvis. Jarvis is the only one who knows ANY of my story. But still, he doesn't know the whole truth about my mother, about the world I grew up in. It's a world that bears so little resemblance to his that we might as well not even live on the same continent. And I don't want him to know!

He wouldn't be sending me cards signed with love if he knew what a liar I was.

I know it's probably premature to say I love him. I don't know him well enough, and he doesn't know me. Right now, he's like Jim, Laura's gentleman caller in *The Glass Menagerie* (Jarvis loaned it to me), a too-good-to-be-true boy with no flaws. I'd have to know him better to see his flaws.

But I know I could love him.

They say adversity shows character. Maybe Jarvis hasn't known adversity like I have, and that's why he can afford to be so good. He's like a child who hasn't been hurt by the world, so he hasn't built up a hard shell like I have.

But he's been hurt, in his own way. And yet, he's still so kind and giving. Maybe he would still love me if he knew my past, but I don't want him to be with me out of charity.

Then I thought about how he said he wasn't sure he wanted to go to MIT, even though that's his dream school.

He doesn't want to go to MIT because he wants to be near *me*, a girl he's known for 2 months and who's lied about everything. He's too invested in me, an investment I can't repay. He thinks he loves me. But he doesn't even know who I am.

And, suddenly, I felt like I couldn't see him again, couldn't go to museums and eat diner food as if everything is okay when it isn't. It never can be, when everything he knows about me is a lie.

I told Phoebe my parents wanted me to come home for a few days. I texted Jarvis the same thing. Then I used part of your gift to exchange my ticket for an earlier one back.

I've been at MAA, studying hard and practicing ever since. I may as well get the most out of this place before I have to leave.

I haven't talked to Jarvis. His texts to me have gotten more concerned. Am I okay? Can I please contact him? He knows I'm not close to my mother, so he probably didn't believe my explanation in the first place. But I don't know what to tell him. I cry every night, not just because I miss him but because I know he must be hurt.

I have to forget him. It's for the best.

But I can't forget the rest of my situation. I love it here! I don't want to leave MAA! I feel like my life has finally begun, and now it is being taken away from me.

Is there anything you can do?

Love, Jacaranda

To: Johnsmith247@dll.com
Date: January 1, 3:59 p.m. Eastern Standard Time
Subject: Thank you

Dear Mr. Smith,

I just got off the phone with Vanessa. I appreciate her calling me over a holiday weekend. She said it might be possible for me to become emancipated, so that even if my mother was released, I would be an adult and able to make my own decisions, such as about school. She said she'd call your attorney on Monday and get back to me.

Meanwhile, I have another sad (and lengthy) text from Jarvis.

Please talk to me. I don't want to seem like a stalker, but two days before Christmas, I had a girlfriend who almost said she loved me and kissed me goodbye on West 54th Street and planned to see me in a few days. So I feel like I have reason to be concerned that she's gone missing. If I wasn't clear, I love you. I didn't say it before but I'm saying it now. Please talk to me, Jackie. . . .

I don't know what to do. I don't know what to tell him.

I'm immersing myself in music. In my nearly empty dorm, I'm singing warm-ups and learning Phoebe's entire playlist. We have auditions for a musical right after break.

Singing is the one thing in which I can take real comfort and pride right now.

Love, Jacaranda

P.S. I wish I could talk to you.

To: Johnsmith247@dll.com
Date: January 2, 10:45 p.m. Eastern Standard Time
Subject: A ray of light

Dear Mr. Smith,

Today is the last day before everyone moves back in. This campus is peaceful and freezing, as if real snow fairies have visited, touching each pine bough with sprinkles of white powder. I went for a late-morning walk, to take a break from thinking about Jarvis.

He hasn't texted since the last long one I told you about. I'm hoping he's given up. But I'm also hoping he *hasn't* given up. You know?

When it was warm enough to leave the dorm, I put on every piece of clothing I own, sweater, scarf, hat, boots, your gloves, all covered by my plum-colored down coat. I headed toward Hobie's Hideaway, where we went for karaoke that night. When they're not serving as a den of iniquity for teen deserters, they make a good chicken chili. Cafeteria offerings haven't been as imaginative over break—there are only so many string beans a person can eat. Or perhaps I got spoiled from living with the Hodgkins family for a week.

On my way back, stomach full, whistling "I Whistle a Happy Tune" from *The King and I*, I felt someone behind me.

I turned, sucking in my whistle. It was a girl from school who I couldn't place at first. Her hood covered her hair and some of her face.

"You didn't have to stop whistling," she said. "It was nice."

I asked if she'd just gotten back, and she shook her head. She'd been here the whole time.

Which was weird because it's mostly only the foreign students who don't go home for winter break. I'd sat with a girl from Sri Lanka last night. But this girl had no accent.

"I've been here a week," I said.

She nodded. "I saw you in the cafeteria."

"I was staying with a friend, but after a while . . ." I shrugged.

"The crust of humility . . ." The girl nodded, knowingly.

I did a double take because the line was from *The Glass Menagerie*, the play Jarvis loaned me. In it, Amanda, a depleted Southern belle, describes women who can't support themselves as "little birdlike women without any nest, eating the crust of humility all their lives." I so related to that line. That's exactly how I've felt ALL MY LIFE. My mother and I lived first with my grandmother, then with boyfriend after boyfriend and, after she was gone, I lived with my aunt April, then in foster homes. And even though Phoebe's and Daisy's families were perfectly nice, I didn't feel like I belonged there either. It felt like, well, being a little birdlike woman with no nest.

"I like that play," I said.

She nodded. "I'm doing an art installation based on that line, about the plight of women and children on the streets."

And that's when I put together who she was, the art and the big brown eyes. It was Falcon, the girl I'd heard about who'd lived on the street before coming to MAA.

As if to confirm this, she said, "Should we keep walking? It's cold out, though I've dealt with worse."

I nodded, and started walking. "You're Falcon?" I said.

"The famous. And you're Jacaranda, right?"

I started at my full name.

"Faculty told me you were coming," she said. "Thought we'd have stuff in common, I guess."

Right. Because we both had sob stories. Except everyone knew her story, while I'd lied about mine. I was such a coward. That's why I'm in this mess with Jarvis.

She kept talking. "I was looking for you those first few days, but when I finally saw you, you had a friend group." She made air quotes around the words "friend group" because it was something a guidance counselor would say. "I thought maybe they didn't know your whole thing, where you came from, and who was I to tell, if you were ashamed."

Did I imagine the hint of judgment in her voice? Was it because I felt I deserved it?

"I'm sorry," I said.

"No, I get it." She pulled her scarf tighter around her neck. "At first I kept it secret, too, invented reasons why I didn't go home for breaks, told people my parents were out of the country. But then it just got too tiring living a lie. You know?"

I nodded. I did know.

Falcon said her mom has an apartment now. But she couldn't afford the airfare to bring Falcon home for breaks. "I'm friends with all the people who stay," she said. "We're like a family. And I get a *lot* of work done."

I said I'd love to see her art sometime. We were near the dorm at that point, and she invited me to her room. Every square inch of the room, every wall, every surface, was covered with her artwork and art supplies. Drawings of children hung from a string across the room. On her desk was a pile of collaged paper birds.

I asked her if people made comments about her situation. Were they mean about it?

I expected her to, idk, equivocate, make excuses. But she said no. "Arty people are just so chill. If anything, they go out of their way to reach out."

Falcon and I sat together at dinner. She knows the Sri Lankan girl, Ayomi. We made plans to meet up other times, and now, I'm wondering if I'm underestimating my friends. If Falcon isn't feeling judged for her situation, maybe I wouldn't be judged for mine.

Except I've been lying all this time.

Love, Jacaranda

To: Johnsmith247@dll.com
Date: January 4, 10:01 p.m. Eastern Standard Time
Subject: New year, new life

Dear Mr. Smith,

It's Monday, and everyone's back. When Phoebe saw me, she actually HUGGED me. Perhaps you've gotten enough of a sense of Phoebe to understand how momentous this is.

"I've missed you!" she said. "I had to spend the rest of break with my *family*." She said it like it was a swear. Apparently, in my absence, she and Jarvis had taken her brother to the play.

I was hoping she'd tell me more about Jarvis, but instead she told me all her different decorating ideas for our suite—complete with Pinterest pages for each. Then Daisy came back and Phoebe repeated the whole thing. By dinner, we'd decided on a tropical sunset theme.

I told them I could probably get Falcon to help us design a mural. As I said it, I realized that I wasn't supposed to have been at school this past week, so how would I have met Falcon? But they didn't seem to have noticed.

Phoebe said, "Falcon? That art girl?"

I nodded, holding my breath. If they judged Falcon, they'd probably judge me too.

Phoebe said, "I didn't know you knew her. Her story is so inspiring."

"Art lifted her up," Daisy agreed, and they started talking about how cool it was. They both wanted to meet her, like she was a celebrity.

Over lunch, I heard all about Daisy's ski trip. She went on her first black-diamond ski trail (whatever that means, but it sounds hard). She also said, "Danny was so disappointed that I didn't bring you!"

I was surprised that Danny cared so much, but it turns out, Daisy and Brent were skiing together the whole time, so I was supposed to keep Danny occupied.

I wanted to be like these people, whose biggest problem was who to ski with.

I checked my email after lunch, but there was nothing from Vanessa.

Then came musical theater class and Harry's long-awaited announcement of the musical.

We're doing *Into the Woods*!

Yay! I watched the movie! It's a bunch of different fairy tales.

Behind me, Brooke was butthurt that it wasn't a dance musical. All the good dancers were. But I'm happy because it has lots of smaller roles. Maybe I can be a stepsister or Cinderella's dead mother. I think Harry likes me.

That is, if I'm still here for the musical.

Phoebe was very closemouthed, but when I asked her what she thought, she said she was "cautiously optimistic" that she could be Rapunzel.

"More like Cinderella," I said. She looks and sounds perfect for it.

She shook her head and said they'd give it to a senior. This girl Ava Tamargo will get it. She already got into NYU early decision.

"You don't know how good you are," I told Phoebe.

Owen was debating which prince he'd be—boys have it so much easier—and David asked how tall I was. I told him 5'4".

"Nah, Nina will be Red Riding Hood," Owen said. He looked at me. "Sorry, Jackie."

Someone asked Harry whether he was going to double-cast the leads. He wiggled his fingers and said all would be revealed and that we needed to have sixteen bars of a ballad and an up-tempo—one by Sondheim—for next Monday.

Since I've been practicing almost nonstop for the past week, I actually have that already. Actually, one of the songs on Phoebe's list is a Sondheim song, "There Won't Be Trumpets."

After dance, just as I was checking my email for the fifth time, Vanessa called. She'd spoken to your lawyer.

The good news (if we're calling it that) is that I'll definitely finish this school year. My mother's case will take several months to appeal, and more time for a new trial, if she gets it. I may even be enrolled as a senior by then, so my court-appointed attorney (called a guardian ad litem) could make an argument that I should stay here for the year, even if my mother gets out.

The bad news is that if she gets a new trial, I'll probably have to go to Miami and testify on her behalf. I was the only witness to what happened, after all. It might be on the news too.

The attorney does think I could file to be emancipated. There are several strategies.

But it's unlikely I'll be able to keep this all a secret. I want to, though. I want to spend the next few months as a normal girl, texting a boy until all hours, worrying about what part I'll get in the musical, and applying to summer programs.

Vanessa says to try not to worry for now.

I wish I could talk to you like a real relative. I wish I could talk to Jarvis too.

But thank you for helping me.

Love, Jacaranda

To: Johnsmith247@dll.com
Date: January 4, 11:09 p.m. Eastern Standard Time
Subject: My story

Dear Mr. Smith,

When Vanessa met with my Publix manager, they said you knew "my story" when you agreed to send me to school. But I'm guessing you don't know exactly what happened that day.

No one knows but me and my mom.

We'd been living with Oscar for about six months. He was a cokehead, which gave him a bad temper. I got in trouble for things like singing, laughing, "talking back," basically, being 11. My mom got yelled at for clinking the dishes too loudly when she washed them. Once, she touched Oscar when he was asleep, and he threw her against a wall.

That day it was my singing. I was watching *The Little Mermaid*. I wanted to be Ariel. I started singing "Part of Your World." Oscar, who was sleeping one off, yelled at me to shut the %@#$% up.

Mom put the sound down so low I could barely hear, but when it got to "Kiss the Girl," I started humming the "sha-la-lalalala" part. Next thing I knew, Oscar was standing over me.

"Run!" Mom said. I bolted for the door just as I felt Oscar's hand. We all ran out the door, Mom with her car keys. "Get in the car!" she shrieked. I had on flip-flops, and I remember them slapping against my feet as I dashed through the parking lot toward our blue Chevy, which was parked too far away. Oscar chased us, screaming names at me, all the names he always called my mother when he was mad. I remember thinking, "Run. Just run." If I got to the car, he wouldn't get me, wouldn't get us. Finally, I grabbed the door handle, but it wasn't unlocked yet. Mom got in on the other side. I heard the lock click.

He caught up with me.

"Get in! Get in!" my mother screamed. I scrambled, but Oscar pulled me back. I kicked him. Mom threw open the door and yanked me in. I lunged for the seat, trying to close the door.

Then, it's all a blur. The car started to pull away. I heard yelling. Oscar was under the car! He was pinned there, screaming in pain. I remember finally getting the door closed. I can still picture my hand on the blue door handle.

Later, the police came and took Mom away. They waited until Aunt April came to get me. I tried to tell them that my mother hadn't meant to hurt Oscar. It was an accident. But I didn't remember exactly how he went from grabbing me to being under the car. Maybe he slipped? Or maybe I pushed him.

My mother got fifteen years. It was worse because a car is a weapon. I've read up on this.

Often, women get worse sentences for killing men (even abusive men) than men get for killing women, because women

usually have to use a weapon while, a lot of times, men strangle a woman with their bare hands—which doesn't allow for as bad a charge.

I'm going to just leave that there, in bold. Also, Oscar's legs got messed up. I'm glad. I hope other parts of him don't work either.

So that's what happened. It's at least partly my fault because, if I hadn't been singing, Oscar wouldn't have gotten so mad . . . that time. But if we hadn't been living with that turd, if my mother had been stronger, if she'd been able to keep a job instead of needing him or some other scumbag to support her, hell, if she had been as brave as Falcon's mom, who lived in a shelter, it wouldn't have happened.

So I blame myself. But that doesn't mean I don't blame her too. And I blame Oscar most of all.

Love, Jacaranda

To: Johnsmith247@dll.com
Date: January 4, 11:20 p.m. Eastern Standard Time
Subject: (no subject)

Dear Mr. Smith,

As I was finishing up my email to you, Jarvis texted me. He's restricted himself to once a day the past few days. But he said he understood that he was going too fast. He suggested maybe we could just text about television or books or something. He wanted to know what I thought of the plays and books he loaned me, if I'd read them. He said he'd refrain from declaring his love.

He said he's lonely and wants someone to talk to.

It's hard to believe someone like Jarvis who has a million friends could be so lonely. But I know what it means to be lonely in your heart, even if you're surrounded by people.

I want to tell him about Falcon and *The Glass Menagerie* and the play. I want to tell him everything, and I want him to understand and say it's okay.

Should I text him back?

Love, Jacaranda

To: Johnsmith247@dll.com
Date: January 4, 11:29 p.m. Eastern Standard Time
Subject: (no subject)

I did.

To: Johnsmith247@dll.com
Date: January 4, 11:58 p.m. Eastern Standard Time
Subject: (no subject)

Not about everything, but I texted him a photo of Falcon's *Crust of Humility* installation-in-progress and told him all about it and about meeting her. He talked about his friend, Stewart, who has a crush on a girl who walks dogs in their neighborhood and wants to adopt a dog in order to meet her. He seemed to be okay with just texting about that and dropping the subject of where I'd been and whether I was mad at him.

He dropped the subject of how much he loves me too.

I'm glad.

To: Johnsmith247@dll.com
Date: January 5, 12:01 p.m. Eastern Standard Time
Subject: (no subject)

No, really. I'm glad.

To: Johnsmith247@dll.com
Date: January 6, 9:04 p.m. Eastern Standard Time
Subject: Secrets

Dear Mr. Smith,

Five days until auditions, and my classmates have become like Vegas oddsmakers, making predictions. There are several potential "cast lists" circulating. I try not to look, but I'm told I'm considered likely to get some part and a long shot for a few of the big roles, like the Baker's Wife or Red Riding Hood.

But I won't worry about that. I just want to be in the play!

Also, I have a math test tomorrow because somehow, algebra is still considered important.

JK, of course algebra is important. I plan on using it constantly in my future.

I'm glad I texted Jarvis because he takes AP Calculus, so he was able to explain Algebra 2 to me. None of my friends here are much better at math than I am.

People think Phoebe might be Cinderella, but we don't speak of it.

Speaking of freaking out, I'm also applying for summer

programs. MAA invited me to stay for their camp with a scholarship. I can also take a paid position here, if I want. The camp has a little shop where they sell smoothies and stuff. And I have sales experience. This would show independence if I want to file for emancipation.

But they're also encouraging me to apply for summer programs, which are mostly 2–3 weeks long. The office helped me get financial aid so I don't have to pay the application fees. Most of the schools require recordings of me singing and a monologue. However, the New England Conservatory has a local audition in Detroit. Phoebe and I and some others are going.

Also, we're going shopping for room décor on Saturday.

I'm happy as I can be, trying to be normal.

Love, Jacaranda

To: Johnsmith247@dll.com
Date: January 10, 11:07 a.m. Eastern Standard Time
Subject: 1 day until auditions

Dear Mr. Smith,

In case you have a burning desire to know, I think my algebra test went well.

More importantly, I've finally selected my songs.

Ballad: "The Music That Makes Me Dance" from *Funny Girl* by Jule Styne.

Up-tempo: "There Won't Be Trumpets" from *Anyone Can Whistle* by Stephen Sondheim. It's a great song about someone looking for a hero. I think of you when I sing it.

Last night, I was leaving the practice building after a marathon session. I planned to take today off to rest my voice and hang out with Daisy and Phoebe to decorate our room. I passed 3 people from my musical theater class and said hi, like a normal person.

No response. Then, when I was at the door, one of the girls said, real loud, "Isn't it funny, how some people think they can just show up here junior year and steal our roles when they haven't paid their dues?"

Okay, so you know I've tried to be very chill and Gandhi-like since I've been here. I haven't fought with anyone, and I even made friends with Phoebe, who started out as my enemy.

But, maybe because of that, or maybe because I'm upset about the whole situation with my mother . . . Well, her comment hit me like an apartment door slamming when your stuff is on the curb because you're evicted. I felt my body get hot, even though the cold air was rushing in from outside. I couldn't breathe.

I whirled around, taking leave of the heavy door. The wind caught it, and it clanged shut so hard that the sound reverberated throughout the building.

On the momentum of that slam, I caught up with them. I got right next to the girl who said it. Brooke. "Was that comment meant for me?"

Her two friends were all denying it, but she said, "Well, yeah. It's not fair that you got a solo in the December show when some of us who've been here longer get nada."

FAIR????

"So you think you've paid your dues, so you're more deserving?"

At this point, her friends were waving their hands, but Brooke said, "What? It's the truth."

I'd had it. I said, "So you paid your dues by going to this fancy school for two years longer, by having rich parents who made sure you had more training and more advantages?"

I waited for Brooke to answer. When she didn't, I went on. "And after all those extra classes and lessons, you aren't better than someone who just walked in off the street. But you think you deserve a pity solo? And that's somehow *my* fault?"

I knew I was out of control. I could feel my heart racing, and I was trying to stop myself because what I'd said was mean. Brooke didn't know about my past. She thought I just didn't care as much as she did. She didn't know anything about me. In the words of Freddie Mercury (of the classic rock band Queen), "I've paid my dues, time after time." But how would she know that?

I finally stopped talking. I stared at Brooke.

She stared back like I'd slapped her. I turned and walked away.

The guy she was with yelled after me, "You can't talk to people like that!"

I didn't answer. What could I say? Four months here, and I've officially become Phoebe.

But maybe Phoebe was treated like that too. Maybe that's why she's so afraid to fail.

And maybe people are trying to psych me out. But I have a scholarship to live up to, and I have your expectations. No one has ever expected much of me, but now you put your faith in me. I won't disappoint you.

I stormed back through the freezing night. I still felt hot, except my face, which had tears frozen to it. I reached my room, threw myself onto my lavender bed, and sobbed.

I guess I must have been too loud because a minute later, Daisy stuck her head into my room and asked if I was okay.

Between gulps and sobs, I recapped the whole experience. Phoebe came in partway through, and when I finished she said,

"Who was it? I bet I know." I told them it was Brooke. Phoebe nodded like it was as she'd expected.

"I shouldn't have gone off on her," I said.

Phoebe shrugged. "She shouldn't have said that. Pretty cowardly to yell it at your back."

Daisy was shocked, but Phoebe said, "I believe it. People can be mean here. You didn't see it because you were new, so people didn't view you as a threat. Now they do."

I said, "Do you see me as a threat?"

"A little," she admitted. "But you make me work harder."

Then she offered to watch me do my songs and give me notes. "But only *after* we order art supplies to fix up our room."

I love my roommates.

Love, Jacaranda

To: Johnsmith247@dll.com
Date: January 11, 9:23 p.m. Eastern Standard Time
Subject: Audition day . . . well, first day

Dear Mr. Smith,

A singer stands before an audience of her peers. She glances around. Not every face is friendly; not everyone wishes her well. She still has her friends, but she has detractors too.

She breathes. It's okay.

And then, she starts singing.

There won't be trumpets or bolts of fire
To say he's coming.

Did I mention it's not a happy, positive song overall?

So I sang the whole thing straight to Brooke. Ha!

I finished. It was the best I've sung that song, maybe the best I've ever sung anything.

And the applause was . . . scattered. David and Owen clapped their hands off. Phoebe and Nina, who are my best female friends in the class (isn't it weird that I'm saying that about Phoebe?), clapped a normal amount. But there were some golf claps, and even some seniors were giving me side-eye.

Which meant I killed it. Phoebe was right. People were nice because they didn't see me as competition. Now they do. Before I came here, no one expected much of me. As long as I showed up and didn't smoke weed on school grounds, it was okay. But now, I have a reputation. I need to do my best because people are counting on me to succeed . . . and others want me to fail.

But I miss the warm, comfortable MAA cocoon. It's broken now, like a real cocoon, when a butterfly emerges. MAA had felt like a family.

But, then again, I guess families have petty jealousies too.

I started my ballad, "The Music That Makes Me Dance." And when I sang, "He'll sleep and he'll rise in the light of two eyes that adore him," the only eyes I could picture were Jarvis's.

I didn't even listen to the applause when it was over. I knew I rocked it.

Tomorrow we read for the parts. More news then. I'm going to bed.

Well, after I text Jarvis to tell him how it went.

Love, Jacaranda

P.S. Phoebe kicked butt, too, not that anyone will admit it.

To: Johnsmith247@dll.com
Date: January 12, 6:14 a.m. Eastern Standard Time
Subject: My mother

Dear Mr. Smith,

I wrote to my mother to tell her I'm very happy that group is taking on her case and that I'll be there if she needs me to testify. But I'm hoping I can stay in school here, even if she gets out of prison.

Also, maybe she could move to Michigan and come live near me. There's certainly nothing for her in Florida other than bad ex-boyfriends and worse memories.

I hope it all works out.

Love, Jacaranda

To: Johnsmith247@dll.com
Date: January 12, 7:29 p.m. Eastern Standard Time
Subject: Second day of auditions—the DRAMA!

Dear Mr. Smith,

Into the woods we go!

Today were the acting auditions.

Harry had us raise our hands for the parts we wanted to read for. Nina chose Red Riding Hood, Owen chose Cinderella's Prince (the better prince), David, the Wolf. Despite saying she'd only get Rapunzel, I noticed Phoebe raised her hand for Cinderella and Brooke for the Witch.

Harry was pacing back and forth, eyeing all of us with his Shakespearean stare. He stopped in front of me.

"What about you?" His voice was thundering, and he pointed a long finger.

"Um . . ." I realized I was the only one who hadn't raised my hand yet. But he'd only mentioned four female parts, Red, Cinderella, the Baker's Wife, and the Witch. I knew I wasn't going to get any of those big parts.

"I'm managing expectations," I said.

Harry's eyes widened. "You want to be in the show?" he boomed.

"Of course . . . sir. If I get in."

Behind me, I heard someone whisper something, possibly mocking my "sir." I once had a foster mom from Mississippi who used to cuff me if I didn't say "sir" and "ma'am."

I said I knew I wouldn't get any of those big parts, since I'm only a junior.

Harry agreed that was probably true, but, "Allow me to make that decision, young lady." He said in the first round, he'd call people up for the larger parts, and then he'd cast the smaller parts based on those auditions. He suggested I try for the Baker's Wife or the Witch.

I chose the Witch. I tried to make my voice sound high and witchy. The other girls all sounded the same, copying Bernadette Peters. The only one who sounded different was Ava Tamargo, a senior, but she was the one Phoebe said would be Cinderella.

Brooke tried for the Witch too. Her voice was too nasal. She tried for Cinderella, the Baker's Wife, and Red Riding Hood too, all with the same nasal voice.

Then Harry asked me to read for the Baker's Wife, but probably just because he wanted to have different people read. He had Phoebe read for Cinderella twice and the Baker's Wife as well.

Then there's a dance call tomorrow with callbacks Thursday (to be posted Wednesday night).

I hope I get a part. I admit that Brooke being such a hater really motivated me.

Love, Jacaranda

To: Johnsmith247@dll.com
Date: January 12, 9:16 p.m. Eastern Standard Time
Subject: Can't sleep

Dear Mr. Smith,

Today, I was almost too tired to go to dinner. My head started nodding onto my music theory homework, and I had to walk around the room to stay awake. I could barely brush my teeth.

But as soon as my lights were out, I was WIDE awake. My mind was racing. What if I didn't get called back? Would I get called back? Would people hate me if I got called back? What if I got a part and then had to leave school?

I turned the lights back on.

This is why Phoebe gets so nervous, because she knows she's being judged.

Now I know too.

Last semester, when I was nervous about juries, the one who talked me down in the middle of the night was Jarvis. Now, we barely talk. I think he's giving me my "space." We text about movies and homework, but we don't have the long conversations we used to have. I know that's my fault. Ever since I got that letter from my mother, I've pushed him away.

Do you think I'm right to? Now, it seems like I might have a chance of staying at MAA. Maybe I can relax. Maybe I can talk to him about something real.

I miss him.

I know you probably won't even read this, but maybe you could give me a sign.

How about this? I'll take a nonanswer as you telling me I should call him. I'll give you until 10:45 to tell me not to.

Love, Jacaranda

To: Johnsmith247@dll.com
Date: January 12, 10:46 p.m. Eastern Standard Time
Subject: Nothing from you

Okay, I'm going to call him. Thanks!

To: Johnsmith247@dll.com
Date: January 13, 12:01 a.m. Eastern Standard Time
Subject: Thank you

Dear Mr. Smith,

. . . for saying I should call Jarvis.

We talked for an hour, until it got too late, and he said I should rest up for dance tomorrow. I love how he worries about me. I feel so much better about auditions and singing and life.

"When we're given a gift, you have the responsibility to understand its value." Jarvis says my talent is a gift. According to him, I have a responsibility to share it with the world.

Somehow, that made me feel better. I'm not fighting against my classmates. Instead it's our mission to spread music and theater to the world.

"That makes me sound like Spider-Man." I made my voice gruff. "'With great power comes great responsibility.'"

I was joking, but Jarvis said, "You do have power. You're so talented, Jackie. You don't understand how talented you are."

When he said it, I believed him. I remembered the show in December, when he said I was "astonishing." He said it like it was a regular word people use all the time.

"I'm so glad you called, Jackie," he said. "I missed your voice so much."

"I missed yours too." I miss more than his voice. I wish he was here, so I could see him, touch him.

We talked longer. He's all worried about Carnegie Mellon. Since he hasn't heard from them, he's realized now that that's the only place he wants to go. He wants to be in Pittsburgh, at the school Andrew Carnegie built. "Did you know he gave away ninety percent of his fortune?" he asked me. "Did you know he came from nothing and became the richest man in the world? And he believed the wealthy were morally obligated to help others? Did you know he gave money to cities to build over 2,000 libraries?"

I didn't know any of that. I also didn't know that the City of Pittsburgh has over 440 bridges or that Carnegie Mellon offers a BS in artificial intelligence, the first in the country.

I agreed it was cool. "You'll get in," I told him.

"And you'll get a part," he said. "Don't let them get in your head."

It made me feel better to worry together. I wish he was here.

I still didn't tell him about my mother. I couldn't. But at least I told him about me.

Love, Jacaranda

To: Johnsmith247@dll.com
Date: January 13, 9:17 p.m. Eastern Standard Time
Subject: Callbacks

Dear Mr. Smith,

Dance call went well. I'm attaching a screenshot of the callback list.

Spoiler alert: I got called back for major parts! The Witch and the Baker's Wife. That still probably means I'll get a smaller part (managing expectations), but some people (coughBrookecough) only got called back for smaller parts.

Phoebe got called back for Cinderella. Nina got called back for Red. David and Owen got called back for pretty much everything. I think David will be the Wolf, which is what he wants. OMG, I'm getting to be like my odds-making classmates.

Going to call Jarvis now and tell him.

Love, Jacaranda

To: Johnsmith247@dll.com
Date: January 14, 3:47 p.m. Eastern Standard Time
Subject: Live, on-the-scene coverage!

Dear Mr. Smith,

I'm at callbacks! I'll give you a live play-by-play.

There are about 30 of us here. Phoebe is frozen solid next to me. I think she's doing deep breathing exercises. She's in the zone. We practiced together, though.

Harry's talking now. I just looked at Brooke, and if looks could kill, I'd be puking up blood right now. I smiled back. I turned to Nina (who's on my other side) and whispered, "I hope you get something!" She said she hoped I did too.

To audition for the Witch, I'm doing a section of her rap song from the opening number. If you're not familiar with *Into the Woods*, the Witch is the one from *Rapunzel*. The rap is about how she took a baby from a couple who stole from her garden, and it's basically a list of vegetables. It's hard not to get tongue-tied, saying things like, "Rooting through my rutabaga, raiding my arugula. . ." especially when you're trying to sound like both a rapper and an old witch at once.

And especially when you're worried about people hating on you.

I remember what Jarvis said about not letting other people get in my head.

I'm going to volunteer to go first!

Love, Jacaranda

To: Johnsmith247@dll.com
Date: January 14, 4:09 p.m. Eastern Standard Time
Subject: I went first

Dear Mr. Smith,

Can you believe it? I went first! I figured the other performances wouldn't get in my head that way.

I thought about the Witch. She's old, old and ugly, but she was once beautiful.

And she's lonely. She only has Rapunzel, who only loves her because she's her captive. How would that feel? She wants desperately to keep Rapunzel with her. But she also wants something else, something the Baker and his wife can get her.

I know what it's like to feel lonely and unloved.

I know what it's like to feel ugly. You might say I'm not, but when the only people you've trusted in life have always rejected you, you feel ugly anyway.

This year, with you and this place and Jarvis, I'm starting to feel pretty again.

So I stood up there and tried to put all that love and tragedy and pathos into it.

Into a song about lettuce.

When I finished, no one applauded. I guess maybe people don't clap at callbacks?

But Nina nodded reassuringly. Phoebe didn't say anything. She's still . . . breathing.

I didn't look at Brooke.

Now Ava's doing the same song. She's great! Of course she is. She already got into NYU.

Would it be wrong if I say I think I'm a *tiny bit* better for this part?

No, she's better. And also taller and more commanding. She has a beautiful voice and might be able to do other songs, like "Stay with Me," better than I can. And she's a senior.

I'm going to stop for a while now.

Love, Jacaranda

To: Johnsmith247@dll.com
Date: January 14, 4:47 p.m. Eastern Standard Time
Subject: On to the Cinderellas!

All the Witches have gone. Tbh, I feel Ava and I were the best, but I know he'll give it to a senior.

The Cinderellas are up now. Harry yelled at everyone to hurry.

Phoebe's breathing must have helped because she was flawless, singing "On the Steps of the Palace." It's a hard song with weird accompaniment.

No one else was as good as she was. She's just meant to be Cinderella.

I hope she gets it. When she sat in her seat, I reached out and gave her a little pat. She looked at me funny.

Now, the Bakers are going. Oh, wait . . .

To: Johnsmith247@dll.com
Date: January 14, 5:05 p.m. Eastern Standard Time
Subject: Still auditioning

Dear Mr. Smith,

Ethan Connover, one of the seniors, tried out for the Baker. He was definitely the best. After he was done, Harry said, "Jackie! Come here and stand by Ethan!"

I obeyed. I heard a few people behind me whispering. But I had no idea what it meant. When I got up, I saw that Ethan is short. Shorter than all the girls trying for the Baker's Wife except me and Nina (who is really short, short enough to be Red).

Then he called up all the wives in succession, to stand next to Ethan.

I remember reading once that when actors like Tom Cruise do movies, everyone else in the movie also has to be short.

Now he's going to have us read in groups.

Love, Jacaranda

To: Johnsmith247@dll.com
Date: January 14, 8:35 p.m. Eastern Standard Time
Subject: And now, we wait . . .

Dear Mr. Smith,

Harry had us read in groups of two or three. Me as the Baker's Wife with Ethan as the Baker. Ava as the Baker's Wife with David as the Baker. And on and on until he'd used every possible combination.

He called me up a lot. I'm hoping that's a good sign.

At one point, he called Phoebe up, and then 3 other girls, including me, and told us to stand around her. Then he swapped Ava for Phoebe.

When I sat down, David whispered, "Stepmother and stepsisters with Cinderella."

The script describes the Stepmother and stepsisters as being "beautiful of face."

Do you think I'm beautiful of face?

AAAAAAAAAAGGGGGGGGGGHHHHHHHHHHHH-HHH! I can't think about this anymore.

Oh! I heard a loud noise in the room next door.

Love, Jacaranda

To: Johnsmith247@dll.com
Date: January 14, 8:42 p.m. Eastern Standard Time
Subject: I'm okay

Dear Mr. Smith,

It was Phoebe, running into her floor lamp.

"It got in my way," she said.

"She punched it," Daisy said. "I *saw* her!"

"It had it coming," Phoebe said, smiling.

Close to 24 hours before I am out of my misery. Harry always puts up the cast list late on Friday, to give people a chance to calm down before he sees them. Smart man.

Love, Jacaranda

To: Johnsmith247@dll.com

Date: January 15, 12:14 p.m. Eastern Standard Time

Subject: 6 more hours

The hours are crawling like the old ladies on scooters at Publix.

To: Johnsmith247@dll.com
Date: January 15, 6:15 p.m. Eastern Standard Time
Subject: I'M IN THE PLAY

Dear Mr. Smith,

I'm Cinderella's Stepmother!

At 6:00, Harry put up the cast list and fled campus through a back door to a waiting unmarked car.

By 6:05, everyone was on the phone to their parents, laughing or crying. I even heard Phoebe shrieking, "Yes! Yes, I got it! Cinderella!" And telling her mother to book plane tickets.

Everyone except me. I have no family to call. I texted the cast list to Jarvis. He tried to call me, but I came back to my room to send this first.

When Phoebe got off the phone, I hugged her. "I'm your stepmother! I get to boss you around!"

I was jumping up and down until I noticed she wasn't. I stopped. "What?"

"You're actually happy for me?" she said. "Like, not sarcastically?"

I said yes, of course. She's my friend.

"That's literally never happened to me in my entire life."

"You deserve it," I said. Maybe this will boost her confidence for when we go to Detroit to audition for that summer program.

I'M SO HAPPY! It's a good part for my first-ever play. Obviously, Harry thought I was funny and "beautiful of face." I get to be in most of the group numbers. All the major female parts except Cinderella went to seniors, so that's fair. Nina is a stepsister, Lucinda, and understudy for Red Riding Hood. David is the Wolf.

I'm also the understudy for the Witch, who is Ava Tamargo.

Brooke didn't get a part. She was crying about having to tell her parents. I'm not saying that adds to my gratefulness for being Stepmother, but I'm not *not* saying that either.

Karma is a thing.

The play is April 1–3, and 8–10 (with both matinee and evening performances on the Saturdays), btw. Make your travel plans.

I'm going to call Jarvis to tell him, because he might actually come!

Love, Jacaranda

To: Johnsmith247@dll.com
Date: January 19, 7:13 a.m. Eastern Standard Time
Subject: The BIG DAY

Dear Mr. Smith,

Yesterday was a holiday, so no musical theater class. Good thing too, since I didn't have to suffer the baleful glances of the uncast.

But today, there's a read-through after school!

I can't wait! Getting this part is proof that I BELONG, that my admission wasn't a fluke. I feel like I got invited to join an exclusive club!

Love, Jacaranda

To: Johnsmith247@dll.com
Date: January 19, 7:10 p.m. Eastern Standard Time
Subject: The BIG day gets bigger!

Dear Mr. Smith,

OMG! This has been the best day so far!

When we met for the run-through, Harry congratulated us all on our parts. "It was a tough decision, as there were many talented students. You should all be very pleased with yourselves." Then he talked about how there are no small parts, only small actors.

In the play, I get to order Phoebe around, telling her she can go to the ball if she completes all sorts of herculean tasks, like picking lentils out of ashes. I tried to be snotty and mean. I sort of channeled Phoebe's New York friends.

After rehearsal, Ava came up to me. I didn't think she was talking to me at first, because she's kind of a superstar, and I'm a lowly junior. But she said, "You were incredible in auditions. I was scared you'd get the part! You'll definitely get a lead next year."

I said I was excited to get a part at all—which is true.

She asked me to walk with her to dinner. She said maybe we could practice together, and she'll give me tips for college auditions next year, kind of like a big sister. She was so nice!

And then I walked into the cafeteria and saw Brooke and another girl who didn't get a part. They were giving me death stares, and when I passed them, I heard Brooke say something about "show her." I wondered what she meant.

Ava heard them, too, and said, "When you're good, you're going to have haters."

Sigh. Still, if it has to be a competition, I'm glad I'm winning for once!

Also, we had chicken divan again for dinner. It never gets old for me!

Love, Jacaranda

To: Johnsmith247@dll.com
Date: January 19, 10:47 p.m. Eastern Standard Time
Subject: Motivation

Dear Mr. Smith,

I'm trying to think about my character's motivation: What makes a Wicked Stepmother into a Wicked Stepmother?

Since Jarvis knows everything about theater, I asked him. "What do you think the stepmother's motivation is, for being so mean to poor Cinderella?"

I've had my share of mean moms in my life, so it was hard to be sympathetic.

He said, "I guess she's worried about her own daughters. She sees they're not as good as Cinderella, and she thinks no one will love them if there's a prettier, sweeter girl around. So she has to take her out of the equation."

That made sense. It also made my character sound like a nicer person, someone who did things out of love instead of just a villain. I thought of my aunt April, who said she couldn't take care of me anymore because she had her own kids. It made me feel so unlovable at the time.

"I like that. She's just a loving mom," I said.

Jarvis said, "I might be getting a stepmother soon."

"Your dad's girlfriend that you spent Christmas with?" I asked. "It's that serious?"

I could almost hear him shrug. "Wendelin, that's her name. I don't care. I'm going away to college anyway, and the apartment's so big, I probably won't even notice her when I'm home. She might even make it look less like a museum."

I didn't tell him it looked more like a law firm.

He said, "She's kind of young, though."

I asked how young, and he said, "Well, not *that* young. Maybe thirty. But they might have more kids or something."

"Would that be terrible?" I asked.

He thought about it and said, "No. It'd be kind of cool to have a little brother. I could teach him to play video games. Maybe he'd come visit me at college."

"You'd be a good big brother," I said.

"You think?" he asked.

"You're a good cousin. Phoebe loves you, and she's not someone who warms up to everyone. Everyone likes you."

He thought about it a second, then said, "Sometimes it's lonely, having everyone like you."

"Why's that?" I asked. I've never had too much love.

"Because, if everyone likes you, it's because no one really knows you. They don't know you well enough to know your flaws."

I got it. I know what it's like to try to be perfect. Every time I went to a new school or foster home, I tried not to be a burden.

"What do people not know about you?" I asked him.

He tried to laugh it off, but I said, "Tell me something embarrassing about yourself."

"Something embarrassing . . ." He thought a second, then said, "I sucked my thumb until I was almost 10 years old."

I said I couldn't picture that. He seemed so confident and self-sufficient.

"Yeah. The doctor called it self-soothing. I didn't do it in public. But, every night, when I tried to sleep, I would start. Or I'd go into the boys' room at school."

"Did you wreck your teeth?" I asked.

He laughed. "Yeah. They stuck out like a window air-conditioner. The dentist told my parents I had to quit, so they bribed me with going to sleepaway science camp. That worked for a while. But when my mom died, I started again. Sometimes I still miss it."

"I still like you," I said.

"Okay, here's another one," he said. "I'm really jealous. When you told me about that guy, Preston, making a move on you at that party, I kind of wanted to go back and kick his teeth in—except he's probably bigger than I am. But this caveman instinct definitely got hold of me."

"You didn't do it, though," I said. My mother's had a ton of boyfriends who would have.

"No, I have self-control. But even at Thanksgiving, when you mentioned your friend Daisy's twin brother, I wondered if he was handsome."

I laughed. "He is . . . but . . ." I didn't finish the sentence. Danny wasn't the one I wanted. I said, "But I like you." I wished he was here. I decided to tell him something embarrassing about me, even though he hadn't asked. So I told him about growing up poor and the Goodwill clothes and the free lunch. "I never wanted to go over to anyone's house after school because then I'd have to invite them to my house, and I couldn't." I didn't tell him part of the reason I couldn't was because my mother or whatever boyfriend she had that week might be passed out on the sofa. But I did tell him about being here on scholarship, and how different I felt from my classmates all the time, how I worried that it would all get taken away from me. It all came rushing out even though I was kind of trying to push the words back in.

It was . . . a lot. But when I finally finished, he said, "That must be hard. But that shouldn't be embarrassing."

I said it was to me.

He said, "You're looking at it wrong, then. You're *better* than other people. It's easy to make it when you've had a head start."

He said, "You want to know something I found out? I thought no one knew about my thumb-sucking at the time. Like, I thought I hid it. But, just recently, my friend Chase—he's been one of my best friends since kindergarten—started dragging me about how straight my teeth are, that my orthodontist was so gifted that you couldn't even tell I'd been a thumb sucker. And that's when I realized he'd known all along. Probably all my friends had. They were just nice about it. Because real friends don't make fun of flaws you can't help."

I heard what he was saying, that my real friends would understand. Obviously, Jarvis has lived this charmed life where everyone's nice to him. But I appreciated that he was saying that *he'd* understand if I told him the truth.

But he didn't know what the truth was, so how could he be sure?

"You always make me feel good about myself," I said.

"Same," he said. He paused and then said, "Are you ever going to tell me why you left at Christmas?"

There was another pause, and I thought about filling it. I wanted to tell him *everything*. Everything about my mother, her creepy boyfriends, Oscar, my life.

"I'd understand, Jackie," he said.

But if I tell him, I can't take it back, so I said I was tired. I want to tell him the truth, but I don't want to lose him.

Should I have told him?

Love, Jacaranda

To: Johnsmith247@dll.com
Date: January 26, 10:47 p.m. Eastern Standard Time
Subject: Rehearsals

Dear Mr. Smith,

The past week has been a whirlwind of rehearsals, preparing for summer program auditions, plus my regular classes. Next week, I'm going to Detroit with 8 classmates (including—ugh—Brooke) to audition for the New England Conservatory. Phoebe already did one live audition for a dance program at the Boston Conservatory, but I'm not applying for that. My early ballet training is not what it could have been.

I sent recordings of myself doing 2 songs, a minute of dance, and a monologue to 10 university summer programs. Carnegie Mellon, NYU, and Michigan are the gold standard, but the reality is, I'll go where I get a full scholarship.

We decorated our room in the tropical sunset theme. We painted one wall of each of our rooms and the entire bathroom a bright pumpkin color then added streaks of red, blue, and gold. Falcon helped us. She suggested adding a darker blue for texture. We hung the ceilings of both rooms with matching colored silks.

It's the most beautiful suite in the whole building!

"You'll have to paint it back white in the spring," Angie warned us when some helpful person complained about the paint fumes. We said we would . . . but we're secretly hoping we can just be assigned the same rooms for next year. Phoebe, Daisy, and I all want to room together again.

I hope I'm still here next year.

At the end of play rehearsal each day, we get notes. The majority—good and bad—are for people with bigger parts. But yesterday, Harry said, "Jackie!"

I jumped at my name, expecting him to say I screwed up, but he said, "Outstanding portrayal. I've honestly never sympathized with the stepmother before."

"Is that good?"

"It's always good for characters not to be one-note. What were you thinking about?"

I told him that, in my elementary school, there were some moms who came in to volunteer in class. One kid named Trevor was a huge bully, who stole my stuff and tipped over my chair every day of his life. But, when his mom came in, she acted like the teacher was being mean by separating him from his friends. She saw him as her sweet li'l dumplin'. I figured that was how Cinderella's stepmother saw her daughters too.

"She's just trying to be a good mother," I said. "A good mother takes her daughters' side over anyone, even her husband."

When I finished, Harry looked like maybe that was more than he wanted to know, but said it was "excellent character work."

On the way to dinner, David said that was the nicest he's ever seen Harry be to anyone!

Next week, I get to play the Witch in rehearsals, because Ava's going to Chicago for something called Unified Aauditions, where you can audition for ten colleges at once. She said she knew I'd hold down the fort.

Love, Jacaranda

To: Johnsmith247@dll.com
Date: January 29, 9:33 p.m. Eastern Standard Time
Subject: Mail

Dear Mr. Smith,

It was a mistake to walk back from dinner with Phoebe. If I'd walked back with Daisy or Nina or Lucky or anyone else, I probably wouldn't have checked my mail. I seldom get anything, so I only go once a week. But Phoebe stopped to check, so I did too.

There was a letter. I stuffed it into my bag real quick, before Phoebe could notice the prison address. But she was too busy poring over *Pointe* magazine, a subscription makeup box, and some other package. Phoebe's mail is definitely #goals for me.

She opened the package and unfurled a beach-themed shower curtain. "Found it online. What did you get?" Phoebe asked, probably just pretending to be interested in my life.

"Oh, nothing. Letter from my mom."

She seemed surprised. "You never talk about your family. I was thinking maybe you were an orphan." She laughed when she said it, but it kind of felt true.

When I got back to our room, I finally sat on the bed and opened the letter.

"I miss you, baby," my mother wrote. And then she told me the appeals process is taking a long time. They're trying to get her a new trial.

I wonder what it would be like to have a mom like Phoebe's, coming to my performances and being all proud in the audience. My mother came to my spring concert once in elementary school. I didn't even know I was lucky. I wonder, if she got out of prison, would she be there, rooting for me, wishing me well?

Do you know what I love most about being at MAA? You might think it's the surroundings or the people or the opportunities. I love all those things. But the best thing is the predictability. Breakfast, lunch, and dinner at definite times every day, tuna on Fridays, lentil soup on Wednesdays. Curfew at 10:00. Angie always says, "Isn't it a beautiful day?" unless there's a thunderstorm, in which case she says, "How about this weather?" The thermostat is always set at 65 degrees. If I put my shoes in the closet, they'll be there the next time I look. No one's late, no one's drunk, the water's never turned off, no one's inexplicably in a bad mood, and other than over break, I never go to sleep in a different bed than I woke up in. I didn't have that type of predictability in foster care, and I sure didn't have it with my mother.

Children need predictability, and it took me a long time to realize I had it here, that it's not all going to be taken away from me.

But human beings need love too, and while I still love my

mother, she isn't here. There's only one person who loves me in real time, in real life, right now.

And I'm going to tell him I love him too. I'm going to tell him everything, and he's going to be okay with it.

I hope.

Love, Jacaranda

To: Johnsmith247@dll.com
Date: January 30, 11:30 a.m. Eastern Standard Time
Subject: I didn't call him

Dear Mr. Smith,

I didn't call Jarvis because when I started to, I heard a knock on the bathroom door. When I opened it, there was Phoebe, holding a bottle of champagne.

She had the cast recording of *South Pacific* on loud enough to muffle our conversation and whispered, "I brought it from home. You missed New Year's, so I thought we could toast together."

I looked at my calendar. "It's almost February."

She whispered, "I know, but they're suspicious right after breaks. Now, they have their guard down." She unwrapped the little wires around the cork then opened it with a big POP!

I followed her into their room. Daisy was waiting with three plastic flute glasses. Phoebe poured champagne into them and handed them around.

"Won't we get in trouble?" I said.

"Not if no one finds out." Daisy raised her glass.

"What are we toasting to?" I asked.

"What else? Our new shower curtain!" Daisy said.

I was a little nervous about drinking at school. But Daisy was right. I took a sip.

The other two drank theirs down and looked at me. I drank mine. But one glass was enough for me. I'd let them have my share.

That was before Daisy suggested a drinking game.

"Good idea." Phoebe refilled our glasses. "We can play Never Have I Ever." When I didn't know what that was, Phoebe (after looking at me like I was raised in a convent) explained that we have to begin a sentence with "Never have I ever" and then reveal something we'd never done before. Anyone who had done it had to drink.

I agreed. What else could I do?

Daisy started. "Never have I ever sung in front of an audience."

Rip. Phoebe and I drank, grumbling that it wasn't fair.

Phoebe went next and returned Daisy's burn. "Never have I ever farted in the elevator." She gave Daisy a look, and Daisy drank.

I went next, trying to think of something they'd done and I hadn't.

"Never have I ever eaten raw sushi."

After they both drank (I was sure they would), Daisy said, "Never have I ever stalked someone online." She stared at Phoebe when she said that.

"I wouldn't call it stalking," Phoebe protested.

"Mmm-hmm," Daisy said, and Phoebe drank. Daisy said,

"Phoebe met this guy at an a cappella festival last year, and she was so obsessed with him she created a fake Instagram just so she could stalk him."

"Turned out he had a boyfriend," Phoebe said.

My turn. I said, "Never have I ever had to be dragged away from a party."

Phoebe drank, but she gave me a look that said not to tell Daisy.

She also drank for Never have I ever smoked weed (Daisy did too), Never have I ever had my heart broken, and Never have I ever kissed someone of the same gender.

Daisy drank for Never have I ever crushed on a teacher and Never have I ever shoplifted (though it turned out she'd chickened out of the shoplifting and left the nail polish near the checkout).

I drank for Never have I ever gotten kicked out of someplace. I didn't tell them I'd been eight at the time, and my mother, her boyfriend, and I got kicked out of the movies because we were too loud.

On her next turn, Phoebe said, "Never have I ever made out with my cousin, Jarvis."

The look on her face was a question.

Daisy said, "Eww, of course you never made out with your cousin." Then she saw Phoebe looking at me and said, "Oh."

I said, "Define making out."

Daisy said, "Omigod, what did you do?"

"Just . . . not that much." But finally, I took a drink.

"I knew it," Phoebe said. "Did he stay over my parents' house that night? Did I hear you sneaking downstairs in the morning?"

I refused to answer, since it wasn't in the rules of the game.

Daisy said, "Never have I ever kept secrets from my friends about who I was dating."

I took a sip and countered with, "Never have I ever made out with a guy named Brent in a gondola." Because I was sort of wondering about that.

"I so did," Daisy said, drinking.

By this point, the bottle was mostly gone, and I was worried about what else Phoebe would ask about Jarvis. So I said, "Let's play a different game."

"Wait." Phoebe refilled her glass. "I'll drink, but I think we should each get to ask one more question." To me, she said, "Are you guys, like, together?"

I said, "I think so?" wondering if that was true but also wondering if she'd get mad.

"Cool," she said, and took another sip.

I said, "My question: What's with you and the stage fright?"

She looked surprised since it wasn't really a secret. Finally, she said, "I don't know. I'm excited at first, and then I worry about people judging me and freak out."

It would have been easy to say she shouldn't, but I knew she knew that, so I didn't. Instead, I said, "You seem to be getting better about it."

"I am," she said.

"I have a question," Daisy said, and she tried very hard to pronounce her words carefully, probably so it wouldn't come out "queshon."

We looked at her. She said, "So you've been dating Phoebe's hot, rich cousin all this time, and you didn't tell me?"

I admitted we'd had dinner the day he'd come to town. Daisy said she understood now why I didn't go to Vermont with her family.

Daisy and Phoebe started searching on their phones for a different drinking game. I pretended to search. I figured if I waited long enough, Phoebe and Daisy would simply drink the rest of the champagne. I don't like drinking. I like feeling in control of my actions. I've spent too much time around people who weren't. Instead, I got sucked in by social media.

And the very first thing I saw was a photo of Jarvis where someone had tagged him.

A photo of Jarvis with some blond girl.

She was hanging on his shoulder.

The caption said, "Jarvis Pendleton enters Lincoln Center with model Faun Montgomery."

Faun? That had to be a typo, right?

But she was sooooo pretty. She looked older than him, but she's probably one of those models who looks 25 when she's 17. She was almost as tall as Jarvis, and she was leaning in toward him, laughing, like he'd said something fascinating. She had the best eyebrows I've ever seen. I've always thought my eyebrows were my biggest flaw. How could I even blame Jarvis for liking a girl with such a high arch???

Also, he took some other girl to a concert at Lincoln Center?

This was my fault. I was the one who'd left at Christmas. I was the one who hadn't wanted to say I loved him, hadn't let him say it to me. He thinks I wanted to keep it casual. We had no commitment to one another. He could go out with whoever he wanted.

I just didn't think he wanted anyone else.

"What's the matter?" Daisy said.

"Nothing." I put down my phone.

It was dumb to expect Jarvis to be sitting at home alone on a weekend night just because I'm here in Michigan.

I just thought he would.

Phoebe, Daisy, and I divided up the remaining champagne, and then I went to bed.

I woke with a killer headache and a text from Jarvis. I didn't reply.

I drank about a quart of water, and now I feel good (well, okay) enough to work on songs for next week's auditions, anything to get my mind off him.

"Art never comes from happiness."—Chuck Palahniuk

Well, Chuck really knew what he was talking about because I rocked.

Love, Jacaranda

P.S. I decided to answer Jarvis's text. I sent him a smiley.

To: Johnsmith247@dll.com
Date: February 3, 9:18 p.m. Eastern Standard Time
Subject: I wish . . .

Dear Mr. Smith,

"I wish . . . more than anything . . ." That's from *Into the Woods,* but it's also a game I used to play when I was a kid. I'd imagine I had 3 wishes, and I'd decide what to wish for. Sometimes, I'd wish to grow 3 inches or for my mother's boyfriend to disappear. Sometimes, I'd wish for more ordinary things, like McDonald's for dinner.

If I had three wishes right now, I'd wish:

1. To get into a summer program for musical theater
2. For my mom to get out of prison but be okay with me staying here
3. For Ava to miss just one performance due to an ingrown toenail

Or maybe I'd wish Jarvis was here and loved me.

No, the toenail is better. I don't want him if he doesn't want me.

I played the Witch in rehearsal the past few days, and I've done really well. Anger helps! We did the opening the first day, and I got a round of applause after the rap. I've been practicing "Stay with Me," and I'll get to sing it tomorrow. It's about how the Witch has no one but Rapunzel, but Rapunzel wants to grow up and see the world. It's so sad.

In a way, it's kind of a metaphor for my mother and me, except in our case, it's her who's imprisoned and me . . . oh, idk. Maybe it's not a metaphor.

Jarvis keeps texting me. He says we need to talk. Is he going to tell me he's dating Faun? I don't know what to say to him.

Love, Jacaranda

To: Johnsmith247@dll.com
Date: February 6, 7:18 a.m. Eastern Standard Time
Subject: The bright lights of Detroit

Dear Mr. Smith,

You know what's scarier than juries?

Summer program auditions.

With juries, I was singing in front of people who were rooting for me.

Here, they'll be total strangers who are looking for people to cut.

No. Calm down. CALM DOWN! They're looking for new talent.

I'm writing from a van to Detroit. We left at 6:00 a.m., 8 of us, packed in tighter than Publix the day before Thanksgiving, and one of those is Brooke, who's in the seat behind me.

Oh! That was the van, screeching to a stop, almost sending my laptop flying. I caught it, but I jostled Phoebe awake.

It was a deer, standing in the middle of I-75. Michigan sure is different from Miami.

"Sorry." I asked Phoebe if she was nervous.

"Not really." She told me she'd read that the best way to combat preaudition nerves was by telling yourself you're excited, not scared. "I'm excited," she said three times in a row.

"Me too," Brooke said from her seat. "I'm excited to have the chance to prove myself, since I never get solos at school."

Phoebe looked at me and rolled her eyes. "Why don't you give it a rest, Brooke?"

I said there was room for all of us to do well.

But I hope Brooke does her absolute best and still doesn't get picked. Am I awful?

The sun is finally up, so I'm going to look over my music one more time.

Love, Jacaranda

To: Johnsmith247@dll.com
Date: February 6, 1:09 p.m. Eastern Standard Time
Subject: Waiting . . .

Dear Mr. Smith,

Waiting. There are about 40 people here. They divided us into two groups and had half of us (including me, David, and Brooke) do the dance call first.

Ugh! Dance is my weakest skill, and I know it. The goal in musical theater is to be a "triple threat," someone who can sing, dance, and act. Phoebe definitely is one. So are Nina and David.

"Smile, baby," Phoebe said when I went in for my dance. I grinned. It's a reference to an old musical, *Gypsy*. Harry says that smiling, acting excited, and acting in general are almost as important as getting the steps perfect.

Almost as important.

But Phoebe's steps are always perfect.

And so are Brooke's. I sort of hate her for that. She thinks she's a triple threat, but that's because she thinks singing loud is the same as singing well.

She's definitely one of the best dancers in our class, though.

When we went into the dance studio, I tried to stand far away from her, so I wouldn't suffer by comparison. But she must have moved right before we started because suddenly she was right there.

The dance instructor, Julie, showed us the steps at 100 mph. I felt Brooke watching me the whole time.

And yet, she did the combination perfectly. I was in back, so I could watch her. She and David took spots in front, the better to showcase themselves.

Not me. At one point, I bumped into the girl next to me, and I couldn't get my arms right.

I did remember to smile.

Then they divided us into three groups of five and called us up.

There was no good group to be in. If I was in Brooke's group, I'd look bad. If I was in a different group, I'd see her snickering.

I tried to be in the *last* group so I could watch it two more times.

I think I got the steps right. I glued a smile onto my face. Still, I saw Brooke whisper to the girl next to her. Why does she hate me so much?

Now we're waiting to sing and do our monologues. I try to remember what Phoebe said about being excited.

I'm excited . . . about blowing Brooke away.

They called me in!

They called me in, and then, when I came out, I spotted Brooke touching my laptop. More than touching—she was holding my laptop.

I yelled, "What are you doing?" Step away from the laptop.

"Oh, sorry," she said, shamelessly. "Some people were walking around, and I was worried your laptop would get stepped on."

She handed it back.

But, when I picked it up, my unsent email to you was right there, not behind some other apps, the way I left it.

What had she been looking at? And how dare she touch my stuff!

The audition went well. The three judges let me do both songs and my whole monologue. I think they liked me.

But I'm still kind of freaked about Brooke touching my laptop. Like what kind of person thinks she can just pick up someone else's stuff?

When Phoebe came out of her dance call, I was shaking. I tried to act normal. I asked her how it had gone.

"The dance? Easy."

"How about singing?" I asked her.

She shrugged. "It wasn't the best I've ever sung, but I did it. How about you?"

I said that dance would be my downfall.

"Yeah, you look upset," she said.

I didn't tell her it was because of my laptop. Instead I said, "I hope we both get in."

I'm going to hit Send and shut down my computer . . . like I should have before.

Love, Jacaranda

To: Johnsmith247@dll.com
Date: February 6, 9:16 p.m. Eastern Standard Time
Subject: Back at school

Dear Mr. Smith,

#%&*!

When we got out of the van, Brooke said, "Bye, Jacaranda!" She's never called me that before.

I've been feeling stabby since we left Detroit, during the 3-hour car ride and a dinner stop where I could barely eat.

What did Brooke see on my laptop?

And how does she intend to use it against me?

Worriedly, Jacaranda

To: Johnsmith247@dll.com
Date: February 6, 10:11 p.m. Eastern Standard Time
Subject: Okay, I'm an awful person . . .

Dear Mr. Smith,

Jarvis just texted me! I'll give you a rundown.

Jarvis: Why are you mad at me?
Me: Mad?
Jarvis: We haven't talked in over a week
Me: . . .
Jarvis: Are you mad I didn't call you last Friday?
Jarvis: I'm sorry . . . I had a family thing
Jarvis: And before that I was a little freaked out.
Me: Family thing?
Jarvis: My dad got engaged
Jarvis: Yeah we went to dinner Friday with him and his fiancée
Jarvis: To celebrate.
Me: Your dad and his fiancée?
Jarvis: Yeah Wendelin and her sister

Jarvis: Whose name is Faun

Jarvis: Can you believe that?

Me: Faun? Like a goat-headed deity?

(I was secretly jumping up and down at this point.)

Jarvis: Right she's a model or something

Jarvis: Torture.

Jarvis: We went out to dinner and a concert.

Jarvis: Because just dinner wouldn't have been long enough

Jarvis: My dad told me to stay off my phone because it was rude

Jarvis: I'm sorry I didn't call . . . .

Me: Your dad got engaged?

Jarvis: I knew it was coming but . . .

Me: It must be hard

Jarvis: I'm being immature

Jarvis: That's what he says

Me: I'm not mad

Me: I was just busy with the play

Jarvis: Really? 😁

Me: I don't think you're immature

Jarvis: Can you talk now?

Me: Yes!!!

Just thought you'd want to know. All those things I was thinking about Jarvis weren't true.

Love, Jacaranda

To: Johnsmith247@dll.com
Date: February 7, 11:00 a.m. Eastern Standard Time
Subject: Jarvis

Dear Mr. Smith,

When I talked to Jarvis, I said, "Remember how you told me you're a jealous person?" And then I confessed I'd seen the photo of him and Faun.

$!%$# was what he said.

He'd seen the photo online and wondered if I was mad about that, but he couldn't think of a good way to bring it up. He texted me another photo someone had taken of all four of them, same clothes, same setting, same everything. Wendelin was holding out a diamond ring big enough to choke an elephant. Faun stood by Jarvis with her hand on his arm, but they were all arm-in-arm for the photo, so it made sense.

"She's 24," Jarvis laughed. "And I'm not even mature for my age, according to my dad."

I said I missed him.

"Same," he said.

There was a sudden silence, and then he said, "Tell me why you left at Christmas," at the same moment I blurted out, "I'm sorry I left at Christmas."

Then we both stopped talking and laughed.

"I *am* sorry," I said.

"Why did you leave? I know what you told Phoebe couldn't be right. You told me you and your mom aren't close."

I couldn't talk for a minute, couldn't even think of what to say, but finally, I settled on sort of the truth. "I was afraid."

"Afraid of me?" His voice shook.

"Not, like, really afraid. But yeah. A little." When he didn't answer right away, I filled the silence. "You're . . . a lot."

"Why?" he asked. "Was it because I gave you that ring? Because I was too serious, and you didn't feel the same way?"

"No." I stared down at the ring, which I'm kind of obsessed with looking at. "I do feel the same way. That's what scared me. We come from such different backgrounds. If you knew everything about me, you wouldn't like me."

He said, "I doubt that." He changed the subject. "I really want to see you. When I'm with you, everything's different. You're not like anyone else."

I remembered that day at Central Park, when he said the other girls he knew would think it was silly to dance in the gazebo. Was that what he meant? But there were so many reasons I wasn't like the other girls at MAA, so many ways I felt less than them.

Jarvis never makes me feel that way, though.

I told him I wanted to see him too.

"I meant what I said in that text I sent you," he said.

I told him to hold on a second, then put down the phone. I typed, *I love you too*. And I sent it to him. "Check your texts," I said.

After a few seconds, he sent me a ☺.

And then a ♥.

"I never said that to another girl, if you're wondering."

I was, but I said, "Same. I mean, I've never said it to another guy either."

"When can I see you?" he asked. "I can come there if you want."

We settled on Presidents' Day weekend, which is *this* weekend.

And it's Valentine's Day too!

So Jarvis is coming to stay in 5 DAYS!

Love, Jacaranda

To: Johnsmith247@dll.com
Date: February 10, 9:48 p.m. Eastern Standard Time
Subject: Jarvis

Two more days.

To: Johnsmith247@dll.com
Date: February 12, 4:00 p.m. Eastern Standard Time
Subject: Jarvis

Dear Mr. Smith,

He's coming today! I'm taking a car to meet him at the airport. Someone from Jarvis's father's company is bringing him a car since he's too young to rent one. I can't wait!

I told Phoebe and Daisy he was coming.

"He's spending a holiday weekend here in the sticks?" Phoebe said. "Boy's in love."

That made me smile.

"How are you sneaking out?" she asked.

I hadn't thought about it. "I was planning on coming back every night at curfew."

"Oh. Well, if you want to stay at his hotel, I could swipe your card for you."

Instead of bed checks, the school uses a card system to keep tabs on us. We check in by scanning our access card before curfew and use the card when we go out. But I hadn't thought about staying over. I wasn't sure where we were in our relationship. When

Jarvis spent the night at the Hodgkinses at Christmas, nothing happened. But Phoebe might not realize that.

"Not tonight," I said. "I want to see how it plays out. Maybe tomorrow."

I probably shouldn't be telling you all this. But you know I'm not some wild girl who sneaks out. I'm a nerd. Also, you probably don't read my letters, so it's more like a diary.

And if you do read them, you know how I feel about Jarvis.

Phoebe suggested that she could let me out Saturday, and I could give her my key to scan. If I came back, she and Daisy would let me in. I said I'd think about it.

But now, I'm off to the airport!

Love, Jacaranda

To: Johnsmith247@dll.com
Date: February 12, 10:22 p.m. Eastern Standard Time
Subject: He's here!

Dear Mr. Smith,

He's here! He's here! When I saw Jarvis at the little airport, coming out from behind the hot dog stand near the exit, the late-afternoon sun lighting his face through the skylights, and the Muzak playing a romantic song, I felt like I was hallucinating. He was too larger-than-life to exist in such a place.

Or maybe he was the answer to one of my wishes.

I said his name, softly at first, to make sure it was him. He turned, his smile like the sun on a bright, cold Michigan afternoon. I broke into a run. It was like a movie. Well, except for the fact that the airport here is tiny, not like movie airports, so there wasn't much space to run. He ran toward me, dropping his duffel bag as he did. He swept me up in his arms and spun me around.

I've always wanted to be one of those airport girls who gets picked up and spun around.

Now, I am.

We went to a diner, a quirky one with hundreds of antlers

hanging from the ceiling. We sat in a corner and talked and kissed and ate French fries until it got close to my curfew and Jarvis took me back to my dorm.

But he's picking me up early tomorrow, and we're going to go sledding.

Yes, sledding.

"You have a sled?" I asked him.

"That's actually most of what's in there." He gestured toward his duffel. Apparently, there are inflatable sleds. Who knew? This Miami girl is learning new things every day.

Jarvis says everyone should try sledding at least once. "I've been researching sledding hills in the area."

I asked him if it was scary, and he said he'd hold me tight. "I'll take care of you."

And I believed him.

But now I'm back in my dorm. It's cold, and I'm thinking that I would be warmer *wherever* he is.

I think I'll take Phoebe up on her offer tomorrow. It's just one night.

Is that okay?

Love, Jacaranda

To: Johnsmith247@dll.com
Date: February 13, 11:49 p.m. Eastern Standard Time
Subject: Lucky

Dear Mr. Smith,

Shh. It's almost midnight. I'm sitting at a hotel-room desk. I can't sleep because the day is dancing in my head like a million snowflakes. I had to get up and write this day down.

Jarvis, on the other hand, is dead to the world. He's so handsome and peaceful when he sleeps, and I wonder how he could love me when no one else has in 16 years? There must be something wrong. Why would someone so perfect be in love with me?

And that's not me having confidence problems. That's just me, having lived 16 years in the world. I know when something's too good to be true.

This morning, I asked him, "Why do you love me, Jarvis?"

And, without even thinking, he replied, "Because you wonder what it would be like if an omniscient narrator was narrating your life, like Dickens."

I remembered that first night, and I smiled.

Today was a beautiful day, Mr. Smith!

Jarvis picked me up before sunrise. We drove to a diner (of course) for breakfast. This one had shiny red tables with maps of Michigan on the surface, shelves full of old milk bottles, and a jukebox full of old Elvis Presley songs. "Heartbreak Hotel" was on when we entered. We ordered (biscuits and gravy for Jarvis, fried eggs and bacon for me). We were the youngest people there. Some guy put on "Jailhouse Rock," and I found myself tapping my foot.

"Elvis fan?" Jarvis said, clearly amused.

I told him my grandma was. I remember me, maybe 6, and her, near 60, dancing around the kitchen to his *Golden Records* album on vinyl. She showed me how to dance like "the sexiest man who ever lived."

So I like Elvis. He makes me happy. You're old, so maybe you like him too.

Jarvis seemed to enjoy watching me dance in my seat and hum along with the line, "Everybody in the whole cell block was dancing to the jailhouse rock," so when the song ended, I asked him for a quarter. He called the waitress over, and she stacked four quarters on my side of the table. I walked to the jukebox. When my first song, "All Shook Up," came on, I didn't sit down.

"All Shook Up" is my favorite Elvis song. I know all the words and can do the King's signature hip-swivel. Suddenly, it was like that day at Publix all over again. I wanted to sing and dance and perform for the sheer love of making people happy, not for grades or adulation. I strutted back to the table, through that sleepy, old-people diner, singing along. Soon, I was getting appreciative whoops, and not just from my boyfriend, who had a huge grin on his face. I noticed a younger guy filming me (déjà vu!). I started swiveling and jiving, leaning in to Jarvis when I sang, "I'm proud to say that he's my buttercup." The old people clapped along, and I loved it.

The song ended, and the whole diner burst into applause. When the next song came on, I offered Jarvis my hand. He knew what to do. We slow-danced around the diner to "I Can't Help Falling in Love with You."

Jarvis is . . . um . . . not a bad dancer. He once said his mother taught him. He waltzed like he was on *Dancing with the Stars*, spinning me around, and he even dipped me! I could have danced danced danced all night.

An old couple got up and danced beside us, and we finished to more applause.

And then my eggs were there, and I sat down to eat them as if nothing had happened.

Jarvis sat too, laughing. "You're an entertainer, Jackie. That was incredible! You're probably tired of hearing how great you are."

I said I wasn't tired of hearing it, not from him.

Someone else put "Blue Suede Shoes" on the jukebox, maybe hoping for a repeat performance, but I was enjoying my fried eggs, and the company. When Jarvis tried to pay the check, the waitress gestured to the couple who'd been dancing and said they'd already paid our tab. As we left, some of the old people leaned over and told us how cute we were.

We drove to a gas station next, and Jarvis insisted I sit in the car while he blew up the giant blue-and-gray sled. Through the window, I could tell he was shivering. He dropped his quarters for the air pump twice, but finally, the sled was inflated, and he managed to squeeze it into the backseat. When he got back into the car, his teeth were chattering. His face felt frozen to the touch.

I put my arms around him. "Are you okay?" I asked.

He said he was fine, but I could feel him shaking. "It's c-colder than New York."

I said maybe it was too cold to go sledding, but he seemed determined. "If I'm going to go to school in Michigan or Pittsburgh, I need to get used to it."

Finally, we decided to drive through McDonald's and get coffee drinks. We warmed up in his car for a while. Then we drove to the sledding hill. There were dozens of kids who'd had the same idea. We finished our coffee, then joined them.

"I'm still scared," I said as we settled onto our sled at the top of the cold hill.

"Remember what I said yesterday," he said. "I'll protect you."

I pulled his arms around me. "Okay," I said. "I'm ready."

He pushed off, and then we were flying. It was the most thrilling feeling I've ever had, the motion, the cool wind in my ears, my face, Jarvis's arms around me, and when we reached the bottom, I said, "Again!" His eyes were shining, and he kissed me.

We flew down that hill maybe ten times, maybe more. Every time, I was afraid. Every time, I felt safe in Jarvis's arms.

"You'll be ready to try free-climbing in no time," he said.

Finally, it got too cold, so we went back to Jarvis's hotel to warm up by the fireplace. Then we ordered room service for dinner (I've never had room service before!).

"I want to change my answer," Jarvis said to me later. "Maybe I love you because you sing Elvis songs in roadside diners."

"And maybe I love you because you take me to such great diners," I said. Tomorrow is Valentine's Day, and I plan to give him a book called *Diners of Pennsylvania,* for when he gets to Carnegie Mellon.

"Is that the only reason?" he asked.

I nodded. "The only reason." But we both know that's a lie.

"What if there was something bad about me that you didn't know?" I asked.

Jarvis said there was nothing in the world that would make him not love me.

"How do you know?" I said.

"Try me," he said. "Tell me what's so awful, and I'll tell you why it doesn't matter."

I shook my head.

"Is it some embarrassing childhood memory?" he asked. "Like my thumb-sucking?"

When I shook my head and said it was worse, he said, "Have you hurt anyone?"

I told him no. He said, "Is there another guy? Are you a spy, sent to ruin my good name? Are you an ogre by night like in *Shrek*?"

No and no and no again. He said, "Do you think Andrew Lloyd Webber is a better composer than Stephen Sondheim? Or you don't believe in global warming?"

Laughing, I answered no to both of those. "I'm not a monster," I said.

His voice became serious. "Did you change your mind about loving me?" he asked.

"Never," I said.

And it's true. Nothing could make me change my mind about Jarvis. Nothing.

"Then I won't change my mind about you either," he said. "Let's just be happy."

I nodded. Maybe that's enough. Maybe after years of being sad, I deserve this, deserve this school, this boyfriend, this life.

Jarvis is stirring. He just beckoned to me to go to sleep.

And I think I will.

Good night.

Love, Jacaranda

To: Johnsmith247@dll.com
Date: February 14, 1:08 p.m. Eastern Standard Time
Subject: Can I talk to you?

Dear Mr. Smith,

Is there any way we can possibly talk? Something awful has happened. I suspect you know what it is. I'm alone and need adult guidance.

Love, Jacaranda

P.S. I'm very unhappy.

To: Johnsmith247@dll.com
Date: February 14, 4:45 p.m. Eastern Standard Time
Subject: What happened

Dear Mr. Smith,

I spoke with Vanessa, and I feel calmer now. She said you were away.

This morning, I woke to snow outside. I was warm and secure in Jarvis's arms, and I could smell bacon cooking somewhere. I know it was wrong to sneak out overnight, but half the school was on vacation with their families on the holiday weekend, and since I don't have one of those, I felt like it was partly justified.

But maybe not. Maybe circumstances have proven that I had no right.

We dressed and went down to the coffee shop in the lobby. It was adorable, with windows all around and a panoramic view of the silver-and-white world outside. We were watching two kids in red snow jackets build a snowman when I realized other people were staring at us.

Jarvis, as usual, ignored them. He's used to being a celebrity. But I had a weird feeling people were looking at *me,* not him. Then a middle-aged woman came over and said, "Excuse me? Are you the girl in that video?"

At first, I thought she meant the Publix video (which I'd never told Jarvis about), but she said, "You know, the Elvis one?"

It took me a second to realize what she meant. Then it came back to me. That guy filming me!

How could this happen twice in a year? When am I going to listen to my grandmother's advice and keep my mouth shut and stop making a public spectacle of myself?

Of course, the first video, people saw because I was talented. This time it went viral because of who I was with!

I told her it was me, and Jarvis said, "Isn't she wonderful?" She started to gush that I was, and meanwhile, Jarvis googled the video. He found it in seconds and showed it to me.

It was as I remembered, me bebopping around the diner, looking adorbs. But when I handed Jarvis's phone back and searched for it on my own, I found thousands of hits for it—many with the headline, "Pendleton Heir Seen with Jailbird's Daughter in Michigan Diner."

"Jailbird's daughter." That was me. I scrolled through the articles. Some connected me to the Publix video. They called me Jacaranda. One noted that an anonymous MAA "friend" first tipped them off about my mother being in jail "for murder."

But who at MAA knew?

My first thought was Falcon. But she wouldn't do that.

Brooke! From my computer that day. She'd seen my emails, all of them.

What did I do to make this girl hate me so much? Was it just because I made her feel stupid that day I talked back to her?

Are people that vindictive?

The articles kept going on and on, calling my mother a "jail-bird" like the guy on the Get Out of Jail Free card in Monopoly, a caricature with no humanity. And the comments! I was a gold digger. And garbage. Or they said Jarvis had been taken in by me, like Jarvis was gullible, instead of being a brilliant guy who got into MIT.

Jarvis held out his hand, trying to cover my phone. "Don't read the comments, Jackie. Don't you know you can never read the comments?"

I wanted to puke. I stood and rushed from the restaurant as fast as I could. Jarvis followed me to the elevator, waving away some people who were getting on. I collapsed against the wall. Jarvis put his arms around me.

"Stop," I said. "I'm awful. I'm taking advantage of you. They all said it."

"Who said it?" His voice was disbelieving. "Internet trolls? I don't care about them."

"But you should care," I said. "They're right. I lied to you." I kept going on, that I was a liar, unworthy of him, and he was trying to calm me down, saying he loved me no matter what. He said he loved me *because* of the hard life I'd been able to overcome, because I was so optimistic against all odds.

I wished I could believe him, but no one is that kind. And, besides, I wanted to be with someone who didn't have to love me due to kindness. Maybe that's why my mother had so many worthless scrub boyfriends over the years. Maybe she knew she wasn't worthy of anyone better. Maybe I'm not either.

The door dinged. I broke away and ran to the room. I began gathering my belongings, with Jarvis begging me to stay. I stuffed everything into my laptop bag and headed for the door. I told him not to follow me. I didn't want a big scene in the lobby. I'd get a car back to campus. I left *Diners of Pennsylvania* on the nightstand.

When I last saw him, he was sitting on the hotel bed. I think he was crying. I felt like a hand was squeezing my heart like one of those stress balls.

He made one final attempt to call me back. "You are the most fascinating, passionate girl I've ever met, and I love you no matter what," he said. "Do you understand, Jackie?"

"It's Jacaranda," I said, heading for the door.

I saw him sink to the floor as the door slammed behind me.

As soon as the elevator closed, I broke down. I wanted to go back and tell him I loved him too. But I didn't. Instead, I blocked his number on my phone. He's better off without me.

I got back to campus somehow. I don't remember. When I reached my dorm, there was more trouble. They'd been looking for me last night, after the video blew up, and found out I wasn't there.

There will be a meeting Tuesday morning about my future here, whether I have one.

I'm sorry. I'm so, so sorry.

Love, Jacaranda

P.S. I want my mother.

To: Johnsmith247@dll.com
Date: February 15, 10:45 a.m. Eastern Standard Time
Subject: Thank you!

Dear Mr. Smith,

I got Vanessa's message, saying she'll be here Tuesday to support me. I guess she'll be here to help move me out if they expel me too.

I didn't leave my room all day yesterday, not even to eat.

I couldn't face my classmates. All those websites reported the story of sweet Jarvis involved with sketchy me. They acted like I was the one who'd been convicted of a crime. They all said I'd lied to him, which was true. But I hadn't lied to get away with something. I'd lied because I didn't want them to sneer at me. I wanted to have friends here.

Now I can't look at any of them without wondering if they're thinking that I'm all those terrible things people posted.

I've been crying so hard that if I cry any more, I'll dehydrate, and there will be nothing left but a pile of Jacaranda dust on the floor.

I'm on my second day of not leaving my room.

Someone's knocking on the bathroom door. Daisy! She has food!

I yelled at her to go away.

She's knocking louder. She just said, "I'm going to keep knocking, so you might as well open it while the waffles are still hot."

I'll write later.

Love, Jacaranda

To: Johnsmith247@dll.com
Date: February 15, 9:15 p.m. Eastern Standard Time
Subject: Daisy

Dear Mr. Smith,

When I dragged myself to the door, Daisy was holding a plate of waffles with syrup and bananas on them. She pushed her way into the room, saying, "I'm your friend even if you didn't trust me with your secrets."

Ouch.

Behind her, I heard Phoebe say something about how she couldn't believe I lied to her. She'd had me staying in her house. Like I might have murdered her in her sleep. Or made off with the silver. Or made off with her cousin!

Daisy pulled the door closed behind her. "She'll get over it," she said.

Daisy went on. "You should have told me. I would have understood."

"You tell people your mother's in jail, and they think they know everything about you," I said. "I just wanted things to be normal."

"I get that," she said, and gave me a hug. "Now eat."

At dinnertime, she insisted I go to the cafeteria. She sat on one side of me, with Falcon on the other. David joined us across the table, and he's tall, so he blocked some of the people staring.

I didn't see Phoebe, but I saw Brooke, holding court at a table across the room, whispering to her friends, some of whom I'd thought were my friends too.

It will probably be better next time. If I don't have to leave school forever.

I'm going to try really hard to stay. At least here, the ice is broken.

Love, Jacaranda

To: Johnsmith247@dll.com
Date: February 16, 7:00 a.m. Eastern Standard Time
Subject: Meeting today

Dear Mr. Smith,

I'm lying in my lavender-and-white bed, typing this on my phone. It's probably my last day at MAA. Where will I go? I've moved so many times, both when I was a kid and we got evicted or when my mom broke up with a boyfriend. Or later, when she was in prison. But this is different. This time, I had hope.

My meeting's at 8:00. I'm too sick to eat breakfast.

I'm sorry I disappointed you.

Oh, God! Someone's at the door! Are they coming for me early?

Love, Jacaranda

To: Johnsmith247@dll.com
Date: February 16, 10:14 a.m. Eastern Standard Time
Subject: Phoebe

Dear Mr. Smith,

It was Vanessa! In a red dress, which she said was her power outfit. I wanted to ask her if she was wearing her fancy red-bottomed shoes (I now know they're Louboutins), like the first day.

At the meeting, they discussed my many sins. I'd snuck out. With a boy! And it wasn't the first time. That time I got dragged out to karaoke counted against me too. They mentioned which rules I'd violated and the possible penalties, including expulsion. Then they asked me if I had anything to say. And they waited.

It took me a minute to say anything at all. When I did, I said I was sorry. I was grateful for the opportunities I'd had, and if they gave me another chance, I'd be perfect. I mentioned that I had good grades in all my classes and had gotten a part in the musical and was going to all the rehearsals. I didn't know what else I could say. There was no excuse.

At that point, someone knocked on the door, one of the ladies who works in the office. When she came in, she said, "Mr. Hudson is here."

Harry walked in.

Why was Harry here? Was he mad at me too?

He looked at me gravely and cleared his throat.

And then he spoke in his melodious voice.

"Jacaranda Abbott is one of the hardest-working students I have ever had the privilege to teach. She started the year two years behind most of her classmates, never having taken an acting class, never having taken dance, completely unfamiliar with music theory, and she has blossomed. Whatever I ask her to do, she does without complaint. She learns from her mistakes, and she improves. She took a small role in the spring musical and has approached it as if she was the star. I wish I had more students like Miss Abbott."

I was trying not to jump up and down in my seat.

"Additionally," he said, "she's helpful to other students. This past semester, I asked her to assist a fellow student who was struggling with a song. Even though the two girls weren't friends at the time, Miss Abbott helped her, and they both improved."

Phoebe! Harry's *Parent Trap* setup!

He continued. "This other student is a young woman who, while very gifted, suffers from such crippling stage fright and anxiety that it has inhibited her progress. Miss Abbott has since befriended her, and this young lady has improved by leaps and bounds, to the point where I have given her a lead role in the musical. I've brought that student to speak on Miss Abbott's behalf."

He walked over to the door, and Phoebe came in. I hadn't cried when I said goodbye to the guy I loved, but I burst into tears when I saw Phoebe.

She gave me a look that said, "Stop crying." Then she spoke to the room. "Harry's right. Jackie's been great. She's an inspiration. And it was *my* fault she stayed out. She was going to come home every night at 10 over the weekend, and I was the one who suggested we could cover for her. If anything, you should kick me out."

Even though she knew that would never happen, it was sweet.

After she spoke, they told me and Vanessa to wait outside while the faculty deliberated. We sat in chairs they'd left for students waiting to hear their fates. Vanessa took my hand. Phoebe took the other hand.

I wanted to thank her for what she said, but I knew it would be weird, so I squeezed her hand and Vanessa's hand too. They both squeezed back, and I felt so much love right then. Maybe it would be okay.

The final decision was to kick me out of the play for the first week's performances. I could play my part the second week. "This is an extremely lenient punishment because of your previous exemplary academics and conduct and Harry's testimony," Miss Pike said. "But if anything of the sort happens again, we'll have no choice but to—"

"It won't happen again," I assured her. "Thank you! Thank you!"

I felt, if anything, sicker than before. Maybe I was sick the whole time, but since I was so unhappy, I hadn't noticed. Now when I stood, I felt the world turn gray, and I sat back down again. Harry told Phoebe to walk me back to my room and get me something at the cafeteria. Before we left, Phoebe asked if she could talk to him while I waited.

"What did you say?" I said on the way up.

"I told him Brooke was definitely the one who told the reporters about you, and that he shouldn't give her your part. That's probably what she wanted all along."

Whoa. I couldn't help but laugh.

Phoebe brought me a muffin. She said, "Jarvis said he already knew about your mother."

He didn't. This was obviously just something he'd told Phoebe so she wouldn't hate me, but I nodded and thanked her for the muffin.

After she left, I lay there, sniffing the cool air, listening to the familiar sounds, someone shoveling snow, a distant trumpet. We so seldom know how lucky we are *when* it's happening, but I do. I am so grateful for still having the right to lie in this bed.

Love, Jacaranda

To: Johnsmith247@dll.com
Date: February 16, 9:14 p.m. Eastern Standard Time
Subject: Brooke

Dear Mr. Smith,

Man, is she mad! I didn't see Brooke before lunch, but I know she saw me in the cafeteria. Still, when I walked into drama class, she pretended to be shocked, exclaiming, "Oh my GOD! How can she even GO here after all the lies she's told!" I heard her whispering that her parents were going to complain to the school.

Can you imagine having parents who would complain if you didn't get your way? I don't think I'd want that.

I don't even care. In class, we're working on scenes now. Phoebe and I are doing one from the play version of *Pride and Prejudice*, a scene between the snotty Lady Catherine de Bourgh (Phoebe) and the plucky Lizzy Bennet (me—perfect casting, right?). Mr. Adams asked if anyone wanted to perform today, and I threw my hand up with the wild enthusiasm of a 7-year-old who knows a spelling word.

"Really?" Phoebe side-eyed me.

"I need a win," I said.

She shrugged and stood up when Mr. Adams said we could go.

To be clear, this is a *great* scene for Phoebe. The character is exactly Phoebe in 40 years. She's a Snooty McSnootface old lady who has come to tell Lizzy not to marry her nephew, Mr. Darcy. She says awful things like, "Are you to pollute the shades of Pemberley?" and talks about how low class Lizzy's family is.

In the end, Lizzy says, "You have insulted me in every possible method. I must beg you to leave." When Keira Knightley played the part in the movie, she spoke so softly and politely. Instead, I pretended Phoebe was Brooke and put some venom behind it.

Owen whooped and said, "Go, girl!"

Finally, Lady Catherine flounces off, saying, "I am most seriously displeased."

My friends burst into applause.

"That was excellent, girls." Mr. Adams looked at me. "What were you thinking about?"

I said, "Um, Lady Catherine's actually doing Lizzy a huge favor because Lizzy thinks Mr. Darcy doesn't love her anymore. But when Lady Catherine comes, she realizes he does. So she's angry at Lady Catherine, but also excited. She's trying to stay in control."

"Very good," Mr. Adams said. "And you, Phoebe? What were you thinking?"

Phoebe glanced at Brooke, looking down her perfect nose at Brooke like she was a piece of poop on the floor. "Some people think they're classy when they're actually pathetic and people are laughing at them."

Mr. Adams nodded. "That is a perfect characterization of Lady Catherine. Brava."

In other news, Harry gave the first week of my part to the freshman who was playing Snow White and then moved another freshman up to her part. Poetic justice.

Love, Jacaranda

To: Johnsmith247@dll.com
Date: February 17, 5:17 p.m. Eastern Standard Time
Subject: Some good news

Dear Mr. Smith,

Today, when I came back to my dorm before rehearsal, there was a little note on my door, saying I had a phone message.

This was strange. No one calls me. Who would call me at school? Still I went down to talk to Angie. She seemed very excited.

"An agent!" she said. "From New York City!"

I thought it must be a prank. But the name of the agency was one even I had heard. I dialed the number Angie gave me. I asked to speak to Debbie Bloom.

"I don't want to sell my story or anything," I told her when she asked if I had representation. I figured that had to be it, that people wanted dirt on me and Jarvis. I mean, that was the whole reason this video had gone viral, because Jarvis was in it.

"Oh, honey, no." The woman had a soft voice with an accent similar to Daisy's mom's. "I totally understand that."

"Okay, then," I said, getting ready to hang up.

"I mean, I could definitely get you that, if you wanted," she said. "But you're right, it wouldn't be the best for your career."

"Career?" I asked.

"You're very talented," she said. "And you've had this exposure, for better or worse. So I'm just saying it might be best to strike while the iron's hot."

I had no idea what she was talking about, but she explained that she represented actors for print and television. She said I was too short for modeling, but I had a good look, and she could find commercial work for me, and maybe more.

"I'm still in school," I told her. "In Michigan."

She brushed this aside and asked if I could put together a demo reel. I had already recorded myself singing and doing monologues, for summer program auditions. I said I could. I think I'll add some of the newer pieces I've been working on. I said I'd send it to her next week.

So, in short, I HAVE AN AGENT!

And all I had to do to get one was be completely humiliated in front of the entire world.

Love, Jacaranda

To: Johnsmith247@dll.com
Date: February 19, 8:23 p.m. Eastern Standard Time
Subject: Stay with me

Dear Mr. Smith,

I got to play the Witch at rehearsal today since Ava had her last audition, at FSU. I told her to say hi to Florida for me.

We did the second act, so I got to sing "Witch's Lament." The part about how children grow "from something you love to something you lose" gave me chills.

It made me think of my mother. Oscar and the criminal justice system took me away from her, and it wasn't fair. She didn't deserve it.

I had to turn away and swipe at my eyes, so I wouldn't get yelled at for crying.

I wonder if she knows what happened. Can they get news from the outside world? What does she think of me?

After rehearsal, Harry came up to me.

"That was spectacular," he said. "And I have had the privilege of seeing Ms. Bernadette Peters in the role."

"Thank you," I said. "And thank you for what you said Tuesday."

"Nothing but the truth," he said.

I said I'd try to be worthy of his praise.

Then I went back to my room and cried until the salty tears rolled into my mouth.

Love, Jacaranda

To: Johnsmith247@dll.com
Date: February 21, 9:18 p.m. Eastern Standard Time
Subject: My mother

Dear Mr. Smith,

I want to talk to my mother. Last time I talked to her was back when I was still with Aunt April. Inmates can make collect calls, and sometimes she did. But none of my foster families wanted that, so I haven't talked to her in years.

Now, I have money (thank you), and I looked up how to get a call from her prison. I sent her my number months ago, to put on her approved list, but since it's a cell phone, she can't call collect. I have to arrange to prepay it. The website said I could get a 15-minute call for $6! I set up an account, and I sent the info to my mother, telling her to call me at night or on a weekend if possible.

I want to tell her everything that's happening in my life, all the good and bad. I want to tell her about Jarvis.

No. I want to tell her about this place and the snow and the cherry trees and all my friends. Especially about singing and how it makes me feel to perform.

What I worry about, though, is maybe if I hear her voice, I'll miss her so much that I'll want to be with her all the time. Over the years, I've hardened myself to not having a mom.

Maybe I'll find out I need my mom more than I need to be here.

Love, Jacaranda

To: Johnsmith247@dll.com
Date: February 24, 7:47 p.m. Eastern Standard Time
Subject: Spring break

Dear Mr. Smith,

I hope it's okay that I've accepted an invitation to go to Daisy's family's vacation home in Stowe for spring break. She invited both Phoebe and me.

Going will make me less sad about not being able to go to New York and see Jarvis. At least, I hope it will. I know you gave me the airline gift card, but I still need Vanessa to sign me out. I'll write to her too.

Also, I sent Debbie my new and improved demo, so she can add me to her website. I've been working on it, in all this free time I have between school and rehearsals.

With Fingers Crossed, Jacaranda

To: Johnsmith247@dll.com
Date: February 26, 3:47 p.m. Eastern Standard Time
Subject: MORE EXCITING NEWS!

Dear Mr. Smith,

I got into a summer program—the New England one! They offered me a scholarship to cover tuition, but I'd have to pay room and board. I'm still waiting to hear from the others, but they want me! They want me!

Of course, the first person I wanted to tell was Jarvis. He was there for all my audition stress. Now, I can't tell him the good news!

I miss him. And miss him. And miss him.

But I'm glad I can tell you and know you'll be happy for me!

Love, Jacaranda

To: Johnsmith247@dll.com
Date: February 27, 7:31 a.m. Eastern Standard Time
Subject: Thank you

Dear Mr. Smith,

Thank you for your offer to pay my room and board for the summer program. Let's see what other offers I get, but I'll keep it in mind. It seems awfully expensive to me, and I hate to ask. I'm not used to asking for anything, really. Maybe it would be better if I worked over the summer, if I can't get a full scholarship.

Love, Jacaranda

To: Johnsmith247@dll.com
Date: February 28, 4:58 p.m. Eastern Standard Time
Subject: Sledding

Dear Mr. Smith,

Today, Phoebe invited Daisy and me to go sledding. I guess Jarvis saw her the day it all happened. That's when he told her that lie about knowing about my mother beforehand. And he left Phoebe the sled he bought. She's had it stuffed under her bed the past 2 weeks.

It's been 2 weeks since I heard Jarvis's voice . . .

I told her that I didn't want to go, but Phoebe wouldn't take no for an answer.

There's a little hilly area near the school, and we set out for it. As we were heading out the door, three of us with a giant sled, Falcon ran up to us.

"Is that a sled?"

When we invited her to come, she said, "Omigod! I've never sledded in my life! I feel like it's important to my development as an artist to experience motion!"

Because she says things like that.

Falcon brought her sketch pad along to draw us, in case it inspired another art installation. She finished *Crust of Humility*. It's on display in the school's art gallery. The local paper even did an article about it.

It was a trek to the hill, and when we got there, it wasn't as high or pretty as the one with Jarvis. But maybe that was better. It wasn't like Phoebe or Daisy or Falcon was going to wrap her arms around me. I wasn't even sure I wanted to go.

Daisy showed Falcon how to mount the sled and push off. When they'd gone, Phoebe said, "Wow, and people say I'm grumpy. You look miserable."

I faked a smile. "Sorry. I was just thinking . . ."

I was thinking I hadn't even TEXTED Jarvis in 2 weeks.

Phoebe seemed to read my thoughts. She said, "You know you've wrecked my cousin, right? He told some reporter that you guys broke up, and they should leave you alone. Jarvis never talks to reporters. He's totally blaming himself for all this."

I said he'd get over it. I didn't mean it to be harsh, but it came out that way.

"Why would he? *You* haven't, and you're the one who did the leaving."

"It's too complicated," I said. "He's, like, a celebrity, and I'm . . ."

"You're WHAT?" she snapped. "You're someone who's had some hard breaks. That's what Jarvis says anyway. He DOESN'T MIND. It's like he thinks you're too good for him, almost, because of what you've been through. He's completely in love with you."

I remembered what Jarvis said that day over break, about my hard childhood making me a better person. But I didn't want my life to be something someone doesn't *mind*, a flaw to be overlooked. "Can we talk about something else?" I asked her.

Phoebe nodded. "But I want to say one more thing. Jarvis is coming to see me in the play next month. But he's not coming to see me. He never came to anything of mine, and now he's come to two shows this year. That's because of you. Because he loves *you*."

Something about the way she said it made me hug her. She had to yell "STOP," and shook me off.

We spent the rest of the afternoon sledding and admiring the sketches Falcon did of the kids on the hill. She said she was thinking about doing a new project about middle-class children doing normal childhood American things and calling it *The Haves*.

I wonder if Phoebe was right.

I remembered what Jarvis said. "If everyone likes you, it's because no one really knows you." He felt like I was the only one who knew him.

Maybe when two people are exactly in accord, always happy when together and lonely when apart, they shouldn't let anything in the world stand between them. I wish I could believe that. But maybe you know better. You probably belong to a rich, important family like Jarvis's, so maybe you can be more objective.

He'll be here in a month, whether I like it or not.

Love, Jacaranda

To: Johnsmith247@dll.com
Date: March 6, 5:18 p.m. Eastern Standard Time
Subject: My mother

Dear Mr. Smith,

She called me. She's tried a couple other times, but I was always in class or rehearsal. But this time, I spoke with her for 15 minutes for the first time in over 5 years.

As predicted, I cried. I tried not to because we had such a short time, but I couldn't stop. And then, when I finally stopped crying and started talking, she started crying.

When we had finally both calmed down, she said she missed me so much. She saw my picture I sent. She said I was so grown-up and she wouldn't recognize me if she saw me. She blamed her sister, my aunt April, for not keeping me with her. That's why I was in @#$# Michigan right now.

I have nothing nice to say about my aunt April, but I told her I love Michigan, and I'm learning to sing.

"Are you good at singing, Randa?" she asked. Randa was her nickname for me when I was little. I'd forgotten. No one has called me that in so long.

"My teachers think so. I have a part in the school play." I wanted to tell her about Harry and all the nice things he said about me, but I knew there wasn't time to explain all of it.

"I wish I could see it," she said.

"I wish that too," I told her.

My watch said our time was almost up, so I said, "Mommy, I miss you so much."

"I miss you too, Randa," she said.

I continued, "I miss you, but you should be happy that I'm learning a lot, and maybe someday soon, you can hear me sing."

She said she'd like that. And then, our time was really up. I told her I'd pay so she could call me again.

When I hung up, I lay on my bed a long time, staring and wondering what she was doing.

I wonder if she wonders about me too.

Love, Jacaranda

To: Johnsmith247@dll.com

Date: March 9, 4:36 p.m. Eastern Standard Time

Subject: Guess who got into two more summer programs?

You guessed it!

To: Johnsmith247@dll.com
Date: March 13, 4:37 p.m. Eastern Standard Time
Subject: The word is out

Dear Mr. Smith,

The whole junior class is buzzing about summer program acceptances. I guess this summer, between junior and senior year, is the most important because it's the last thing before college auditions next year. Phoebe got into the New England program and the Boston Conservatory musical theater dance program. She's waiting for a couple of others. David has gotten in everywhere he tried. It's nice to be a guy, since they are scarcer in musical theater, but he's also super talented!

The good thing now is that people are talking about the girl who got into three summer programs instead of the girl whose mother is in jail.

Even the lady dishing out scrambled eggs congratulated me on my big news.

"Thanks. Does that mean you're going to make me some celebration grits?" They're the only food I miss from my past life.

She wrinkled her brow and said maybe I could teach her. I plan to.

I love this place, and I love you for sending me!

Love, Jacaranda

To: Johnsmith247@dll.com
Date: March 21, 10:00 p.m. Eastern Standard Time
Subject: Me on skis

Dear Mr. Smith,

Here's a photo Danny took of me in my ski outfit, which Daisy loaned me because she has 5. This is a beautiful town, with red brick houses and tall-steepled churches. If you haven't been to Vermont, Mr. Smith, I recommend it.

Today was my first day of "ski school." I'm the only one here who isn't 6 years old. Floridian problems.

After my lesson, Danny volunteered to stay with me on the "bunny slope," a tiny hill for children, so the others could go on harder runs. Danny was very patient. I told him he didn't have to stay with me if he didn't want to.

"I don't mind." He said he'd like to go to college somewhere near a ski area, maybe University of Denver or University of Utah (which also has a football team), and be an instructor someday like his dad was. He says by tomorrow, I should be able to go on a longer green trail, and by the end of the week, I'll be on the gondola.

I didn't think so. The gondola is the enclosed lift that goes to the higher parts of the mountain (you probably know this).

"When I was little," he said, "our mom didn't realize that one of the easier trails used it. She thought it was only the hard trails. So one day, my dad went on it with us. He took our picture and sent it to her. She was all shocked, saying, 'My babies!' It was funny."

I laughed, picturing it, but that turned to a frown when Danny said I could do the same thing, send my family a picture and freak them out . . . then he realized his mistake and stumbled all over himself for misspeaking.

I said it was fine and asked him to take this photo to send to my guardian.

"You look cuter in that outfit than Daisy did," he said as he took it.

"Could that be because she's your sister?" I asked.

He said maybe and then asked if I wanted to race down the hill. He'd give me a head start.

When he finally caught up, he said, "You're good. If this theater stuff doesn't work out, maybe you can be an Olympic skier."

I laughed. "I think I'll stick to theater."

"You're good at that too. I saw that video."

We smiled at each other. Daisy says Danny likes me. I wish I could like him that way too. Maybe I could. He's funny and nice.

Maybe if I wasn't constantly thinking about Jarvis.

So I said, "Let's race again!" and took off, quick as I could, toward the lift. Maybe later in the week, I'll send *you* a picture of me on the gondola.

Love, Jacaranda

To: Johnsmith247@dll.com
Date: March 26, 10:36 p.m. Eastern Standard Time
Subject: I rode the gondola!

Dear Mr. Smith,

It was beautiful! And long and peaceful. There is just something so *powerful* about being above everything.

Danny was right. The trail isn't really harder, just longer and more satisfying. I pretended I was an Olympic skier, and I didn't fall even once.

When I was finished, I was so jazzed about having done it that I wanted to go again.

But Danny's friend Brent said he was cold and wanted to go to the lodge, so of course, Daisy was cold too. And Phoebe wanted to get one last run in on a harder trail since tomorrow's our last day.

Danny offered to go with me, and we boarded the gondola.

We were all alone in there, looking over the quiet mountain. I said, "Isn't it pretty?"

And then he leaned toward me, and I thought he was going to kiss me.

"Oh, no!" I said, taken off guard. I like Danny so much! And Daisy too! I didn't want to ruin everything!

But I also didn't want to kiss him.

There's only one guy I want to kiss.

I remembered how sweet Jarvis was, asking if he could kiss me that first night. It wasn't that Danny was presumptuous, exactly. Or maybe most guys are.

He jumped back. "Oh! I wasn't going to . . . !"

"No, it's me," I said. "I like you so much, but . . ."

"Daisy said she thought you still liked that rich guy," he said.

I nodded even though he was wrong. I don't like Jarvis. I love him.

Danny continued. "I said I didn't think you did because *you* broke up with him. If you still liked him, you'd be together."

I shook my head and said it was because of my family and everything.

Danny raised an eyebrow. "Only a jerk would care about that kind of thing."

Then, thankfully, it was time to get off the lift. I skied down without falling in a heap on the exit and waited for Danny.

When he got there, I said, "I really wish . . ."

Danny waved his hand at me. "Nah. I'm sorry. I shouldn't have made it awkward. I hope we can still be friends."

I told him of course we could.

The whole way down, I thought about Jarvis. It would be so much easier if I could just like Danny. But that's not how I feel. Everything that happens to me, what I want to do is tell Jarvis.

I think when he comes to school to see me, I'll tell him we should talk.

Love, Jacaranda

To: Johnsmith247@dll.com
Date: March 28, 10:36 p.m. Eastern Standard Time
Subject: Tech week

Dear Mr. Smith,

Back at school. It's tech week! You can see me April 8–10, matinees on Saturday and Sunday at 2:00 and evenings on Friday and Saturday at 7:00.

You know, if you happen to be in the area.

Pleadingly, Jacaranda

To: Johnsmith247@dll.com
Date: April 4, 11:58 a.m. Eastern Standard Time
Subject: Guess who called

Dear Mr. Smith,

I wasn't going to write again until after this weekend's performances because I'm ABOUT TO DROP with exhaustion. How do real theater actresses do it when they're playing 9 performances per week?

But today, just as I was thinking about going to the theater, my phone rang and . . .

It was my mother. Again, for the second time. I feel so guilty. She must really have missed me!

She asked me what was happening in my life, and I told her about the play and summer programs and that I'd visited my friend for spring break. I downplayed Vermont because talking about open spaces seemed mean to someone who is incarcerated, especially in hot Central Florida. But she wanted to know about the play.

And then she asked me to sing!

Mr. Smith, I never sang for my mother. I've never sung for any member of my family unless you count singing with my grandma before she died. For a second, it felt like juries all over again. I drew a blank on every song I ever knew.

Then, for some reason, I thought of Phoebe, singing "Hallelujah" that first day, and how that song has all the angst of my heart, so I sang that, and when I finished, my mother was crying. She said, "Was that really you, Randa?"

She said she couldn't believe how grown-up and talented I was, "Like a star. You're a star, Randa," and asked me if I remembered watching *American Idol* when I was little. I did!

And then she said, "Your father loved to sing. You get your voice from him."

Mr. Smith, I never met my father. My mother never mentioned him. I assumed she didn't really know him, or worse. So this was a revelation.

But, just as I was going to ask her about it, the call dropped.

My father could sing! Imagine.

Love, Jacaranda

To: Johnsmith247@dll.com
Date: April 6, 2:17 p.m. Eastern Standard Time
Subject: Incredible news!

Dear Mr. Smith,

Well, good news for me, anyway.

Ava Tamargo has mononucleosis! She wore herself out with rehearsals and auditions and flying all over the country, and the doctor has prescribed at least a week in bed.

I'M GOING TO BE THE WITCH!

We have extra rehearsals after school today and tomorrow. I asked Harry whether all the publicity and controversy about me would be bad for the show. He said, if anything, it would sell more tickets. "You've been through so much, and you're still devoted to your art. Who your parents are makes no difference. It's all who you are."

Have I mentioned I love Harry?

That made me remember Angie on the first day, saying I'd be fine if I just did the work.

Maybe Jarvis was right all along. What some internet trolls or even jealous, awful people like Brooke think doesn't matter. What matters is people who have my back.

Like Jarvis.

I've been needlessly cruel to him. As Elvis so wisely said, "Don't be cruel." Why wouldn't I let him make his own decision? Harry's right. I'm awesome. And Jarvis *wants* to be with me, no matter what my past.

Phoebe says Jarvis is coming to my performance Saturday. I'll tell him how I feel, how I've always felt.

Please come see me. I want to make you proud!

Love, Jacaranda

To: Johnsmith247@dll.com
Date: April 9, 12:11 a.m. Eastern Standard Time
Subject: I didn't see you at my performance

Dear Mr. Smith,

I looked and looked for some sign of you. Well, your loss. I was AMAZING.

Before the show, Harry announced, "The role of the Witch will be played tonight by Miss Jacaranda Abbott." There was a gasp from people who recognized my name, but no one left.

And then, when I walked onstage, another murmur, probably from people trying to decide whether it was me. The Witch wears heavy makeup in the first act.

But it calmed down, and I played my part well. People laughed at the funny lines, like they're supposed to, and got a little weepy during "Stay with Me." In the end, when I transformed into my beautiful, glamorous, young self, people applauded maybe a little more than they should have. Some people whooped and yelled, "JA-CA-RAN-DAH!" and someone even yelled, "I love you!"

The applause at the end was genuine. I wished you could have been there. Also, I wished my mother could have been there too.

But, as Jarvis said, I'm an entertainer. That means laughing through the tears sometimes.

And at tomorrow night's performance, I'll see him, and it will be even better!

Wish me luck!

Love, Jacaranda

To: JJarvisP3@gmail.com
Date: April 10, 12:03 a.m. Eastern Standard Time
Subject: I can't believe you!

Dear Jarvis,

I was so looking forward to seeing you tonight. Phoebe said you were coming. I'd made up my mind to talk to you, that what happened wasn't your fault and maybe you even loved me.

Little did I know . . .

When I came onstage, I instinctively searched for you. It wasn't hard to pick you out, the tall one with flowers. What was hard was not directing every song, every line to you.

Finally, the show ended. I rushed backstage, knowing you'd be at the stage door.

Outside, you looked at me tentatively, as if you wondered how I'd react. But I suspect you knew. I threw myself into your arms. For one moment, two, it was so wonderful to feel you close to me. I saw people taking pictures, but I didn't care. I heard your voice in my ear. "Jackie . . . Jacaranda . . ."

And then you said, "I knew. I knew all along. Don't you see?"

I was confused. You'd told Phoebe you knew about my mother.

But that was a fib. How could you have known unless, maybe, you'd investigated me?

"How? How would you know?"

You gestured to the roses in your hand, to the card attached. You held them toward me.

I took them, opened the card. A business card fell out. Your father's.

It said, *To Jacaranda, With warm regards, Mr. John Smith.*

I still couldn't comprehend it for a moment. How could you, Jarvis, know about Mr. John Smith? None of it made sense.

Then I realized what you'd said. You'd known all along. Didn't I see?

And suddenly, it all made sense. All the pieces came together, and I understood that you were—or maybe your father was—Mr. John Smith. I was some charity case your family was sending to school because they were so high, and I was so low.

I dashed the flowers to the ground and ran to my dorm room. Even though you ran after me, I couldn't face you. When Phoebe knocked on the door, minutes later, I pretended not to hear, but I'm sure she could hear me sobbing.

I can't believe you lied to me. You knew everything and you lied. You got your father to pay for my schooling. Then you used what you knew to make me fall in love with you. Did I get that right?

Did you think I needed a sugar daddy to pay my way through school? Do you believe that's what I wanted? The poor are not pets, nor were we put on this earth to assuage your guilt about being wealthy. We have lives just as worthy as yours, even though you might not think so.

Take your love, Jarvis, and take your money. I don't need either of them. I'll go back to Miami where I belong.

Jacaranda Abbott

Century Hotel
11 Main Street
Rolling Hills, Michigan
April 10

Dear Jacaranda,

First, I'm sorry. You have to believe I had innocent intentions. I saw your video. You were so talented, and I thought you should go to this school, which I knew about from Phoebe. My family foundation donates scholarships there. I told my father about you. The foundation helped you because you deserved it. Yes, you're right that I've always felt guilty about how much I have. There's no way my family deserves a hundred times more than someone else's family. But I didn't help you out of pity.

And I didn't plan to fall in love with you.

Yes, I read your letters at first. They were your idea, but I didn't object. I felt like someone should read them, in case you needed something. I thought maybe I would just read one. Or two.

I didn't know you'd write so often or in such detail. I didn't think I'd read them all. But you snuck into my mind at odd times, as I studied or went out with friends, checking and rechecking *my email for something new, wondering what you were doing at that moment. Were you singing? Were you in French class? How did your voice sound in French? Had you seen some new tree or flower, eaten some new food? Were the leaves beginning to turn where you were?*

I didn't think I was treating you like a pet, but maybe I was.

That first day, you said, "I want to be like other girls, like everyone else here except me."

But you were like no one else, at least no one I'd ever known. Maybe you'll say there are lots of girls out there like you: strong, smart, talented girls who keep their optimism despite terrible difficulties.

I didn't think I'd want to meet you. But I fell in love with you, like some old Nora Ephron movie my mom would make me watch, You've Got Mail *or* Sleepless in Seattle *or the musical* She Loves Me, *where the couple is in love, but they haven't met.*

I never realized I was lonely until I was lonely for you.

So, when I went to Ann Arbor to tour UM, I took a side trip to see my cousin, and to see you. I loved you even more in person. Just watching you eat a lobster gave me life because it was all special and new to you. But I went slowly. I didn't want to take advantage. You have to believe I loved you, Jacaranda. I still love you. That's why I'm writing this.

I wanted to tell you the truth. I tried to. I just didn't know how. We were both lying to each other, weren't we, neither of us knowing how to stop?

I promise that I stopped reading your letters to "Mr. Smith" once we met, once you started writing about me and writing to me as me. I told Vanessa to change the password and to read them all herself, in case you said anything Mr. Smith would need to know, like when you asked to go away for Thanksgiving break. That's also why I gave you the airline gift card for Christmas. I wanted you to be able to decide whether to come see me or not. So I put the choice in your hands.

I wanted to know you as just Jarvis, the way you knew me. I wanted not to have the advantage of knowing your thoughts, though it was tempting. I wanted to let it unfold.

I wish I could have met you completely innocently, as Phoebe's cousin. Because that was what you deserved.

This isn't meant to justify what I did. I was wrong to lie to you. I could use the excuse that I'm "just a kid" and didn't know what I was doing, but I should have known. I don't plan on writing you a hundred letters or trying to wear you down. I wish you'd give me another chance, but I understand if you don't. I hope you'll think about it, though.

I know you think it's best, but please, please don't leave school. Take the money, Jacaranda. It's only money. My father's money. Vanessa can help you apply for financial aid, but if it's too late to do that for next year, take the money. There's no conflict of interest if we aren't dating.

Take the money, and leave me.

So often, people tell me I get everything I want. But the only thing I want is you. I know I've thrown away your love. So be it. I want you to be happy. I want you to be successful. I want you to *have the future you deserve. If never speaking to me again is what it takes to make that happen, I can live with that.*

But I wish I didn't have to.

Love,

Jarvis

To: JJarvisP3@gmail.com
Date: April 11, 11:28 p.m. Eastern Standard Time
Subject: Please don't write anymore

Jarvis,

I got the letter you gave Phoebe. I've been hiding in my dorm every minute I don't have classes. Except I don't even know if it's *my* dorm anymore, because your family is paying for it. I want to go home except I don't even know where home is.

You say, "Take the money, and leave me." But I can't keep taking your money.

I think it's too late for me to leave MAA before the end of the year. I told Vanessa I want to go back to Miami for the summer. I asked her to contact my case worker.

At the end of *My Fair Lady*, Eliza tells Henry Higgins that when he took her in and taught her to speak correctly, he changed her. "I sold flowers," she says. "I didn't sell myself. Now you've made a lady of me, I'm not fit to sell anything else."

I know how she felt. Before, I wasn't exactly happy, but I didn't know all the opportunities I was missing. I thought maybe someday I'd be a cashier at Publix or even a manager! That was my dream, and it was a fine one. Now, you've made me too good for it. You've ruined me.

But I'm not going to be ruined. I can go to Miami where it's sunny and beautiful all year long, and the jacarandas are in bloom. I can work at Publix and apply to colleges. It might take longer, but I can do it.

I don't know how I'll manage without writing to you, *either* you. But I will.

Please don't write again.

Jacaranda Abbott

To: JJarvisP3@gmail.com
Date: May 6, 2:07 p.m. Eastern Standard Time
Subject: Open window?

When the Lord closes a door, somewhere He opens a window.
—*Maria,* The Sound of Music

Jarvis,

It's been almost a month since I saw you. I've written so many emails I haven't sent. But, almost every day, I think, "I wish I could tell Jarvis this" or "I should write to Mr. Smith."

I miss you both.

I'll send this one because it contains the story of how I became independent.

Monday, just two days after the door closed on us, a window opened.

I got a message from Debbie. That's my agent.

She seemed all excited and told me the school had just gotten a phone call from a casting director who wanted to talk to ME! Hands shaking, I called her back.

As soon as I stopped trembling enough to understand her, she said this:

The Shake-It Burger Company saw my video—our video—online, and they wanted me to be in a commercial for their restaurants.

A NATIONAL COMMERCIAL! Which means everyone would see it!

"What do they want me to do?" I asked Debbie.

"Just exactly what you did in the video," Debbie said, except they wanted me to sing "Don't Be Cruel" instead of "All Shook Up," and there would be dancing waiters involved and dancing milkshakes. Shake-It Burger is really famous for their milkshakes.

We talked about SAG-AFTRA (actors' union) and something called Taft-Hartley (I am so knowledgeable about the business now), but I barely heard her because I was already humming "Don't Be Cruel" in my head.

Which made me wonder if I was cruel to you.

But just for a minute because I was soooooo happy! Blakely, who does modeling, always says commercials can pay a lot of residuals! Maybe enough to be independent.

Debbie was still talking. Since Shake-It Burger has a lot of locations in the Midwest, they were going to film the commercial at their Cadillac location, not far from here, "if they can find dancers in this part of Michigan," Debbie said.

I told her I knew dancers. "They have a dance program here. And musical theater. You should have auditions here!"

So that is exactly what they did. They hired some older people, but they chose like six students from the dance program and four from musical theater, Phoebe and Garret, David and . . . Brooke!

Okay, I wasn't thrilled about that last part, but I'm so happy I can afford to be generous.

Phoebe is a dancing milkshake.

"They wanted to cover my figure, because I'm too pretty," she said in her Lady Catherine voice. "They didn't want me to upstage the star."

A few months ago, this would have been a typical Phoebe-ism, but when I looked at her, she cracked a smile and pointed her finger at me like "gotcha."

The star. Me. *I'm* the star.

We filmed this week. It took three days, a day of learning the dance and two days of filming. The premise is a girl at Shake-It Burger with her boyfriend. He refuses to give her a sip of his shake. "Don't Be Cruel" comes on the jukebox, and she sings and dances with the waiters. All the customers (and dancing milkshakes) join in. Finally, he orders her her own shake. Happiness!

I think we can agree that the differences between Shake-It Burger and Shake-speare are minimal!

It was so much fun!

When I got back to school after the second day of filming, I sat with Falcon, Phoebe, and Daisy at dinner.

"Do you feel awesome?" Falcon asked me.

"Like a real actor," I said.

Falcon nodded. "When that lady at the shelter looked at my art and thought it was good enough to send me to this school, that was the first time I ever thought of myself as an artist. Not just some dreamer who drew a little."

I nodded, knowing what she meant. For me, it was the day Vanessa came to Publix and told me that Mr. John Smith wanted to send me to boarding school. Before that, I'd thought I was just an ordinary girl. Mr. John Smith changed my life.

You changed my life, Jarvis. Other people complimented me because it didn't cost them anything. But you were the one person who saw my talent and did something about it. You thought I was special, and you wanted the world to know.

I sometimes forget that.

That's not the only thing that happened.

Yesterday, my mother called. She said she had bad news. She's not getting a new trial. Not enough "new evidence," and without something like DNA, it's hard.

She'll be in prison another 9 years. For running over someone who probably would have killed both of us.

And what made me the saddest is that I knew I couldn't help her.

I said, "I'm sorry, Mommy," and I meant it.

Because I actually *want* to go to Florida and tell them what happened.

When I told her that, she said, "No, baby, you keep singing." Then she told me about my father.

His name was Chris, a dark-eyed boy who climbed a tree to pick her jacaranda flowers and brought them to her at school. He liked to play the guitar and sing and wanted to start a band and move to California.

But he was shot a few months later when the pizza place where he worked was robbed. Then she found out she was going to have me.

I said, "I never knew about this. I always assumed—"

"A one-night stand?" she said. "Yes, I let you believe that, because it made me too sad to think about him, and I didn't want you to be sad too. But maybe you'd be sad either way. Your father, he was the only one who was kind to me."

And then she gave me maybe the only good piece of advice she's ever given me.

"Randa, always be with the one who's kind to you. If I'd been with your father, none of this would have happened."

I'm not sure if that's true, but she believes it, and I'm sorry for her. Too soon, it was time to get off the phone. I told her I wanted to visit her over the summer.

After the conversation, I thought about what she'd said. "The one who's kind to you." For me, that's been you. But were you kind to me when you didn't tell me the truth?

I looked over the letter you wrote me. I was so angry when I first read it. I wanted to rip it up into a million pieces. But something made me keep it. I understand what you're saying, how it all just happened. Time has softened the edges of my feelings. I was mean to you. Cruel. I said things you didn't deserve. We both lied to each other, neither of us knowing how to stop.

"Take the money, and leave me," you said. You were saying you cared more about my well-being than about us being together, more than your own happiness. I appreciate it, but I don't want to take your money.

I don't want to leave MAA either.

But now, I'll be making some money with the commercial. I also took your advice and spoke with the financial aid office. They're giving me money for next year. Someday, I'll pay your family back, so you can send another girl to school.

My mother taught me one other thing by being a bad example. She taught me never to be dependent on a man for my support. Dependence is the death of love.

I'm grateful to you for introducing me to all these opportunities. I apologize for what I said about Eliza Doolittle and you ruining me. It was kind and generous, what you did. *You* are kind and generous. You introduced me to a world of opportunity I never knew existed, like when Henry took Eliza to the Embassy Ball. But I don't want to be beholden to you.

In *My Fair Lady*, Henry Higgins talks about growing accustomed to Eliza's face. He sings, "I was serenely independent and content before we met . . ."

But the audience knows he wasn't really happy before Eliza, and I wasn't happy before you, or you before me. So I think th

Oh my God! As I was typing, Phoebe pounded on my door. She said you've fallen from a cliff!

J

To: JJarvisP3@gmail.com
Date: May 6, 5:06 p.m. Eastern Standard Time
Subject: (No subject)

Dear Jarvis,

I know you won't see this, but I have to do something, and writing calms me down.

I'm sitting in the airport with Phoebe, waiting for an airplane to take me to Aspen, to you.

I pray I'll see you when I arrive . . . and I don't pray often.

There's nothing like having your ex fall from a cliff to make you focus on how much you still love him.

Okay, you fell while climbing the *side* of a cliff, but it still sounds bad. It's on the news right now, and it's pretty scary.

How, Jarvis? How could you think it was a good idea to go rock climbing in such poor weather and so far from home? Seriously! Just because you can afford to fly to Colorado to climb rocks doesn't mean it's a good idea! And, if you're going to do it, maybe make sure your phone gets decent service so if you fall and tear a massive hole in your leg, you can call for help!

Thank God you had Chase with you and he was able to climb down and call.

Graduation trip! Celebrating getting into Carnegie Mellon! Never thought I'd say this, but maybe you have too much money and not enough supervision!

They're calling to board now. I hope there will be good news when we land.

Love, Jackie

To: JJarvisP3@gmail.com
Date: May 6, 6:37 p.m. Central Standard Time
Subject: (No subject)

Dear Jarvis,

O'Hare Airport now! What a busy place this is, even compared to Detroit! Phoebe updated me that they were able to save your leg (!!!), but you're still in intensive care!

Phoebe says you'll be fine. "With his money, he has the best care."

I think she's trying to convince herself. I've been thinking that rich people have also been known to die, but I didn't say it. I'm saying it to you now because I know you'll only read it once you're safe and sound, but GOD, I'm scared!

And it didn't help that Phoebe told me, "He only did this because of you." As if you'd thrown yourself from a cliff due to spurned love.

"He's been talking about rock climbing for months," I told her, though I'd had the same thought, that you were taking unnecessary risks after we broke up. And, truly, if you'd come to Michigan, you'd have been strolling through cherry blossoms, holding my hand instead of tumbling from a precipice!

I know I was angry. I was embarrassed to realize you'd known my secrets all along. I felt spied on. But Vanessa confirmed your story, and I can see how it would be hard for you to confess the truth.

It's not like I never lied to you.

You did the kindest thing anyone could do. You believed in me, in my talent, in dreams I didn't even know I had. It's like Falcon said: You made me see myself as an artist. You, Jarvis.

I was so disappointed that Mr. John Smith wasn't a real person. But you are, my love. Soon, I'll be stuck on a three-hour flight with no word. I hope when I arrive I'll be able to tell you in person.

I love you. And I'm frightened.

Love, Jackie

To: JJarvisP3@gmail.com
Date: May 6, 11:01 p.m. Mountain Standard Time
Subject: Are you okay?

Dear Jarvis,

It's close to freezing here, and Phoebe has no new information. No one in your family is answering their phone. No one in her family knows anything new.

Do you know it was almost exactly a year ago today that I sang at Publix and some stranger recorded that life-changing video? That has to be lucky, right?

I pray we can celebrate together!

I'll be there soon, soon, soon.

Love, Jackie

To: JJarvisP3@gmail.com
Date: May 7, 2:27 a.m. Mountain Standard Time
Subject: My darling, Jarvis

Dear Jarvis,

I know you can't read this now, in your doped-up sleep. But I wanted to write anyway. Writing is the closest I can get to being with you.

When we arrived, Phoebe asked for your room. The horrible front desk man laughed. "You and everyone else! No-o-o-o fan-girls. Mr. Pendleton isn't up to visitors. They weren't sure he'd make it for the first 6 hours."

My chest tightened, but Phoebe's hand found her hip. "We're family."

"Suuuure you are," said the awful guard. "What are you, his sister? He hasn't got a sister! I'm sorry, but he can't . . ." His eyes fell on the ID Phoebe had slapped down onto the counter. With a gloved finger, she pointed to the word "Pendleton" in her name.

"Pendleton. Pen-dle-ton," she said in the voice that used to scare me.

The guard stepped back. "How about you?" he said to me.

I started to fumble for my school ID, but Phoebe said, "She's with me."

Then Vanessa showed up. "Jarvis's cousins," she told the guard. We followed her.

"How is he?" I asked Vanessa.

She said you'd been better, and that your father and Chase and Wendelin were there.

Wendelin seems sweet, by the way. She looked like she hadn't combed her hair, and there was about an inch of eyeliner collected under each eye. I think she'll be a good mom to your someday half brother.

She held out her hand to me first. "He asked for you."

"So he's . . . ?" I didn't know what to say? Awake? Coherent? Not going to die?

"They've got him on some good drugs," she said, "so he goes in and out."

Which didn't seem like the type of thing you'd say about a dying kid.

Phoebe pushed me ahead. I parted the curtains, and there you were.

When I saw you, I gasped. Your body was covered in blankets, but your face was scraped and bruised, and you had every type of tube and wire connected to you, even one of those heart monitor things they use on TV. I don't even know what the other things were. At least your heart was beating. For a moment, I couldn't tell that your eyes were open.

You spoke softly, and I jumped.

"What?" I said.

"Are you real?"

"Yes." I was scared to come too close. You looked like I might hurt you if I breathed on you wrong. "What happened?"

"I . . . fell." The last thing you remembered was your hand, about to make contact with a rock. When you came to you were on a ledge, maybe fifteen feet below, in agony. You could hear Chase yelling above you. And then you looked down at your leg, which was all red blood except something white. Bone and maybe muscle. You'd scraped it against a rock when you fell.

I shuddered, thinking of it. I'm shuddering now, writing this!

You told me more about making a tourniquet with your jacket despite your broken arm. It was hard to listen. Still, I heard you when you said, "I just wanted to see you, Jackie. I wanted to see you and apologize for what I did, for lying to you. I'm so sorry. You'd be right never to forgive me, but I had to see you."

You smiled, which managed to be charming somehow, despite the bruises, and I thought about what would have happened if you'd fallen a little differently, if help had taken a little longer. If, if, if . . . that angry letter might have been my last communication to the one person who gave me everything.

If that had happened, the world would have cracked open and swallowed me up.

"I forgive you," I said.

"Really?" Your voice was the barest whisper.

"Yeah." And then I decided to be less cautious. Still trying to avoid the wires and the tubes, I crouched beside you and kissed your bruised face, gently. I heard you sigh, or maybe that was me.

When I'd kissed every inch of your face that wasn't covered by bandages, you asked me if I was leaving MAA.

I said no. I told you about the financial aid and the commercial, that I'd be able to stay as an independent person, one who isn't taking your money.

"That's the most romantic thing I've ever heard," you said, your eyes crinkling at the sides.

"It is," I said. "I love you. Now that we've been truthful with each other, we have nothing to fear."

"I wanted to tell you the truth all along," you said. "I didn't want to lose you."

I nodded. "I've learned a few things about losing you, this past 24 hours. I don't want that to happen either."

"It won't." You squeezed my hand with your one good hand.

You sounded happy, but also tired and a little delirious, so I let you sleep. Phoebe never did get to see you, but we'll come back tomorrow. And over the summer. And next year and the year after and the year after that. Because you did change my life, Jarvis. Now, I want to change yours.

I won't sleep a wink tonight, but you must. You have to sleep so you can get well so you can come to me.

Love, Jacaranda

P.S. This is the first love letter I ever wrote. Isn't it funny that I know how?

To: JJarvisP3@gmail.com
Date: May 12, 5:38 p.m. Eastern Standard Time
Subject: The cherry blossoms are in bloom!

Dear Jarvis,

This afternoon, as soon as classes were over, Phoebe, Falcon, Daisy, and I walked into town to see the cherry blossoms. Spring has finally reached Northern Michigan!

It was a glorious pink-and-white day, the kind that makes you glad to be alive. We all held hands and ran through the falling blossoms. It was a day to Instagram, but we just lived it.

When we got back to the dorm, there was a crowd of people standing in the lobby, watching something on TV. "There they are!" said someone. Nina.

She shouted to pause the television. We walked closer to see.

It was me! Well, me and Phoebe and David and about 20 other people—the Shake-It Burger commercial! We were dancing, and I was singing. I looked happy and confident and much like every professional singer on every commercial I've ever seen in my life.

BUT IT WAS ME! ME!

I wonder if you've seen it.

Nina rewound, and we watched again. Everyone clapped.

If I close my eyes now, I can still see myself, happy and confident.

I know you're on your way back to New York. Thank you for your invitation to see you "walk" (or whatever it is you'll be able to do by then) in your graduation. The Hodgkinses have invited me to stay, and I accepted happily.

After that, I'll be back at MAA. They've offered me a job at their summer camp. So I'll be here when the cherry trees bear fruit. I'll work at the little shop, selling ice cream and souvenirs to spoiled middle schoolers. I'll live on campus and receive a small stipend. That and the money from the commercial will fund me for the fall. I hope maybe you'll want to fund the education of another MAA student in my place. It's fine if it's a girl, but no letters, please.

Falcon is staying to work during the summer program, too, and we'll room together. We also plan to be roommates next year, with Phoebe and Daisy in the other half of the suite. Somehow, I'll have to make room for her art supplies, but that means I'll have her art everywhere too!

And I know you saw the commercial because you just texted me from the airport to say it was on the TV there. My agent says she's gotten other calls about me, which brings me to . . .

One summer program offered me a full scholarship, including room and board. And it's in NYC, so maybe I can go on some other auditions. I'll be in New York for 3 weeks in July!

Don't get too excited. I plan on working hard, probably even nights and weekends, and I can't slack off to be with you. But maybe you can go by the school and throw a pebble at the window, and I'll know you're there. And some weekend, we can take a walk in the park again, and dance and kiss like the first time.

But, before any of that, I'm taking the last of the airline gift card you gave me to visit my mother for the first time in six years. Vanessa has generously offered to accompany me.

When I spoke to you before you left the hospital, you sounded healthy and happy and excited for the future. I am too. One day this week, Phoebe and Daisy and Falcon and I plan to walk into town to visit the sweet tearoom where we went that first day, and I'll think of you.

I can't wait to see you again in three long weeks. We belong to each other. Even when we're apart, I'll be yours, and you'll be mine. Always.

Love, Jacaranda

ACKNOWLEDGMENTS

Thanks to the following individuals for helping me with this book:

Alyson Day for her loving editing, Megan Ilnitzki for all her help, my agent, Elizabeth Bewley, a great ear and sounding board. I thank my critique group—Gaby Triana, Danielle Cohen Joseph, Christina Diaz Gonzalez, Alexandra Alessandri, and Stephanie Rae—for listening to early bits of this. Thanks to Debbie Reed Fischer and Flora Stamatiades for info on agents, unions, and commercials. Special thanks to my daughter, Meredith Flinn, whose idea it was to go to the *Daddy Long Legs* musical, which reminded me how much I'd loved this book, and who let me share her high school musical theater experiences.